A LOVER'S DISGUISE

"I shall be glad when I can put off this disguise. I don't want to be a man any longer!"

"Well, if you won't be a man any longer, then you could pose as my wife, as I suggested before." Angus put a hand at the back of her waist and pulled her hard against himself so that they touched at all points from chest to thigh.

"What are you doing?" Blanche whispered, her forehead almost touching his shoulder.

"Trying to throw myself at your feet."

"Feet?"

"Well," he laughed softly, his breath tickling her ear as he buried his nose in her hair, "in a manner of speaking."

"A foolish way to speak. . . . Why bother?" She lifted her head to stare up at him. His hands continued to caress her warmly.

"To add some spice to our adventure. Why else?" He pulled her even more tightly against himself and lowered his head, gazing at her mouth . . . and slowly touched his lips to hers.

ELEGANT LOVE STILL FLOURISHES –
Wrap yourself in a Zebra Regency Romance.

A MATCHMAKER'S MATCH   (3783, $3.50/$4.50)
by Nina Porter

To save herself from a loveless marriage, Lady Psyche Veringham pretends to be a bluestocking. Resigned to spinsterhood at twenty-three, Psyche sets her keen mind to snaring a husband for her young charge, Amanda. She sets her cap for long-time bachelor, Justin St. James. This man of the world has had his fill of frothy-headed debutantes and turns the tables on Psyche. Can a bluestocking and a man about town find true love?

FIRES IN THE SNOW   (3809, $3.99/$4.99)
by Janis Laden

Because of an unhappy occurrence, Diana Ruskin knew that a secure marriage was not in her future. She was content to assist her physician father and follow in his footsteps . . . until now. After meeting Adam, Duke of Marchmaine, Diana's precise world is shattered. She would simply have to avoid the temptation of his gentle touch and stunning physique – and by doing so break her own heart!

FIRST SEASON   (3810, $3.50/$4.50)
by Anne Baldwin

When country heiress Laetitia Biddle arrives in London for the Season, she harbors dreams of triumph and applause. Instead, she becomes the laughingstock of drawing rooms and ballrooms, alike. This headstrong miss blames the rakish Lord Wakeford for her miserable debut, and she vows to rise above her many faux pas. Vowing to become an Original, Letty proves that she's more than a match for this eligible, seasoned Lord.

AN UNCOMMON INTRIGUE   (3701, $3.99/$4.99)
by Georgina Devon

Miss Mary Elizabeth Sinclair was rather startled when the British Home Office employed her as a spy. Posing as "Tasha," an exotic fortune-teller, she expected to encounter unforeseen dangers. However, nothing could have prepared her for Lord Eric Stewart, her dashing and infuriating partner. Giving her heart to this haughty rogue would be the most reckless hazard of all.

A MADDENING MINX   (3702, $3.50/$4.50)
by Mary Kingsley

After a curricle accident, Miss Sarah Chadwick is literally thrust into the arms of Philip Thornton. While other women shy away from Thornton's eyepatch and aloof exterior, Sarah finds herself drawn to discover why this man is physically and emotionally scarred.

Available wherever paperbacks are sold, or order direct from the Publisher. Send cover price plus 50¢ per copy for mailing and handling to Zebra Books, Dept. 4336 , 475 Park Avenue South, New York, N.Y. 10016. Residents of New York and Tennessee must include sales tax. DO NOT SEND CASH. For a free Zebra/ Pinnacle catalog please write to the above address.

A Midnight Masquerade
Meg-Lynn Roberts

ZEBRA BOOKS
KENSINGTON PUBLISHING CORP.

"True love is like ghosts, which everybody talks about and few have seen."
    —*François, Duc de La Rochefoucauld (1613–1680)*

In the story, the ruined monastery on the outskirts of Carlisle is a product of the author's imagination.

Chapter 1

. . . ten . . . eleven . . . twelve. Midnight.

The sound of the bell tolling in the church tower adjacent to the Hen and Feathers Inn died away abruptly, drowned out by the howl of the wind and the spattering of the rain against the roof and walls of the old stone building.

A fitting night for All Hallows' Eve, Blanche Charolais thought wearily as she saw the flimsy curtains at the open window of her shabby second-story bedroom blowing inward. The threadbare fabric was being twisted and turned this way and that by the gusts of wind accompanying the fierce rainstorm. The dead might walk tonight, but surely no living being would want to be out in such a tempest.

The floor of the room was becoming wetter by the minute as the howling gale blew the spray of cold rain in through the open window, but Blanche didn't care. She couldn't manage to make the effort to get up and shut the window just at the moment. She

7

closed her eyes as she lay on the lumpy bed in the sparsely furnished room and groaned.

There was a sudden discordant noise above the sound of the wind and rain that distracted Blanche from her worries. She opened pain-filled eyes and glanced toward the window. In the dim light of the single candle flickering on her bedside table she saw a figure silhouetted for a moment in the open window. Then there was a flurry of movement. The booted and spurred figure leapt through the window into the room, a long black cape billowing out behind him as he did so.

Her heart gave one feeble leap in her breast at the sight.

"Who's there?" she called. "Are you a man or a spirit to venture out among the other poor wandering souls on this All Hallows' Eve?"

"Aye, 'a spirit of no common rate,' " the masked figure said as he removed his wide-brimmed hat with a flourish and swept a bow in Blanche's direction as she raised herself up on the bed. The old-fashioned hat, complete with a long, dashing white feather and trailing black ribbons, was now sadly bedraggled by the rain. "Just a 'merry wanderer of the night,' Angus Dalglish, at your service, ma'am." He sprinkled raindrops about him as he made the extravagant gesture, some even falling on Blanche as she still half-sat up on the bed.

"Some call me Black Angus," the apparition said in a deep, resonant voice, rich with humor.

"Oh, do they? How vexing for you," Blanche remarked dryly, as she lay back down after her first start of surprise.

He laughed as he tossed his outdated hat aside and reached into his pocket.

"I'm glad to see you aren't the type of female ready to set up a screech at every trifle, for I would hate to have to use this," the masked man said, waving a small silver-chased pistol he had cupped in the palm of his hand in her direction. He strode forward, his spurs jingling on the bare wooden floor as he did so. Blanche turned her head where it rested on the pillow to watch his approach. His silver spurs and the silver chasing on his pistol were the only points of light about the dark figure as they caught the flickers of the weak candlelight when he moved.

"What good would 'setting up a screech' do?" she asked. "Except to bring even more strangers bursting in, invading my private chamber."

"You're remarkably cool under the circumstances, ma'am," the man said admiringly.

Blanche remained silent. She didn't feel up to sparring with the stranger. As he came nearer, she felt a bubble of laughter well up in her throat as she got a better look at her midnight visitor. The figure *must* be in costume, she decided. This was the *nineteenth* century, after all! Men didn't wear their hair in long, black curls nowadays, or sport such curling, sinister mustaches!

Her "spirit," she realized in a flash, had affected the style of a seventeenth-century cavalier from the court of Charles II, complete with knee-length cloak

9

thrown back over his shoulders, and a long flaring black coat-jacket embellished with gold-threaded jet braid was buttoned to the waist and fell almost to his knees. The jacket was worn over full, gathered, black breeches that were tied with ribbons just below the knee. The long, wide lace cuffs of his white shirt protruded from his jacket sleeves and fell over his hands, while at his throat he wore a fine, white lace cravat. Soft leather boots with deep turndown cuffs and encircled by the jingling silver spurs completed his costume.

"You look to be a tasty armful," the man said, unhooking his wet cloak at the neck and casting it aside as he looked down at Blanche where she lay on the coverlet.

"Either it's a trick of the light or your eyesight is failing you, sirrah," Blanche said coldly.

"You don't look to be vastly alarmed by my presence, my dear. Perhaps you would welcome ravishment," the figure teased lightly, grinning devilishly behind his mask.

"Ravish away, then, if you must. I have the toothache."

"Good God! You don't say so!" Taken aback, Angus rocked back on his heels and looked more closely at the female who lay on the bed before him with her long, silver hair spread out over the pillow. She had closed her eyes and thrown an arm across her forehead. His dramatic entrance had been for naught, then, he realized with a grin.

"I wouldn't dream of troubling you, under the circumstances, ma'am. A toothache is the devil's own torment. Accept my sympathies, my dear young lady.''

There had been too many disasters that day for Blanche to be overset by the sudden, highly irregular appearance of a masked man in her room. Blanche's troublesome charge had given her the slip late that afternoon while she lay on her bed at the out-of-the-way inn nursing a toothache. Her charge—her seventeen-year-old cousin, Prudence Wilmont—was a featherheaded but determined chit of a girl who had decided to elope with her equally foolish young swain, Bartholomew Waddle.

Blanche and Prudence were on their way back to Prudie's home at Heywood near Manchester. Prudie had been sent to Harrogate, the Yorkshire watering place, by her father to stay with his sister-in-law, Lady Lottie Wellwood. Blanche had gone along with her cousin to play duenna as usual, and Prudie's maid, Sukey, had accompanied them. Prudie's father, Sir Horace Wilmont, was Blanche's uncle and, more importantly, her employer.

Sir Horace had foolishly hoped that the good, but remarkably muddleheaded, Lady Wellwood could, by some miracle or other, mend his daughter's willful temper and ill-bred manners. He had decreed that there would be no London season for his daughter unless she returned home ready to obey her papa and be guided by him in all things.

11

The fact was, Prudence Wilmont was not at all a biddable girl. After four years as her companion, Blanche was resigned to the fact that there was little hope of mending Prudie's headstrong, foolish ways. Not to put too fine a point upon it, Prudie was a coquette and a spoiled baggage; she had not a particle of sense in her imprudent, but undeniably beautiful, head.

Sir Horace had made some little mention of Prudie making a match of it with their neighbor, Jebediah Lodestone—a forty-year-old bachelor whose fine manor adjoined Sir Horace's acreage—but Blanche was persuaded her uncle was not serious. Prudie, however, liked to pretend differently, so that she could assume the airs of a tragic maiden being coerced into marrying against her will.

Blanche knew that what her uncle really wanted was for Prudie to go to London and take the *ton* by storm. He wanted to show off his beautiful daughter. Sir Horace was convinced that Prudie would catch a title. But he wanted her to learn a little conduct first. Prudie, being as determined to have her own way as her father was to have his, refused to knuckle under to any of his suggestions.

Prudence and Uncle Horace were forever locking horns over everything under the sun, Blanche recalled with a sigh. It didn't matter whether the issue at hand was of major significance or some minor matter, father and daughter were constantly trying to best the other in their contest of wills. Blanche had decided long ago that they were both too stubborn by half.

Blanche's mother, Anne Wilmont Charolais, had been estranged from her older brother Horace because of just such stubbornness on his part. Horace Wilmont had refused to acknowledge his sister's marriage to Jacques Charolais, a French emigré, and the two siblings had not met again since the day Anne Wilmont became Anne Charolais. Blanche supposed she was fortunate that at least her Uncle Wilmont had provided her with employment and a roof over her head after her parents died.

That employment was now in grave jeopardy.

Lady Wellwood had written to her brother-in-law, informing him of Prudie's unsuitable attachment to Bartholomew Waddle, a young man she had met at one of the assemblies in Harrogate. Sir Horace had sent a scalding letter posthaste to Blanche, accusing her of neglecting her duties as a chaperone, and ordering her to bring Prudie back to Heywood immediately.

After her first tantrum on hearing her father's decree had subsided, Prudie had been suspiciously meek in agreeing to give up her acquaintance with young Waddle and return home. Now Blanche could see what lay behind her cousin's uncharacteristic compliance, *and* what lay behind her plea to take the ''scenic'' route back to Heywood across the hills and moors of the Pennines. The indirect route from Yorkshire back into Lancashire had taken them treacherously closer to the Scottish border.

The rundown Hen and Feathers Inn, where Blanche had been forced to take rooms, lay in the town of

Skipton, a mere eighty miles from Scotland. And Blanche made no mistake that *that* was where her headstrong charge was headed. Although Prudie's note had not mentioned their destination, the foolish couple had undoubtedly decided to flee across the border into Scotland where they could be married over the anvil in some dusty blacksmith's premises in Gretna Green. Blanche knew her little cousin well enough to know that Prudie would have insisted upon such a "romantic" course. And Prudie's actions were all to thwart her father, not because she had fallen head over heels in love with the unprepossessing young man.

The axle on the coach Lady Wellwood had lent them for the journey to Heywood had cracked just outside of Skipton late that morning.

"Lucky for you ladies," Lady Wellwood's coachman had said, "we're near a largish town. Shouldn't 'ave no trouble finding a wheelwright 'ere. This 'ere ve'icle should be fixed up in jig time."

"Jig time" in Skipton apparently meant three days, Blanche had surmised, to judge by the wink the wheelwright gave the coachman after a friendly farmer had given them a lift into town. She had determined to hire a vehicle and continue on their way, but at Prudie's pretty pleading to stay a few days in the attractive town, and her own increasing misery from the toothache, she had decided they would spend at least one night in Skipton.

Blanche had had to make do and take rooms in the less agreeable Hen and Feathers Inn because there was not a spare inch, much less an entire room, to be had at the more exclusive Swan a few streets over. At least the Hen and Feathers was not overrun with leering gentlemen, she had congratulated herself as the Hen's landlady led her and Prudie up the stairs to their rooms that afternoon.

She had stopped first at the well-maintained Swan Inn to inquire about accommodation before going on to the Hen and Feathers. She had been uncomfortably aware of several pairs of male eyes turned her way when she had stepped into the lobby of that rather exclusive establishment to speak to the proprietor. The landlord had informed her that all the gentlemen were gathered at the Swan to participate in a rather unconventional card party that evening.

The garrulous innkeeper had been ready to tell Blanche all the details. The gentlemen were to draw lots that would determine in which of several rooms set aside for the purpose in the inn they would present themselves. As it was All Hallows' Eve, it had been decided that everyone would be masked and costumed. No one was to know anyone else's identity. At the stroke of twelve midnight, all gaming was to cease and everyone was to unmask.

Blanche had assumed this was just another hey-go-mad amusement for those gentlemen who had too much leisure and too much money, but too little sense. As she spoke with the Swan's landlord, Blanche had been aware that wagers of one kind or another were already flying thick and fast. No doubt other forms of low behavior were going on as well, she had thought with a disapproving glance around at several garishly dressed and obviously painted ladies occupying the inn's large anteroom.

The collective leers of the miscellaneous group of swells, nobs, lesser gentry, and locals had become even more pronounced when they had caught a glimpse of her exquisite little cousin. A few catcalls were even heard when Prudie stepped over the threshold into the room.

Prudie had disobeyed orders to stay with her maid and the coachman at the wheelwright's shop adjacent to the Swan's yard and had waltzed into the inn several moments after Blanche entered. She had given herself time for a grand entrance. Prudie had stood with a pretty pout on her face, attracting the eyes of every man in the vicinity of the lobby, and sly looks from the lightskirts, too. Blanche was unhappily too well accustomed to her cousin's tricks for Prudie's conduct to occasion any surprise.

Prudie was a beauty, from the top of her shining gold head, past her peaches-and-cream complexion, pouting red lips, and quite maturely rounded figure, down to the tips of her dainty kid half boots. One of her adoring admirers at home had once said fulsomely that had Miss Wilmont been present at the legendary competition among the three goddesses to decide who was the fairest of them all, Paris would undoubtedly have awarded the golden apple to Miss Prudence over Athena, Hera, and even Aphrodite herself.

And Prudie, without any shame at all, had accepted his fatuous comparison as no more than her due. She loved to be the cynosure of all eyes.

Blanche could not deny that her cousin's disposition did not match her lovely looks, however. Prudie's strong determination to have her own way in all things could not be thwarted by her stubborn father, her long-suffering cousin-companion, or her doting Aunt Lottie in Harrogate.

Her cousin's willfulness was the bane of Blanche's life. Blanche did not allow her annoyance to show on most occasions, merely correcting Prudie with a well-placed word of admonishment or a disapproving glance and slightly uplifted eyebrow, knowing this was the best way to avoid the loud, childish tantrums that Prudie affected when her will was crossed. Blanche had learned to control her emotions and studied to maintain her cool composure on the surface, but frequently she had to fight to keep her anger at Prudie's behavior from boiling over.

If only Prudie hadn't met young Bartie Waddle at that dratted assembly in Harrogate. The boy seemed to be ineligible on every count. Despite close questioning of all her gossiping cronies, Lady Wellwood had been unable to determine if young Waddle had any funds of his own, and his connections remained a mystery. His manners were rather unpolished—as might well be expected of an unlicked cub of a boy, for he could not have been a day above one and twenty. And even in the matter of looks, Blanche would have thought he had little enough to recommend him to her cousin, for Bartholomew was a thin, pale, blond young man, not much more than an inch or two taller than Prudie herself. And he must be a perfect ninny to boot, Blanche decided, if he had allowed Prudie to talk him into running away with her. It was folly to expect that a match between two such babes in the woods could succeed.

Now Blanche faced a bleak prospect. With no Prudie, there would be no employment, no money, no home, no future.

Blanche lay quietly with her eyes closed, trying not to move about too much and jar her face. The ache in her mouth would become fearsome if she did so. She was lost in her own thoughts and it was little wonder she ignored the midnight presence of a costumed, pistol-brandishing, masked man in her room.

Angus closed the window and pulled the tangled, wet curtains across to conceal the dim light in the room from anyone who ventured into the courtyard below, then stepped closer to the bed. "What is your name, my dear?" he asked, putting the pistol away in his belt as he peered down at the woman in the weak light of the one flickering candle. He was satisfied for the moment that the lady had no intention of calling for help and revealing his presence.

"Blanche Charolais," she answered automatically, opening her eyes and looking up to see the stranger standing over her. He extended his hand toward her and Blanche unthinkingly put her own slim hand in the man's firm clasp. Then, realizing her error, she tried to snatch her hand away.

"Though why I'm telling you this, I don't know," Blanche said in exasperation, giving up the fight to reclaim her hand from his firm clasp.

Angus managed to retain her hand and bent to kiss it with warm lips, proving that he was no spirit of the night after all but all too human flesh and blood.

"Ah, Blanche," he said, savoring the sound of her name on his tongue, drawing out the soft cee of the French pronunciation in a long, sighing breath. "You must have been named for a white flower. Not a daisy, though," he said, looking down at her critically. "A lily perhaps? I shall call you Fleur."

"Indeed, you shall do no such thing! Release me and begone from my room at once, sirrah!"

"Ah, I'm afraid I cannot honor your command, my dear Fleur. Though it goes much against the grain with me to be forced to refuse to honor a lady's wishes. And even though it *in*commodes you, I'm much afraid the consequences of such an action do not bear thinking of." Angus shuddered, all unseen by Blanche.

"You have a glib tongue, sirrah," she scoffed. "Why, pray, can you not honor my request?"

"I do not wish to alarm you with the tale, but I must beg your indulgence for the nonce. Spirits of another sort—arch fiends, I would call them—seek my blood, my dear young lady. They are armed to the teeth and exceedingly dangerous. If they were to find me, I fear they would think nothing of putting a period to my existence. You would not have a man's blood on your conscience, would you?''

''What have you done that such villains are out for your blood?'' Blanche asked, her curiosity aroused.

''Accused a rather notorious—and extremely powerful—member of the nobility of cheating at cards, which he was doing so blatantly that a babe would have seen it. Unfortunately for me, the Earl of Wolverton has powerful friends and, er, muscle-bound henchmen, only too willing to do his bidding at his every whim, no matter the right or wrong of the matter.

''The other members of our card party would not believe me, of course, nor would they credit the evidence before their very eyes—though they were victims of the earl's cheating as much as I. I have a rather, ah, uncertain temper, I'm afraid, and perhaps I acted somewhat precipitously when I exposed the marked deck in Wolverton's face. His men were upon me in the next instant.

''There was a nasty moment when I thought Lady Luck had finally decided to desert me. Fortunately, with my usual quick-witted acuity in such situations, I was able to devise a plan of escape.''

''What did you do?'' Blanche asked, listening in rapt amazement to the tale.

''I assumed a look of horror and pointed to the empty fireplace on the opposite wall. 'Look!' I cried. 'A lost soul of the dead walks here among us on All Hallows' Eve!'

20

"We were all masked and costumed, you understand," he said, gesturing to the clothes he wore.

"Yes, I had noticed that you were not attired in what one would call the *modern* mode," Blanche murmured.

His teeth gleamed white in the dark as a large grin split his masked face. "It was to be a select card party befitting the occasion. And no one was to know the identity of anyone else. There was no mistaking the notorious Earl of Wolverton, however, no matter that he wore a domino and half mask, he took little care to conceal his identity.

"There had already been much jittery laughter about it being a devilish night to be abroad. And when they all turned to stare at the figment of my imagination, I pulled my pistol from my pocket and fired once at the candelabra, putting out most of the light in the room, and dove for the window. Two of them fired after me. Fortunately, one missed and the other only put his bullet through my hat." He bent and picked up that article and inspected the bullet hole briefly. He absently twirled the hat about on his finger for a moment, then carelessly tossed it aside and continued his story.

"The fiends raced after me in hot pursuit, but again fortune smiled. As I dodged into the inn yard here, I saw your open window . . . and *voilá,* it was a simple matter to climb the drainpipe and cast myself upon your mercy." At these melodramatic words, Angus bent down on one knee on the damp floor and folded his hands together in supplication.

Blanche thought she could detect that distinctly humorous note in the stranger's voice again, and his dark eyes glittered mischievously behind the black silk half mask as he made the extravagant gesture.

"How affecting! Especially as it seems I'm to be given no choice in the matter. . . ."

Chapter 2

"You seem to derive a certain pleasure from this adventure, Mister Dalglish. It would appear that you live an exciting life if you must always be prepared with a pistol up your sleeve," Blanche said dryly as he rose to his feet.

"In my profession, one must be prepared for emergencies in *any* situation."

"What *is* your profession?"

"I am a knight of the green baize, ma'am."

"Ah, a gamester, are you? That is no profession— it's a life of dissipation."

"As much as it wounds me to contradict your charmingly frank assertion, dear lady, in my case, it is distinctly a profession. It's how I make my living, you see."

At Blanche's skeptical look, Angus said, "I see I must tell you the sad story of my life and try to tug at your heartstrings a little . . ." He negligently rested one booted foot on the wooden frame of her bed, propped his elbow on his knee and launched into his story.

"I was born to an ancient and respected name. My father was the youngest son of a—er, a titled gentleman of property. When grandfather died and my Uncle Maurice inherited the title, my father was given a rather ramshackle manor house with some unprofitable, marshy acreage attached to it from which he was meant to eke out a living. Alas! My father had trouble reconciling his new life with the extravagant one he had enjoyed while his own father was alive. So he mortgaged his property and made investments, most of them unwise, in order to support his former way of life.

"In next to no time, we—my father, mother, and younger sister, Frances, and I—found ourselves reduced to living in our former gamekeeper's cottage on the edge of our marshy estate. My mother was soon prostrate under the strain. A year later my father was killed in a hunting accident. My uncle, for reasons of his own, did not see fit to help us after Father died. Though I was in my final year at boarding school and had hoped to go up to university at term's end, there were no longer funds available to pay the tab. I was sent home in disgrace.

"My sister Fanny was shunned by all the local gentry, our formerly toad-eating neighbors. She had to help out with the housekeeping and take in sewing to eke out enough to feed and clothe herself and my mother. To do something for them, and myself, I joined the army as soon as I could. A friend from school bought my commission and I've since paid him back, you'll be pleased to hear. But when the forces were cut after Waterloo two years ago, I decided to sell out and ply the trade I learned while I was in the army."

"Trade? You learned a *trade* in the army?" Blanche inquired. "I would have thought your *trade* would have been fighting Napoleon's army."

"Indeed, it was. But, you see, my dear, you can't be fighting every hour of the day. In order to while away the time between battles, we fellows had to find something to do, apart from sleeping and eating and drilling the troops. As it happened, in my unit at least, most of my fellow officers and I derived a great deal of pleasure from playing cards—endless games of cards. Took one's mind off the, ah, more unpleasant duties of army life—fighting battles and so forth." He waved an airy hand.

"And, of course, it always made the game more interesting if one could stake a bet or two on the outcome. With most of my pay going home to my mother and Fanny, I needed to live by my wits in order to stake myself. You'd not believe how paltry the pay is for a junior officer. Of necessity, I became quite good at most games of chance, and learned to hedge my bets. Soon I was joining in games where the stakes were for more than a penny a point. I was able to supplement the meager pay I received and could send home enough to keep Mama and Fanny from landing in the poorhouse. Well, I ask you, what else was I to do?" Angus concluded with an innocent look.

"You couldn't soil your noble hands by farming

25

your land or earning your living by honest means, I don't suppose.''

Ignoring her sharp comment, Angus explained patiently, ''Our land is under long-term lease. Alas, it is not mine to farm for the next twenty years, unless I can somehow manage to pay off the rather hefty mortgage my father took out on it before he was killed. So . . .'' Angus spread his hands in a wide, helpless gesture. ''Seems I must tarry here awhile with you, dear lady.''

''I suppose you would like to hide beneath my bed, my fine cavalier,'' she said cuttingly. ''I wonder a man of honor would stoop to such a thing.''

''It's a sharp tongue you have there, Fleur . . . but *under* the bed would be *much* too uncomfortable . . .'' he said suggestively, with a twinkle lurking in those dark eyes behind the concealing silk mask.

''I suppose they call you Black Angus because of your bovine manners,'' Blanche said with disgust. Even as she spoke, she closed her eyes again. She was too fatigued to keep them open.

''Too true, my dear. How did you guess?''

''You're a wild man.''

''Wild and woolly.'' He grinned rakishly, ready to continue their banter. But at the groan of pain Blanche couldn't suppress, he winced. ''You really are ill, aren't you? I would call for some assistance for you, but alas, I dare not risk being discovered here with you.'' He spoke with concern, for he couldn't bear to see a fellow creature suffer so.

At this Blanche opened one eye, ''Ah, you recog-

26

nize the impropriety of being caught here with me and fear you'll be forced to wed me? Well, put aside your fears, Mister Dalglish. I wouldn't marry a common gamester even though I am at my last prayers.''

"Last prayers, ma'am?'' Angus asked disbelievingly as he gazed down at her delicate features and at her long, silvery hair spread out over the pillow where it gleamed in the candlelight, then down along her slender figure as she lay over the coverlet. "I should rather say if you believe that to be the case, you've been hiding your light under a bushel for far too long.''

"Fustian!'' she exclaimed mildly, easily dismissing his teasing words of flattery.

But the gray hair was unexpected on a *young* lady, Angus thought, despite his light words. And the pale woollen gown she wore was sadly outmoded and spinsterish, giving her the look of a nun. Perhaps this serene, shabbily clad lady was his elder by several years. That didn't mean that he must give up his effort to turn her up sweet, however, so that she wouldn't feel she had to call for help or take some other action to force him from her room. He judged he was relatively safe from his pursuers for the time being in this unlikely refuge.

"And I'll have you know I'm no common gamester, Fleur,'' Angus told her with mock severity.

"Oh?''

"No. I'm an *un*common gamester. For, you see, I have a master plan. I began by investing half of all my winnings when I left the army—''

"Invest? What kinds of investments does a hard-ened gamester make that are not another form of gambling? I wonder. What kinds of risks would you not take in your investments?"

"None. My investments are quite sound, I assure you! Well, to be scrupulously honest, only a quarter of my winnings are invested in ventures that have the least risk. Only consider how unexciting otherwise," Angus said dryly.

"Is that why you decided to participate in this masked gambling party, then, for the excitement of it?"

"Partly. I can't lay my hands on the money that's tied up in investments, you know. And, you see, I had just sent all the cash I could spare home to Fanny so that she and Mama could have a proper Christmas. When I learned a gathering was to take place in this out-of-the-way place on All Hallows' Eve, I thought it would provide a good opportunity to replenish my pockets."

"How could you be so confident that you would win?"

"Oh, I'm good at my profession, my dear."

"That good?"

"Yes."

"But it seems you've come to grief instead."

"I shall come about, never fear."

"I wish you would cease your chatter and go away now," Blanche said fretfully, as she turned on her side away from him. She had to stifle another groan

28

as the movement sent a ripple of pain through her face.

Angus gently laid his hand on her shoulder. "Toothache is the very devil!" he said compassionately. "In another hour Wolverton's men will have given up hunting for me in this vicinity and it will be comparatively safe for me to step downstairs and summon a servant. I'll send him for someone to see to you. I suppose you'll need a toothdrawer," he said, gnawing on his lip in concentration.

"Much good that will do me when I don't have the means to pay for his services. Prudie took all our blunt when she gave me the slip this afternoon, you see."

"Ah, an appeal to my better nature—but I'm afraid it will do you little good, my dear. They took my purse, you know. It was resting on the table and one of Wolverton's men grabbed it up as soon as I challenged his master. But I have a few coins left in my pocket," Angus remarked casually as he settled himself in a ladder-backed chair a little way across the room from the bed.

"Something else up your sleeve for emergencies," Blanche remarked coolly. But she was amazed at the nonchalance of the man, hiding, as he was, from men seeking to kill him. He had told her rather casually that his life was forfeit, should he be discovered, and here he sat bantering with her.

"Perhaps I could be persuaded to part with some of the ready in return for certain, ah, considerations."

29

"Don't be a fool! I won't sell my body, even if I'm dying."

"Tempting as the thought is, my dear, I need a different kind of sustenance at the moment. . . . Have you any food?"

Blanche gave a gurgle of laughter. "What a strange fellow you are! There are a few things in the tapestry workbag near my traveling case, over by the wardrobe."

Angus laughed, too. It was not often he felt he could trust someone on first acquaintance, but here he was trusting this lady with his life. He not only trusted her, but he had swiftly come to admire this cool creature who maintained such a calm, collected demeanor despite having her room invaded by a masked, pistol-waving stranger in the middle of the night while she was suffering agonies from the toothache.

He went over to check the articles she mentioned and found half a loaf of bread and a wedge of cheese along with two apples. He knelt down on one knee to rummage around in the bottom of the workbag and found a small knife, took it out and cut himself a thick slice of bread and a hunk of the cheese, then proceeded to eat it ravenously. "Are you sure you don't want to share? I wouldn't want to deprive you."

By way of answer, Blanche made an inarticulate sound in her throat that Angus took for a decided negative.

"I suppose it's too much to hope that you have some strong drink concealed in the bottom here,"

Angus spoke even as he reached down into the work-bag again.

"No, there's only the water here." Blanche indicated the pitcher on her bedside table.

As she spoke, Angus lifted a prettily wrapped box of chocolate bonbons out of her bag. The box had been opened and just one chocolate taken out.

"Ah, dessert," he said with relish, as he lifted one of the bonbons out of the box and popped it into his mouth. "How about a chocolate?" He came toward the bed, dragging the chair he had been sitting on with him. "They are quite soft. Wouldn't take much chewing. You could almost swallow them whole," he remarked as he turned the back of the chair to the bed, straddled it with his long legs, sat down and extended the open box to Blanche, resting his arms over the chair back as he did so.

"No, no," she said forcefully, pushing his hand away as he held the box toward her. "That's where the trouble started—when I bit into one of the chocolate creams Lady Wellwood presented us with before we left Harrogate this morning."

"Ah, most unfortunate for you. I love chocolate creams. Who's Prudie, by the way?" he asked conversationally as he stood up to remove his jacket and boots. He turned the chair about, sat down and rested his stocking feet against the bed, tilting his chair back so that it teetered precariously on two legs as he did so.

He seemed to be wholeheartedly enjoying his makeshift picnic with the last of her food, Blanche thought disgustedly. Oh well, there was no way it would be of any use to her in her present condition. She couldn't manage to eat a bite.

Somehow Dalglish's easy manner won her over. Besides, she realized that while she talked with him she was not as aware of the pain in her mouth.

"Prudie—Miss Prudence Wilmont—is my cousin and my charge. Though there could not be a more foolishly named girl in all of Christiandom! She doesn't have a prudent bone in her entire body. She is rather—*willful*—and a more troublesome minx you'd never want to meet."

"And what about you, Fleur. Do you follow suit? Do you have no prudence, either?"

"I make up for what she lacks in spades."

"Ah. Remind me to take great care in my dealings with you, then, if you hold all the spades. I shall have to be on my mettle if we should happen to play cards and make sure that I hold enough winning hearts, diamonds, and clubs to take a few tricks myself. . . . And why did your imprudent cousin hie off on you with all your money, then?"

Blanche sighed. "I see I shall have to tell you the whole story," she said, repeating his earlier words to her. "I'm Prudie's companion, you see, hired on to earn my daily bread by my uncle, Sir Horace Wilmont . . . of the Wilmont banking family. You may have heard of him."

"The name does ring a vague bell," Angus murmured with a considering look on his face as he bit into another one of the chocolates. "Your last name is Charolais, you said, not Wilmont?"

"Don't get your hopes up. I can't provide you with a chance to improve your 'investments.' It's my cousin who is the heiress, not I. I'm only a penniless spinster. Uncle Horace is my mother's brother. My father was a French emigré—and disapproved of by my mother's family. She was cut off without a sou."

"Ah. As affecting a story as my own. And so this heiress you've been hired to guard gave you the slip?"

"Yes, she did. Prudie and I were on a visit to her aunt, Lady Wellwood, in Harrogate—a dull enough watering place, I'm sure you'll agree. But there was a young man—"

"Yes, isn't there always. . . . How old is your Prudie?"

"Just turned seventeen, and a prettier little picture you couldn't hope to see with her golden ringlets and big blue eyes. She's a small girl but exceeding well, ah . . ." Blanche hesitated. She had inadvertently fallen into a comfortable but decidedly overly familiar way of speaking to this swashbuckling adventurer and took herself to task for it, blaming her lapse on the extreme discomfort she was feeling from her troublesome tooth and the oddness of his midnight presence in her room.

"Well formed is the description you were searching for, is it not?"

"You're very perceptive, Mister Dalglish."

"Angus, please, my dear."

"Well, Angus, then. Why not? I suppose I'm ruined already—ruined and penniless. I shall have to apply for a job in an orphanage after this episode, for my uncle will be sure to turn me off now, what with losing his precious Prudie and her more precious fortune to that gauche schoolboy.''

"Surely it can't be that bad? What happened exactly?''

"Lady Wellwood wrote to Uncle Horace when she saw that Prudie had formed this decidedly *imprudent* attachment to a most unsuitable young man. Naturally, Uncle ordered me to bring Prudie back to Heywood forthwith. But young people being exceeding foolish—''

"And you being ancient yourself," Angus interposed wryly.

"Ahem. As I was saying, unbeknownst to me, Prudie got in touch with her young man—Bartholomew Waddle he's called—and he evidently followed closely behind our carriage on horseback—''

"Not of the Sheffield Waddles, by any chance?''

"Er—no . . . I don't really know, actually. . . . Anyway, the axle of our carriage cracked just outside Skipton this morning. There was no choice but to stop here. I did not feel up to accompanying Prudie around town. So I allowed her to go out for an hour with only her maid, Sukey, to accompany her while I rested here. I thought she had returned to her room, until I forced myself to get up and check at dinnertime. I found her gone. She left me a note telling me she 'had to take desperate measures' because 'everyone was so cruel.' Prudie saw my indisposition as a golden opportunity—and she took it, along with all our money, leaving me to my misery."

"A very enterprising young man."

"Enterprising young *man?* Not at all. 'Twas Prudie who planned and plotted the whole. The young man is a very nodcock!"

"I assume they're heading for Gretna."

"Prudie didn't outline their plans in her note, but that would seem to be the obvious conclusion," Blanche said dryly.

"You're taking this all very calmly, I must say. I would have expected you to have had the vapors under the circumstances; any other female would have."

"Vapors? An affectation of little use to me. I would go after her, but I can do nothing until this pain subsides."

"She took her maid with her?"

"Yes. At least she had enough sense to take Sukey, so she is not quite, *quite* ruined, I suppose." A wry smile curved Blanche's mouth. "Though Prudie did not take her maid along to preserve *propriety,* you know."

"Did she not? Why take a maid along on one's elopement then?"

"Why, because Prudie can't dress herself without assistance," Blanche said with a straight face.

Angus gave a crack of laughter. "Your cousin is an heiress, I think you mentioned?"

"A considerable one."

"Well, it seems her father can kiss her fortune goodbye now. Young Waddle will have complete control once they tie the knot. Your Prudie and her fortune will be irretrievably lost before too many more hours have passed."

"Well . . ." Blanche said, looking over at Angus consideringly. "Perhaps there *would* be a way to retrieve her . . . if I could shake off this toothache, I could go after her—with your help. Would you help me recover her, Mister Dalglish?"

"My help? What do you mean?"

Even in the dim light of the candle Blanche could see the alarm in Dalglish's dark visage.

"I'm not a marrying man, my dear. I couldn't marry her for you, if you are proposing that as a way to escape ruin."

"You!" Blanche exclaimed in surprise. "That would be worse than marrying her to young Waddle—marrying her to an adventurer, a hardened gamester, like you. Put your alarm away, Dalglish, I wouldn't dream of such a preposterous solution."

"Then what form would my help take?"

Blanche thought for a moment. "You mentioned your need to earn your income. Would you consider doing something other than gambling to make money?"

"What have you in mind?" Angus asked. He fingered his chin with his long, slender fingers and looked at Blanche consideringly.

"I think I can speak authoritatively when I say that I'm sure my Uncle Horace would make it worth your while, were you to help me recover my cousin and restore her to him unwed." Blanche looked over at

Angus hopefully. What made her trust this unknown stranger, she didn't know. It was hardly a cautious move to ask him to help her, but she was at point-non-plus.

Angus folded his arms across his chest and looked down at his lap as he considered. Wolverton, whose reputation was decidedly unsavory, was not known to forgive his enemies lightly. Angus was not sure if he had been recognized. The earl would not have known him, but there were several men around the table whom he had played cards with before in London. At least Angus knew that the earl's certain attempt to bribe the innkeeper to learn the identity of the Black Cavalier would be fruitless. He had not been staying at the Swan, and no one there knew his identity. The disguise he had worn tonight had been almost impenetrable.

So Wolverton would pursue a phantom, a ghost, who would disappear without a trace. Still, Angus knew he could take no chances while Wolverton's men hunted for him. He would have to cover his tracks from this area, in any event. It was no good going home and bringing danger to Fanny. Even in the unlikely event that someone *did* learn his identity, no pursuer would think of looking for him heading toward the Scottish border. Especially not to Gretna Green! With his reputation as a confirmed bachelor well known to one and all, it could be the ideal place to take himself off to, he decided with a self-mocking grin curving up his lips.

He raised his head and looked over at Blanche.

"Bluntly, my dear, how much of a reward are we talking about here?"

"Prudie's fortune is in the neighborhood of thirty-thousand pounds, so I should think Uncle Wilmont would come down quite handsomely. Say in the region of a thousand pounds," Blanche said without a blink, though she crossed her fingers under the folds of her skirts, not knowing if her uncle would pay *anything* to have his troublesome daughter returned to him, especially if he considered that Prudie had been compromised beyond redemption. But Blanche desperately needed to convince Angus to help her. If she couldn't recover Prudie and take her back to Heywood, Blanche herself would have nowhere to go, no means to earn her living.

"Hmm. It would be a rather unusual adventure. You tempt me," Angus said at last, and Blanche let out a breath she didn't realize she was holding.

"Good." She sighed in satisfaction. "I hope you will succumb to the temptation, then."

Angus grinned. "Always. I hope she's worth it."

"It's settled then." Blanche extended her hand to shake his on the bargain.

"You're in no condition to go hying off after your impetuous relative and her foolish swain just yet, though," Angus said, retaining her hand for a moment after they had sealed their bargain.

"Give it another hour, if you can bear it, then I shall summon a servant to go for a toothdrawer," he ordered with a fierce look that would brook no refusal from her.

Chapter 3

Blanche awoke from a fitful sleep when Angus gently shook her shoulder. It was still dark to judge by the misty moonlight coming in through the curtains. The storm must be over, she thought groggily.

"The toothdrawer awaits just outside, Fleur," the man said in a low voice as he bent over her.

She gave a start of surprise at the sight of the dark stranger standing over her with his hand on her shoulder. She tried to clear the cobwebs from her brain and recollect just what this man was doing in her bedchamber. But then she remembered how the masked man had leapt into her room and how he was to aid her in recovering Prudie. She had been too tired to work out the details of pursuing Prudie after Dalglish had agreed to help her and she had gone to sleep.

"I've told the man you are my sister—to save our reputations, you know. So remember to answer to the name of Miss Dalglish."

Blanche nodded her head slightly in agreement,

fuzzily noting that he had removed his mask and mustache while she slept—and he had cut his hair.

Afterward Blanche had only the haziest recollections of the events that followed. She remembered an elderly man bending over her and poking about in her mouth. He had located the source of her trouble without any difficulty. She had literally bitten into her lip to stifle her cry of pain when he had withdrawn his wicked-looking instrument. "This tooth will have to come out," the toothdrawer had proclaimed in a loud baritone.

"You'll have to hold her down, lad," he had said to Angus.

As the man turned away to prepare his instruments, Dalglish had leaned over the bed, forced her to sit up, and tipped a large glass of brandy down her throat against her sputtering protests. She remembered the surge of warmth that coursed through her veins when Angus had held her tightly in his arms and said in a fierce voice to the elderly toothdrawer, "Don't hurt her any more than you have to!"

"You've naught to worry about, young man. I know what I'm about. Your sister will be safe enough in my hands," the man had assured Angus. Then she slowly sank into unconsciousness as the toothdrawer took hold of her tooth with his instruments and began to pull. The last thing she remembered was Dalglish's voice saying heatedly, "Damn your eyes! I told you not to hurt her!"

* * *

Now Blanche was awake and although she still felt some residual pain, she noted with considerable relief that the agonizing ache was gone. There was a glass of water and a bottle of laudanum on her bedside table. She found that she had been tucked up under the bedclothes, but thankfully she found that none of her clothes had been removed.

In the faint light coming in through the curtains, she looked over to see Angus tipping back in his chair with his head leaning against the headrest. He appeared to be asleep. His mouth was open slightly and his dark head was lolling on his shoulder. Blanche took frank stock of his appearance.

He had removed his concealing mask and costume, including the old-fashioned black wig and false mustache, before he summoned the toothdrawer. Looking at him now, she could see how thoroughly he had been disguised last night. Now that he had shed his fantastic garb, it was as though he had peeled away the layers of another century. A new nineteenth-century man had emerged from the ghosts of the past.

In the early morning light, Blanche could see his features more clearly than she had been able to when he had awakened her in the shadowy room during the night. Dalglish was very dark, his complexion, with a day's growth of beard to shade it, appeared almost swarthy. She could well see why he had earned the sobriquet *black* Angus.

Without the wig, she saw that his hair was gleaming black, thick and wavy, and worn long, falling over the open collar of his white shirt. Long, dark lashes formed a shadowy semicircle under his closed eyes. His full lips were surprisingly soft-looking in sleep. Indeed, there was a softened look about his whole face as he dozed unself-consciously in the chair.

How old was Dalglish anyway? Blanche wondered. Last night he had sounded dangerous—definitely an experienced man of the world. But looking at him now, Blanche doubted he was as old as she was. He looked a mere boy. He could not possibly be more than three and twenty, she decided, dropping her gaze from his face. Her eyes trailed over his muscular physique.

No—not a boy, after all.

The black silk breeches he wore looked rather comical. They were rather voluminous from the waist down to where they were gathered and tightly banded just below the knee. Below them, his hard-muscled calves were encased in black silk stockings. He had removed his long jacket, and the frothy white lace cravat he had worn at his neck last night lay in an untidy heap on the floor. More silky dark hair was visible, curling softly at the open neck of his wide-sleeved, white lawn shirt where he had untied the ribbons, Blanche noticed with some embarrassment.

Her eyes skittered away from him and she inspected the room. His black silk half mask lay on the dressing table where it had been carelessly tossed, and the dark jacket was draped over the ladder-backed chair near her bed. The long, full-skirted jacket was made of heavy wool and elaborately trimmed with jet black braid picked out with gold threads along the neck, front opening, and over the high turnup cuffs.

Dalglish had told her that the participants in the card game were all masked and costumed. How appropriate that he had chosen the garb of a roistering cavalier! Her mouth quirked up in a half smile. Yes, from their conversation last night, she had learned that he was an adventurer who loved the drama of his own existence. From all the seventeenth-century history she had read, Blanche decided that Angus Dalglish had much in common with the larger-than-life gentlemen of that era. She had to stifle a small laugh as she spotted the outrageous wide-brimmed, cocked hat, bedecked with trailing black ribbons and long white feathers, he had doffed to her. It was resting on the floor where he had tossed it.

It was almost as though he had appeared through a window in time from another era, leaping to the rescue. She *hoped* he would rescue her, at any rate. She *must* have his help, if she were to stand a chance of recovering her cousin.

She continued to smile as she studied Angus's costume and thought how foolish she was to trust such a reckless gentleman. She sighed. It appeared she had no other choice.

His long legs, stretched out and resting against the dressing table, gave a clue as to his height. He must be well over six feet, Blanche calculated. She glanced at his arms folded across his broad chest encased in the sleeves of his billowy shirt. She remembered the strength of those arms holding her while she had had her tooth extracted.

She gave a guilty start. This stranger was altogether an exceedingly attractive man, if one liked dark and dangerous-looking men. Blanche was not sure if she did. She flushed and averted her eyes, reaching for the glass of water on her bedside table.

She took a sip and swallowed uneasily. She had had no idea last night that she was entertaining such a handsome swashbuckler in her bedroom. Well, her calm good sense and unemotional temperament would just have to serve her now, as they were always used to do. She *would* make use of Dalglish to track down Prudie. She must, if she were to have any hope of retaining her position and her means of livelihood. If her Uncle Horace should dismiss her, she had no other relative to call upon. She had no money of her own and nowhere else to go.

Angus awoke with a start and nearly tipped over in the teetering chair. He looked over at Blanche and blinked. "Ah, you're awake. You look amazed to see me still here. 'Fraid I shan't vanish like an evil spirit with the coming of day, my dear. . . . How do you feel this morning, *sister?*"

"Sister? Ohh!" Blanche put a hand up to her jaw as she felt a sharp pain from her recent extraction. She quickly put her hand down and clenched her fists, determined not to show any reaction before this stranger.

. Angus got up and came over to her. He put his hand on the top of her silvery head and said, "I'm

44

sorry you're in pain, my dear. But I've been assured it will pass off soon, now that the troublesome tooth has been removed.''

She was mortified that she had allowed herself to show so much emotion and modulated her voice, injecting a note of cool detachment, as she thanked him for his concern. ''You've been very kind. I'm sure you're right. As soon as the immediate pain wears off, I'll be right as rain.'' She smiled up at him with something of her old insouciance returning. She threw off the bed covers, and sat up on the side of the bed.

Angus stepped back at the sight of her brilliant smile. It quite transformed her careworn, pale features and lit up her odd, silvery eyes to disturbing effect. Perhaps she was not as old as she had appeared last night, with her gray hair and sedate demeanor. His first assessment underwent a speedy revision. First impressions were often deceiving, Angus smiled to himself as he looked at her more closely and saw that not only did she have a brilliant smile but that she had a flawless complexion of pale alabaster, a classically shaped nose atop a firm mouth and chin, and perfectly arched black eyebrows in striking contrast to her long, silvery hair. Yes, her hair was definitely silver, not gray, as he had thought last night, Angus decided.

It was that silver hair that had deceived him as to her age. The girl couldn't be above two-and-twenty, at a guess. Three or four younger than he was, he realized in surprise. Those oddly lit, light-colored eyes were her most striking feature, however. Why, they were not gray at all, but almost silver like her hair, he mused. He had never seen the like before, with the pale irises edged in black, causing the eyes themselves to stand out in an arresting fashion.

But, for all that, the woman was too thin for his taste, he decided as she stood up and shook out the folds of her wrinkled woollen gown and twitched her skirts into some semblance of order. After she had run her hands over her skirt to smooth it down and pulled her hair back over her shoulders away from her face, she calmly folded her hands over her skirt and stared across at him with a challenging light in her eyes.

"Have you finished your examination, Mister Dalglish?" Blanche asked tartly, as Angus unconsciously leaned toward her. "Pray, may I ask your conclusion?"

Angus, realizing he was staring quite rudely, recollected himself. "I beg your pardon, but your eyes— I've never seen the like before." No, she was not in his usual style at all. He liked curvaceous, pouting, little armfuls of femininity, not self-contained, statuesque, regal creatures like Blanche Charolais.

"Yo—you've not slept in here all night, have you, Mister Dalglish?" Blanche asked, trying to insert a dispassionate note into her voice as she fought to remain unperturbed under the scrutiny of those disturbing black eyes. Blanche was afraid she knew the answer to her question even without asking.

"No, indeed. How could I get any sleep with you tossing and turning all night," Angus answered with an innocent look on his black countenance as he sat down again and pulled on his boots. "And you're to call me Angus. Remember?"

Blanche frowned at his teasing words. "What will the landlord think? Why did you not take a room of your own, once the toothdrawer had done his work and left me for dead?" In truth she was worried about the impropriety of the situation and trying her hardest to make light of it.

"We can't afford it, my dear. We haven't a feather to fly with. The dibs ain't in tune, as I told you before, but I daresay you were in too much pain to attend properly. I couldn't risk venturing too far abroad and being found by Wolverton's men, now could I? I refuse to risk my skin in this venture. Dark and disreputable as it is, it's all I've got. And I'd much rather have a whole skin, thank you very much, if I'm to help you chase after your cousin. . . . And, besides, you had to have someone with you, you know. Such a symphony of moaning and groaning," he said with his black brows raised in exaggerated fashion.

"I take it you drugged me," Blanche said, ignoring his dramatics and indicating the bottle of laudanum on the table near her bed.

"Aye. When you awoke with the pain, I tipped a spoonful of that concoction down your throat and you finally slept like a babe. I did manage to get forty winks after that, but, Lord, I could have done with ten times that amount," he added, yawning and stretching his arms above his head. He walked over

47

and picked up his long jacket, shrugged it over his shoulders, and bent to retrieve the ruined neck stock.

"Well, thank you very much for your concern, Mister Dalglish," Blanche said doubtfully, wondering if he hadn't taken monstrous advantage of her. But she didn't *feel* that she had been taken advantage of—she felt, rather, that she had been cared for. A strange feeling for one of her independent nature. She had been caring for herself for close to ten years now, since her parents had died in a carriage accident when she was only fifteen, in fact.

With his mouth quirked up in a half smile, Angus folded his arms across his chest and gave a slight bow. What an admirable creature, he thought, remarking her self-control. In his experience, most females would have already made a scene.

"*Where* did you manage to get your, er, 'forty winks'?" she asked, glancing at the still damp floor. She knew he could not have made a bed for himself down on the hard, wet boards, and surely he had not been able to *sleep* in that chair he had been teetering in when she awoke.

He waved a hand to that very chair.

"Not the most comfortable 'bed' I've ever known, but beggars can't be choosers, you know." He changed the subject. "You must be famished. I know I am. I shall fetch us some breakfast."

"What will they think? A strange man in a room taken for a single lady?"

"No need to worry about that. I passed the word to Samuel, the boy apprenticed to the landlord of this

48

establishment, that I was your brother, arriving late to meet you here so that I could escort you home. The lad will undoubtedly have relayed the gossip to the others belowstairs. And then, too, servants are a superstitious lot. No doubt they were much too concerned with lost souls of the recently expired wandering about on All Hallows' Eve to take much notice of any, er, irregularities, in our sleeping arrangements. No one will wonder that a brother takes such care of his sister." He smiled at Blanche, a flashing, brilliant smile, that disturbed her in some indefinable way, and left her wondering if she were wise to trust her midnight intruder after all. She lowered her dark brows at him.

"So you hope to convince everyone that I'm your sister, do you?"

"Well, my dear, you wouldn't pass for my mother," he quipped outrageously with a definite twinkle in his eye.

"I may be older than you, but not *that* much older," Blanche answered, irritated at his joke.

"I doubt that you have more years in your dish than I do. Anyway, it was all I could think of on the spur of the moment to account for us sharing a room. We shall have to continue the charade as we chase after young Prudie."

"We are too dissimilar to pose as brother and sister," Blanche said consideringly, noting again the contrast in their coloring as she looked up at Dalglish's swarthy complexion, knowing her own skin was pale by comparison, not to mention his midnight black hair set against her own prematurely gray locks. "It wouldn't work. You're so much darker than I, and our features are nothing alike."

"Then husband and wife it must be!"

"Husband and wife?" Blanche sputtered, losing her customary composure at the scandalous suggestion. "Don't you dare entertain using such an outrageous idea for even a moment, sirrah! Besides," she said as she collected herself somewhat and added in a more prosaic vein, "they would never believe us. I *am* older than you."

Angus laughed.

"I doubt it. 'Twould be no impediment even if you were. . . . If you want me to find Prudie for you—and I take it you mean to accompany me, for I wouldn't know the chit from a needle in a haystack—then you'll have to accept that we must travel fast and we must travel economically. I can't lay my hands on any blunt at the moment. We will have to wait until we've put a considerable distance between ourselves and Wolverton's men so that I can find a suitable card game to exercise my, er, professional skills. So, you see, my dear, the problem that lies before us."

"Yes," Blanche admitted tentatively, not liking the sound of Angus's plan, but feeling she had no other choices. She refused to be intimidated by the man, and managed not to blush as she said boldly, "I would rather pose as your sister than your wife, if I must conceal my identity."

"Hmm." Angus looked at her critically from head to toe as she moved to the dressing table where she sat down on the stool and took up some hairpins, pulled the mass of her gleaming hair back, and formed it into a neat coil at the base of her neck. Her appearance was changed dramatically by the rearrangement of her hair.

As he watched her movements, Angus had an idea. "I'll tell you what. How would you like to pose as my companion?"

"I, sir, would *never* consent to such a thing," Blanche assured him with icy contempt heavy in her voice as she gazed back at him through the looking glass.

Angus gave a sharp bark of laughter. "No, no! Not a *lady* companion. . . . You're tall enough—and thin enough—to disguise yourself as a young man with your hair pulled back and concealed under a hat. Yes, the more I think on it, the more I see that such a disguise would be the way to avoid certain, er, complications as we travel."

"Avoid complications? It seems to me to be adding to my—*our* troubles," Blanche said.

"I wouldn't have to hire a coach for you. We could move faster, both on horseback. You do ride, don't you?"

"Yes, of course," Blanche answered with a lift of her chin.

"I would have to fork out less of the ready," Angus continued, "and we might have a chance of catching them, though they will have over a day's start on us, as it is."

"Less than that. Prudie did not leave until late afternoon yesterday."

"Less than a day, then. No doubt your cousin took the coach that conveyed you both here?" he asked.

"No," Blanche told him. "The broken axle on Lady Wellwood's carriage won't be mended for a day or so, according to the wheelwright."

"Ah. Would it be too much to hope that the only conveyance available to them was a rundown coach with a pair of bone-knockers to pull it?" Angus raised one black brow in humorous query.

Blanche gave a half smile. "Knowing the pair of them, that hope may well be justified, Angus. But surely they will change their team at the first convenient inn, and who knows what kind of animals they'll be able to obtain there."

"Just how much of the ready did Prudie abscond with, anyway?"

"All of it," Blanche said, lifting her reticule from the dressing table and turning it upside down to show that it was indeed empty.

Angus whistled through his teeth. "Not very considerate of Prudie, was it, to leave you ill and with not a sou to your name? Are you sure you want to recover the little minx? If she were my cousin I would be tempted to give her a sound thrashing for playing such a trick. How much exactly was 'all of it'?"

"Almost all of the ten guineas Uncle sent us for the journey, plus the three I had saved from our sojourn in Harrogate. I only dipped into our funds to give Lady Wellwood's coachman enough for the coach

52

to be mended and for our luncheon yesterday—and the rooms for Prudie and myself here, of course."

"Not a vast amount for such a journey."

"No," she admitted. "Uncle Wilmont is something of a, er, skint."

Angus grinned at her plain speaking.

"I must recover her. I will have no hope of a home, otherwise. . . . When will you be ready to leave?" Blanche asked. Her anxiety to pursue the foolish youngsters pushed the lingering effects she was experiencing from her tooth loss completely out of her mind.

"I'm going to find us some riding attire first. I can't be seen again in this damned costume. I'll try to procure a set of clothes that will fit you, too. Perhaps the groom will have some spare togs he could be persuaded to donate to a good cause," Angus said with a twinkle in his eyes.

Blanche wrinkled her nose at the thought of wearing the groom's cast-off clothing, but, nodded her head slightly, nevertheless.

"Perhaps we should extend our masquerade and I should dress in your skirts until we're well clear of here and not take any chance that Wolverton's men are still hanging about town looking for me."

Blanche leveled a glacial stare at him. "You are surely in jest, Dalglish."

"Not at all," he assured her with a straight face. He folded his arms, crossed one booted leg over the other and leaned against the wall as he watched for her reaction. He had a sudden irresistible desire to provoke this cool creature and startle her out of her calm composure.

"Then feel free to help yourself to one of the garments in my valise. I doubt that my skirts will reach to your ankles, though," she remarked serenely. "The sooner we disguise ourselves, if you are indeed set on this masquerade, the sooner we can be on our way."

Angus laughed. "We'll both need some nourishment first," he said practically. "Do you think you can manage to eat this morning?"

"I think I can manage some soft toast, eggs, and tea," Blanche said deliberately after running her tongue over her teeth and the inside of her mouth. "And perhaps some soup, too, if it's not too greasy."

"I shall just step down to the kitchens to ask them to send up a suitable tray for us, then. You'll be all right while I'm gone?"

Blanche smiled ironically. She had managed to look after herself perfectly well for years before Angus Dalglish leapt into her life a few short hours ago.

"I'm perfectly fit now," she said, standing up from the dressing table stool abruptly, then swaying on her feet. She put a hand up to her head. Angus moved forward agilely to catch her before she fainted. Strong arms closed about her as he picked her up and carried her back to the bed where he deposited her unceremoniously.

"Now you see what comes of being silly. You haven't eaten in what?—over two days. Rest here and don't move," he wagged a finger at her as he straightened up. "I shall be right back."

"Why are you showing so much concern?"

"You forget. I can't claim your uncle's reward without his daughter in tow—and you're the one who can recognize the little darling. And the one who can recognize her improbable beau, for that matter."

"Angus."

"Yes?"

"Take care, won't you."

"Don't worry about me, I have the devil's own luck," he said with a wicked grin lighting his face as he left the room.

Chapter 4

Encountering nary a soul, wandering or otherwise, Angus carefully made his way down the back stairs to the kitchens where he used his charm on the serving wench to order up breakfast. After instructing buxom young Betsy to send the food up to the room he was sharing with his "sister" as soon as it was ready, Angus cautiously peered round the back door into the deserted inn yard. He slipped out and stealthily made his way to the stables where he found the head groom and one of the stable hands amenable to an early morning game of chance.

Angus was not best pleased that the game the lads wanted to play was dice. Dice was too unpredictable, depending entirely on luck. He preferred card games that required some skill. After several see-saw rounds Angus lost the few coins he had left in his pockets after paying off the toothdrawer. He saw that he had nothing left to put up, except his clothes. So, with an inward groan, he wagered his new boots of soft Spanish leather that he was excessively fond of. He had had them made specially as part of his disguise and did not want to part with them. Luck shifted and the old bones rolled several times in his favor. He managed to throw enough winners to regain the few shillings he had lost.

"You've the devil's own luck, guv'nor," the groom whistled through the gap between his front teeth when Angus threw a seven again. Angus found that he liked the lads. He didn't want to chouse them out of their modest wages. And so he proposed that they abandon the game, calling it even. He asked if they would be willing to trade some of their working clothes for his outmoded, but rather costly, jacket and breeches. They were amenable to this idea.

He decided to keep the cloak of fine new wool he had worn last night. It would come in handy against the chill beginning to set in during these late autumn days. Although it was black, it had no other particularly distinguishing feature that anyone who had participated in last night's revels could recognize.

The groom brought out a rather ragged and stained set of old clothes that Angus knew would not please Blanche. Nevertheless, she would have to make do. For himself, there was a pair of stained buckskins and a heavy, rough jacket as well as a torn, old oilskin to provide protection should the weather turn rainy.

The few shillings he had left would just have to see them through the day. If they were not able to come up with the runaway couple this day, he would have to find a card game when they stopped for the night, if he were to finance this mad dash that might take them all the way to Scotland.

Angus knew it was no good trying to retrieve the hard-going sorrel he had ridden into Skipton from the stables at the Swan with the possibility of Wolverton's men still milling around. But he managed to talk the Hen and Feathers's groom into hiring him a pair of hacks in exchange for the pair of spurs he had worn over his boots. He could not continue to wear them—they had attracted attention last night and he had to conceal them or dispose of them anyway.

When the stable boy led out two rather broken-down-looking nags from the back of the Hen and Feathers's stables, Angus groaned.

"Not what one would call high-blooded bits of flesh and bone, are they?" Angus muttered under his breath as he ran his hand down the left flank of the flea-bitten gray mare Blanche would have to ride.

"Nay, they ain't high-blooded cattle. But they's good goers, guv'nor," the lad assured him.

Angus returned to the bedroom clad in the buckskins and the rather worse-for-wear riding jacket to find Blanche sitting at the dressing table, sedately eating her small breakfast of toast and egg, and consuming a pot of tea. He grinned to see how she stiffened and thrust her chin in the air as he came into the room after only a preemptory knock.

Angus leaned his wide shoulders back against the

door he had just closed, watching with amusement at the changing emotions flitting across Blanche's face.

"Don't go all starchy on me, now, Fleur. Just when I thought you were a right 'un."

Blanche's breath caught in her throat as she gazed up at the sight of Dalglish standing with his shoulders spanning the doorway. He was freshly shaved and the buckskin trousers he now wore stretched tightly across his long, muscular legs. She was impressed by his solid strength. He filled the room with his presence, bringing the fresh, brisk air from outside into the room with him. A small voice in her head, barely a whisper, told her that here was a man she could rely on.

"I don't know what you mean," she said in a cautious tone.

Angus laughed and threw the clothes he held in her direction. "Here. Change into these when you've finished eating . . . I'm starved. Where's my food?"

Blanche indicated the tray on the small table near the bed.

"Splendid!" he said, walking briskly across the room and rubbing his hands together with anticipation as he saw the tray loaded down with a beef steak, gravy, half a loaf of bread, a slab of butter, a pot of marmalade, a tankard of frothy ale, and a steaming pot of coffee standing ready for him. Angus dug in with relish and quickly wolfed down the food. Blanche watched him eat with amazement.

"Are you always so ravenous? It was only a short time ago that you finished off the food I had with me." Blanche held a flowered teacup daintily in one hand as she turned to stare at him. She primly sipped at her tea.

"I'm not the one who has been suffering from the toothache. My appetite is a healthy one, in food and, ah, other things, as well, which you'll find as we travel together," Angus quipped when he could speak again.

"Your manners, Mister Dalglish, leave something to be desired. They are quite—"

He put a hand up to silence her. "I know—bovine. So you've said before. You must blame it on my inadequate education, interrupted as it was when I was still only a callow youth. Whereas you, Fleur, have the manners of a queen!" He lifted his tankard of ale in a toast and bared his white teeth in a wide, mocking smile, then began to drink thirstily.

"The manners of a queen? Despite the impropriety of allowing you to remain in my room all night? I think not—unless you compare me to the consort of our Regent, in which case your compliment is a decided set down."

"Ah, but such regal creatures as queens are a law unto themselves. They make the rules, they don't have to follow them. They are such exalted beings that they can afford to overlook the conventions that apply to lesser mortals."

"You, sir, are a sophist and a tease," Blanche said with a slight smile.

"I'm happy to see you're feeling better, at any rate."

Seeing her quirked brow, Angus continued provocatively. "I do have a stake in your health, you know, if I'm to earn that generous reward you promised. All the more chance of catching your Prudie before the youngsters tie the knot, if you're feeling fit as a fiddle. I've arranged to hire mounts for us, and I'll be ready to set out as soon as you've changed into those togs."

Blanche put down her teacup and picked up the bundle Angus had thrown at her feet. She lifted the garments gingerly and held them away from her nose. She could detect the strong odor of horse and sweat permeating the clothing. "I suppose I must wear these filthy things!" She shook her head despairingly.

"Certainly!" At her doubtful look, Angus continued, "Dam—dash it, you want to catch up to your cousin as soon as may be, don't you?"

"Of course."

"Then, you must dress as a man so that we can make faster time."

"They smell most vilely of the stables," Blanche said, wrinkling her nose and glancing disparagingly at the articles.

His smile flickered briefly. The regal creature before him reminded of nothing so much as a kitten as she stood there with her noble nose wrinkled up.

"Would you excuse me, please?" she asked politely and waited for him to leave the room.

"What for?" Angus asked obtusely, still chewing his food.

"I have agreed to wear these—these *rags,* now I must change into them."

61

"Is that all? I'll turn my back. No need to go all missish."

"I am not *missish!*" Blanche insisted through clenched teeth. "But a woman does like to have *some* privacy when she is changing her clothes."

"Come on, Fleur. I won't look," Angus said, getting up from the chair where he had been sitting astride. He turned the chair around, swung his legs over, and sat down so that his back was to her and began addressing his food again.

It was only because they must make haste, she told herself, that she abandoned all modesty and actually pulled on the foul clothes in his presence. First, she kicked off her shoes and pulled on the worn and soiled leather breeches over her own stockings under her skirt. Then, cautiously, with several peeps at Dalglish's back while she was about it, she reached behind her and unbuttoned her woollen dress, let it fall to the floor, and quickly slipped the groom's dirty gray smock over her head and with deft fingers tied up the ribbons at the neck. Then she wound the spotted neck scarf about her throat and knotted it. She hastily thrust her arms through the stained brown leather jerkin, pulled on the short, square cut, corduroy coat, and shrugged it over her shoulders.

The down-at-heel ankle boots presented a problem. They were at least two sizes too big. She solved the problem by stuffing a spare pair of stockings in the toes.

"May I turn around now?" Angus asked politely, after he finished his mammoth meal.

"You may," she answered.

"Ah," he said, putting his hand over his heart and trying to stifle his laughter. "You look ravishing, my dear."

"No need to be sarcastic. I know I must look like a performer in a raree-show."

Angus stepped forward to hand her the groom's cocked hat of moss green felt, and watched critically as she tried to push her hair up underneath. Despite her efforts, a few strands fell down and Blanche impatiently tried to tuck them up again.

"We may need to do something about your hair."

Blanche sent him a withering glance. "That's what I'm trying to do."

"Ah, ha. I've got it!" Angus snapped his fingers. He took two quick strides across the room and grabbed up the wig he had discarded the previous night.

"You can wear this!" He smiled with unholy glee at the expression on Blanche's face.

"You must be mad! Do you expect me to be a figure of fun? Those long, black curls would look ridiculous! I would attract the attention we're seeking to avoid."

"No, no. We'll cut the curls off. You see." Angus took a small, sharp knife from his pocket and proceeded to hack at the curls.

"Stop! You'll ruin it!" Blanche protested. "Here, let me." She took the wig from his hands.

"Why, it looks and feels like real hair!" she exclaimed as she picked up the wig and walked over to

63

her tapestry workbag. She produced a pair of embroidery scissors, and proceeded to trim and cut the hair until she had produced a somewhat natural-looking shape to resemble a modern style.

"It *is* real hair! The last time I played cards, I scalped my victim," he said with a leer as he watched Blanche concentrating on her task.

She looked up at his mockery. "Did you?" she asked in feigned astonishment. "What a mess that must have made!"

"I never do things by halves, you see, Fleur."

"Remind me never to play cards with you!"

"Ah, yes. Quite in the modern style," Angus teased as she finished snipping at the wig. "Byron himself would not disdain to wear your creation."

Blanche shot him a triumphant glance and stepped over to the pier glass to adjust the wig over her hair.

Angus came up behind her and reached out to tweek the curls in place round her cheeks. "No need to take such care," he said. "You're not dressing for a ball, you know. Since you'll be riding a hot, sweaty horse for hours on end with the wind in your face, I daresay it won't matter by the end of the day."

She blanched at his words. Although she had told Angus she could ride, it was several years since she had ridden hard and long. She hadn't done much more than amble along behind Prudie, who was a poor rider, for the past few years and the prospect of a day in the saddle was suddenly daunting. Despite her anxieties, she put aside her qualms, lifted her chin in the air, and said with an admirably lighthearted air, "Lead on, Macduff."

"Let's see you walk first."

"Walk?"

"Don't want to give away the show, now do we, if you walk with too much of a wiggle?"

"Wiggle!" Blanche uttered in low, stilted accents and lifted her head to stare up at him. "I have never walked with a *wiggle* in my life."

Angus concealed a smile behind his hand to see so much emotion from his cool, silver lady. "Unless I miss my guess, you've never walked around in breeches before in your life, either! Now show me how you can walk with a bit of swagger."

She cast him a withering glance and walked across the room.

"Too stiff by half. Relax. Let your shoulders roll a bit. . . . That's better," he said as Blanche began to imitate the gait of a certain handsome, young farmer she remembered who always came strutting up to her uncle's manor house to pay his quarterly rents.

"That's good!"

"Just mimicking you," she said sweetly, looking back at him over her shoulder.

Angus gave a shout of laughter.

When Angus deemed she had mastered the swagger, Blanche threw her few belongings into her valise, along with the incriminating black half mask and false mustache Angus had worn last night, and they departed. She hastily scribbled a note to Lady Wellwood's groom, informing him that she and Miss

Wilmont would be visiting friends in the neighborhood for a time and that those friends would convey them both to Heywood. He was to return home to his mistress in Harrogate with Lady Wellwood's carriage when it was mended.

It was scarcely more than an hour since they had awakened when Blanche and Angus left the Hen and Feathers. Blanche was thankful that she had paid the shot when she had arrived yesterday before Prudie had nipped away with their money. She didn't know how she could have faced the landlord with an empty purse, never mind how she could face him in her disguise.

It was well before eight o'clock and none of the other guests were yet stirring. Blanche straightened her spine, pulled her shoulders back, and tried to walk like a man, the way Angus wanted her to. From the way her companion's shoulders were shaking, she judged that he was laughing at her, but she rolled on anyway.

When they reached the stables and she saw her horse, Blanche belatedly realized that she was expected to ride astride in her disguise. With a muttered "oh dear!" and a whispered "I hope you're an easy goer, girl," to the mare, she put her left foot in the stirrup, swung her right leg over, and mounted the animal.

Betsy, one of the serving girls, came running out of the inn with a large bundle in her arms, as Angus and Blanche were walking their horses out of the inn yard.

"Here ye be, surr," the blushing girl said, smiling up at Angus as she handed him a basket covered by a large checkered cloth. " 'Tis the food ye wanted, surr—the chicken and bread and cheese."

"Ah, you remembered our picnic, Betsy. Good girl," Angus said, leaning down from his horse and pinching the girl's apple-red cheek after he slipped her one of his precious few coins. He smiled down at her easily.

Blanche, chaffing at the delay, saw how the bold, buxom girl dimpled up at Dalglish's attentions and thrust her chest forward. The girl's blouse was very low cut. Blanche almost blushed to see how the girl wore her woollen shawl tied beneath her assets, leaving herself sadly exposed to the early morning chill.

"I hopes ye and yer young friend will call in 'ere on yer return journey, surr," Betsy said flirtatiously, hoping the handsome gentleman would remember her and stop at the Hen and Feathers when he was next in these parts.

"Save a bed for us, Betsy," Angus said with a gleam in his eye.

Blanche looked on with disgust at this bold byplay.

Betsy slid a curious, interested glance in Blanche's direction, wondering if she should solicit the young gent's custom, too. To judge by his dress, the lad didn't look as if he had two ha'pennies to rub together, though. Pity, Betsy thought. Why, the young lad was almost *pretty,* he was so handsome, with his midnight black curls and striking light eyes. The two gents were as handsome as they could hold together, in Betsy's opinion, despite their rather worn dress. She glanced again at the younger man's pale, downy-soft cheek and sighed. The lad was even more appealing to her than his darker and more rugged-looking companion. She gave Blanche a bold smile.

Blanche looked completely disconcerted. Good lord! Blanche thought, understanding Betsy's actions, she takes me for a man!

"Ah, Fleur, I see I shall have to warn you about the propensities of barmaids and serving wenches— for your own protection," Angus murmured as he watched this bit of action with an amused smile on his face. He turned his horse about and rode out into the road. When they were through the gates to the inn yard, Blanche brought her horse up and they rode side by side once they reached the road.

"What does a man like you want with a girl like that?" Blanche asked genuinely perplexed.

"When a woman indicates her, ah, interest, it would be churlish of me to spurn her, now wouldn't it?" he answered. His dark eyes were gleaming with laughter, she saw.

"And do women indicate their, 'ah, interest,' often?" she couldn't stop herself from asking.

"Now how can I answer that, without you thinking me either an arrogant coxcomb or an unconscionable braggart?"

Blanche realized her error in alluding to the subject and turned her head away without answering.

They quickly reached the outskirts of town and all conversation was at an end as Angus quickened their pace and they rode away at a fairly fast clip. The horses weren't worth much but, being fresh, the animals did have a certain amount of go. Blanche and Angus left Skipton behind and rode out along an open country road heading for higher ground, leaving Yorkshire behind and heading into Cumbria.

They stopped twice in small towns not far from Skipton to inquire about the runaways, but with no luck. Soon they were again in open country and miles from any towns where Prudie and Bartie could have procured a change of horses. They rode on.

"I wish we could change these two slugs at the first decent coaching inn we come to," Angus said to Blanche when they paused briefly to water their flagging horses. "However, until our fortunes come about, I'm afraid we'll have to make do."

"This mare is a friendly animal, at least," Blanche said, as she leaned forward and gave the flea-bitten gray a hard pat and a good scratch on its neck.

"We need a name for you, halfling," Angus said easily. He took a drink from a flask he had had the forethought to refill at the inn and handed it to Blanche. "Here. Drink."

"I'm afraid that I can't help you there. I've not your experience of making things up." She put her lips to the flask and took a large swallow, longing for a drink of water. "Ugh!" she sputtered, "what is this?"

"Brandy. It will do your sore mouth good. How about Flowers?" he asked, ignoring her set down.

Blanche handed the flask back to him with a cool look and considered his name for her. "If you must," she said with a resigned air, deciding that she was in this game of concealing her identity so deeply already that she couldn't object to this further subterfuge.

"You know, you're younger than I thought," Angus said, studying her face and seeing in her smooth white complexion more youth than age. He could not see a wrinkle nor any other kind of flaw. "How old are you anyway, Fleur?"

"Five and twenty," Blanche admitted candidly. She bit back a smile at Dalglish's look of astonishment. "An aging spinster firmly on the shelf, you see."

Angus made an impatient, inarticulate note in his throat. "No one would take you for an aging spinster."

"It's my disguise that makes you say so."

"Yes, that black wig quite changes your looks."

"Ah, but you know the truth of the old, gray-haired woman who hides beneath this wig."

"No. The black curls round your cheeks do make you look young—eighteen or nineteen—but your own hair gives you the look of beauty fully matured." He surprised himself with this fulsome compliment, but it was no more than the truth. The black wig did emphasize the youth of her face, but her own silver hair gave her a more regal, dignified appearance and brought out the beauty of those striking eyes of hers.

"With the emphasis on the word *mature*," she said,

70

dismissing his words as so much Spanish coin. "And you, Angus?" she asked, in truth quite curious to learn his age. "How old are you?"

"Seven and twenty. I could have sworn that . . ." he left the rest unsaid, realizing almost too late how undiplomatic it would have been to give utterance to his thought that last night he had been sure she was *years* older than he.

"You thought I was your senior by a dozen years, no doubt," she accurately guessed his thought anyway.

"Not that many," he assured her.

"No doubt I am your senior in good sense," she issued the icy set down with nary an expression marring the perfection of her pale alabaster features. She was thinking of his hot-tempered behavior at the card game the previous night and his unconventional life.

"Aye, no doubt you are," he said, irritated for a reason he couldn't fathom.

He kept looking at her. "Why are you staring so?" she asked finally.

"I keep seeing a boy instead of the woman I know you to be. It's damned disconcerting to see a woman transformed so thoroughly into the opposite sex. Especially a staid and proper lady like you."

Blanche's silvery laugh rang out. "Serves you right, then, for turning me into one. 'Twas your idea, after all."

They rode on through the crisp late autumn day. Blanche recalled that it was the first day of November, All Saints' Day, and she was amazed that it was

71

so mild for this time of year. There were gray clouds hanging low over the almost barren hills, but the sunshine was doing its best to break through. The patchy mists floating above the little river they were following were lifting higher with each mile they covered.

They rode on over hill and through dale until Blanche thought she would collapse from exhaustion. She no longer felt the soreness induced by the unaccustomed motion of the horse that had plagued her after the first hour. Her hinder portions had long since become numb. There was a tingling in her toes that told her her feet must still be attached to her legs, though she couldn't feel them. And her mouth was still tender but she fought against the need to call to Dalglish to stop for a rest. They must press on and perhaps they could even overtake Prudie today, she told herself optimistically.

Just as Blanche thought she could not bear to sit her horse a moment longer, Angus called to her, "Over there. Across that hedge there's a stream where we may have our picnic and water the horses." And he wheeled his horse away before she could vouchsafe a yea or a nay.

She watched in amazement as Dalglish urged his mount to take the rather low hedge in a fluid jump, horse and rider merging as one. He pulled up on the other side, waiting for her, urging her on, not knowing that she had never jumped a hedge before in her life, nor anything else, for that matter.

Blanche would never admit that her besetting sin was pride; she was bound and determined not to let

72

Dalglish see her flag. After all, speed was of the essence if she were to succeed in recovering Prudie before her cousin and young Waddle could be married over the anvil in Gretna Green, and to let her companion see that she could not "go the pace" she was bound and determined not to do! Therefore she set the flea-bitten gray at the hedge and with great surprise she felt the animal rise beneath her for the jump. She closed her eyes and clasped her arms about the mare's neck, holding on for dear life.

Despite her efforts, Blanche found herself on the ground a moment later.

She landed in a pile of brightly colored autumn leaves covering the soft turf. But even with such a cushioned landing, the shock to her system rendered her almost insensible for a few moments.

Angus was beside her before she could sort out what happened, putting his hands gently on either side of her face and stroking across her cheeks with his thumbs. "Are you all right, Fleur?" he asked anxiously.

Her eyes flew open and she looked up to see his black eyes wide with concern only inches from her own. She was too stunned to speak for the moment but managed to nod in answer to his question.

"Oh! I've lost the wig!" she exclaimed, putting her hand up to the back of her head.

"Yes, but that doesn't matter. Are you hurt?" he asked.

She was glad to look away from his concerned gaze. She tested her various limbs and found that all in all, it was her pride that was bruised more than anything. To retrieve her dignity she complained, "That was a very tall hedge, Dalglish, almost a small tree. It was foolishness for either of us to attempt to jump such an impossible obstacle." She glared up at him as he continued to hold her head between his hands, his long fingers gently moving over her forehead and down the sides of her face. A smile crept into his eyes at her words.

" 'Twas a mere bush you jumped. How came you to fall off?"

"Probably because I've lost the feeling in the lower half of my body," she said with a small smile.

She pushed his hands away and sat up, then reached for the wig and her cap that had fallen nearby. She arranged them neatly on her head, then attempted to rise. When Angus saw the difficulty she was having, he came to her assistance, took hold of her elbows and heaved her to her feet.

A suspicion of the truth dawned on him. "You're not a very experienced rider, are you, Fleur?"

Blanche turned a determined look upon him. "I can ride well enough when I have to. 'Tis just that I have not had much practice lately. And I have never before ridden astride."

"But that should have made it easier to hang on!"

She attempted to move away from his supporting arm but her legs refused to obey her and she staggered against him. He was nothing loath to receive her in his arms.

"If it's embraces you would prefer, my dear, you

74

have only to say so." He leered down at her, though he was immediately taken aback to see the "boy" gazing back at him with cold eyes.

"I thought we had decided that I was beyond the age for dalliance. Besides, you hardly have time to waste on a penniless spinster when there's that reward to claim. We must rescue Prudie before she and Waddle are married!"

Blanche pulled herself out of his grip and managed to recover the use of her numb legs. She walked determinedly, if stiffly, to the little river where her horse had wandered for a drink. "No need to overdo your concern for me, Dalglish," she threw over her shoulder as she went. "My uncle will amply reward you if you help me recover Prudie, and I know you don't want to miss your chance at that reward."

"Aye, no doubt you're right, ma'am. I'm a heedless fellow—except where my pockets are concerned." Angus clamped his lips shut on an angry retort. The icy lady would spurn his concern, would she? Well *he* certainly had nothing to gain by dallying with an aged spinster like her, he thought with a flash of temper.

He watched her retreating back broodingly. Those long, shapely legs of hers showed to advantage in breeches, he had to concede. She presented quite a tempting picture from the rear, even dressed in such disreputable garments. What would she look like in a proper pair of tight-fitting pantaloons? he wondered, his temperature rising as he imagined the sight. When the dibs were in tune perhaps he would purchase a pair for her, just so he could have the pleasure of looking at her in them.

Although she had first appeared to him in the guise of a plain, elderly spinster, Miss Blanche Charolais was not without charms that would stir a man's blood despite the frosty, staid exterior she presented. It began to dawn on him that perhaps he was not as immune to her as he had thought last night and this morning. Otherwise, perhaps he would not have agreed to accompany her on this journey that was bound to throw them together so intimately.

The masquerade he had proposed as a lark, as much as anything, had not been such a good idea, either, for he was likely to find himself hoist with his own petard. His companion was his opposite in many ways—as cool as he was hot, as serene as he was restless—yet he was feeling irresistibly attracted. He could only hope that they would find her cousin, the imprudent Miss Prudence, before too many more hours had passed.

They wasted no time eating their small picnic by the stream. As she thanked Angus for remembering to provide them with food for the journey, it was on the tip of Blanche's tongue to request that they ride more slowly, explaining that she wasn't up to anything too strenuous. But pride held her back. She refused to admit any weakness to him. She had been shaken, too, when he had comforted her after her ignominious fall. She didn't want to admit it, but she had enjoyed the feel of his warm hands caressing her face. Her mind clamped down on the thought; she *would not* allow herself to become attracted to this adventurer, no matter how blessed he was with good looks, or how much concern he showed for her.

They were soon on the road again, riding doggedly through the rough countryside, meeting few travelers along the way.

"We shall stop for the night in the next sizable town," Angus said after a while, turning his horse and bringing the animal alongside Blanche's gray.

Fallen leaves crunched under their horses' feet. The sun was beginning to sink behind the hills in the late autumn afternoon and the air had grown distinctly chillier.

"What!" Blanche protested perversely, immediately taking issue with him, though moments before she had been longing for Angus to call a halt to their ride this day. "You can't mean to stop now. We must catch up to them as soon as possible. We've undoubtedly gained on them today."

"Yes, I'm sure we have. We've ridden hard—harder than you realize. It will be dark before too long. We must either change horses or give these nags a rest. And you know that we have no means to hire a new pair of hacks until I've had a chance to recoup."

"But, then, how can we afford to stop? Shouldn't we just keep these mounts?" Blanche asked, puzzled.

"These bone-knockers have had it. Just look at them." He pointed to the two horses walking along, both covered with a light sheen of sweat, their heads hanging down under the slackened reins. "Besides, it's November now, remember? It's too dark and cold to go much farther this day. Come now. Don't be perverse, woman. Admit you would welcome a rest and some substantial fare as much as I." A dangerous light flared in Angus's eyes as he spoke. He didn't care to argue about this matter. His companion must have an iron constitution—or an iron will—he marveled, if she could make such a fast recovery from her ordeal of the previous night. He was bone tired himself.

Blanche saw the folly of arguing with him and admitted to herself that she was exhausted. She straightened in the saddle and said reasonably, "Perhaps you're right, Angus. We can start out all that much earlier tomorrow morning." Then she dropped her reserve and turned a worried look on him. "We will catch them tomorrow, won't we?"

Angus, realizing how important her quest was to her own future, knew that she must be living on her nerves at the moment, however good she was at concealing it. He reached over and covered her hand with his where it rested on her horse's briddle. "I hope so. I certainly hope so." He removed his hand after gazing at her averted profile for a moment. "Now, remember, you're a boy. Act like one when we stop."

"Yes, Mister Dalglish, sir," Blanche said, reaching up to tug on her cap. She dipped her head in his direction and promised to be inconspicuous.

"I'll take rooms for us, then I must locate a card

game so that we can pay for our accommodations and an evening meal.''

"Gamble for the money, you mean?''

"Of course. How else are we to come by any blunt? You have nothing to sell to finance this journey, do you?''

Blanche gave him a glacial stare. "You ask such an improper thing just to get a rise out of me, but I refuse to give you the satisfaction." She turned her chin up and looked away from him.

"Brrr! You're a cold one, my dear, not to mention prickly as a pear. A man would freeze if he came too close to you." At his words, Angus shuddered dramatically.

"And you, sir, are too hot. A woman would be burned to cinders if she stayed overlong in your vicinity.''

"Touché! So we're opposites, heh?''

"As black and white.''

"They say opposites attract, my dear Fleur.''

"Do they? How perverse of them. I would have thought that opposites repel.''

"We shall have to put it to the test sometime soon," Angus said, looking at her with such a fiery glance that Blanche's cheeks flushed uncomfortably.

Chapter 5

Blanche and Angus walked their tired horses into a moderately sized town in the fading light of late afternoon. They had covered a goodly number of miles and they were tired, thirsty, and hungry, not to mention chilled to the bone.

Angus was again cautioning Blanche to remember the role she was playing and to keep her voice low when he spotted a men's haberdashery shop just about to close up for the evening. The proprietor was even then extinguishing the lantern hanging from the shop sign over the door.

Angus quickly dismounted and threw his reins to Blanche. "Hold my horse. I'll be right back." With openmouth surprise she watched him dash into the shop.

When Angus emerged a few minutes later, he wore a new bottle green hacking jacket over charcoal gray riding breeches, and had a clean, white cravat hastily tied round his neck.

Blanche stared to see the smart town buck grin widely and give a wave in her direction. Dalglish was completely refurbished from head to toe in fashionable gentleman's togs, and he was carrying a large parcel under his arm. Her night spirit had again changed his appearance, she mused wryly.

"Well, that's it. I've spent our very last penny to reoutfit us both," Angus said as he gathered his reins from her hands and remounted his horse. He hoped Blanche wouldn't notice the absence of the gold signet ring he usually wore on his left hand. She wouldn't have known that he always carried the crested watch he had inherited from his grandfather in his pocket, and thus wouldn't realize that it no longer resided there. He had pledged both items in exchange for the new clothing, promising to return on the morrow to redeem them, confident that he could do so after a successful night at the tables.

"Reoutfit us *both?*" He must be mad, she thought incredulously. "But I have my own clothes, my gowns and the other things I will need when I throw off this disguise in my traveling case. Why have you bought me new things?" Blanche asked, puzzled by his odd action.

"Well, you've let it be known that you are none too pleased with the shabby togs you're wearing now. You'll look, and feel, more the thing in these," Angus said, tapping the package he carried with one long finger. "Should be easier to carry off your disguise, too."

"You've bought me a set of *men's* clothes? Why on earth—?"

"You'll see," Angus said a little sheepishly. He couldn't admit to her that it was for the pleasure of seeing her in form-fitting pantaloons that he had made the extravagant purchase. A slight flush crept along his cheekbones as he said, "I've no desire to play a down-at-the-heels hedgebird for longer than needs be. And any companion of mine must look the part of a well-set-up young swell."

"You're certainly impetuous, Dalglish." Blanche shook her head at him. "How are we to afford overnight accommodations, not to mention engage in that activity you're so fond of—eating—since you've spent our last penny?"

"No need to worry your bewigged head about it," Angus teased, flashing a wide grin at his companion. "I'll win enough at the card table this evening to see us through, else my name isn't Angus Dalglish Sincler, just leave it to me," he recommended with casual confidence.

He guided them to a large, well-kept inn set flush along the main roadway through town. The heavy, swinging sign of a brightly colored jeweled crown hanging out over the door proclaimed the hostelry to be the Golden Crown. Angus and Blanche road through the open doors of the great gateway of the inn, tall and wide enough for a coach to pass through, into the courtyard where they found well-maintained stables. The inn yard was a beehive of activity. A large number of carriages and wagons of all descriptions crowded the area and attendants and grooms were moving to and fro, leading out fresh teams and taking away spent ones while many travelers stood about talking or consuming glasses of ale or cups of tea brought out to them by the solicitous inn staff.

"There's nothing like an English inn, you know, Flowers," Angus said with a sigh of satisfaction as he glanced about him. "Take my word for it, I've been on the continent and they've nothing like our own homegrown variety of hostelries for good food, pleasant accommodations, and friendly innkeepers dedicated to their guests' comfort."

"I hope so," Blanche said fervently. "After the time I've spent on this horse's back today, I would like nothing so much as a soft, comfortable bed to sleep in and a well-cooked meal beforehand."

"Yes, it's a shame that English roads do not compare with English inns. Hmm. Perhaps there's a cause-and-effect relationship here. If the roads were better and travel easier, we would make better time and there would be no need for the number and variety of inns, and the solace and good cheer to be found therein."

"You sound like an expert on the nature of such accommodations."

"As a man who must travel frequently to make his living, I am."

Blanche glanced around a bit uneasily. The sight of so many people abroad, any one of whom might well discover her disguise, caused a nervous fluttering in the pit of her stomach. She stiffened her spine and composed her features, allowing no sign of her inner perturbation to show, and followed Angus as he walked his tired mount into the stables.

She had great difficulty in dismounting, so stiff was her lower body. But at a look from Angus, with one of his black brows raised in warning as much to say *I can't help you, you know,* she managed to maintain her balance and her dignity as she threw one leg over the mare's back and dismounted in admirable imitation of a suitably masculine style.

"You're pluck to the backbone," Angus whispered *sotto voce,* before turning away to hide a grin. He did feel a concern for her aches and pains, however. Damn, he hoped their quest would soon be rewarded.

Angus needed to find out where men assembled to play cards over a friendly bottle or two of wine. With that goal in mind, he struck up a conversation with a garrulous groom. He made his usual inquiries about the runaway couple. The groom had been away all day and had just come back to work so he didn't know if a couple such as Angus described had stopped at the Golden Crown. But he was a goldmine of information about when and where to find a good card game. Angus watched Blanche from the corner of his eye while she untied her valise from the back of the saddle and then turned to tell the stable hand to rub down the two horses.

"Slouch, Flowers, for God's sake. Keep your eyes on the ground and walk behind me. You're my companion, remember," Angus reminded Blanche as he motioned for her to follow him into the inn. He didn't want her marching in ramrod straight and fixing the innkeeper with that frosty, regal eye of hers and giving away the game.

"Your best dinner and rooms for the night for myself and my companion, if you please, landlord," Angus said in a hearty tone to the beaming, moon-faced innkeeper.

"I'm sorry, sir. There's a pugilistic contest to be held hereabouts tomorrow. We're almost full up," the friendly innkeeper informed him apologetically.

"A boxing match? I wish I could stay to witness it. I assume wagers are being taken," Angus said in an interested voice.

"Oh, yes indeed, sir. Why, some's got wagers as high as five-hundred guineas riding on the outcome."

"Oh? There's been heavy betting on the match, has there?" Angus queried. "I would like to get in on the action, then. Have you any suggestions to offer about where my, ah, young friend here and I could find overnight accommodation nearby? We've spent a weary day in the saddle and are not anxious to ride on to another town."

The landlord's glance shifted to Blanche. He ran his eyes over her in a knowledgeable manner, though he did not penetrate her disguise. Even in the borrowed stable hand's togs, there was something about her carriage that bespoke quality, if only the quality of an upper-class servant. The landlord's respect for her companion, or master as the case might be, therefore increased.

Feeling the landlord's eyes upon her, Blanche immediately allowed her shoulders to slump and nonchalantly looked away from his keen gaze, letting her eyes wander about the room.

"Well," said the landlord, scratching the stubble on his round chin, "there's a small room at the back of the stables that'll be free. But I doubt that it would do for the likes of your honor—it won't be what you're used to, sir. Nor, I daresay, your companion, either."

Without a glance at Blanche, Angus said, "Seems we must make do with what's to hand, then. I'm too weary to go farther tonight when we must be off at first light tomorrow. Yes, I think we really must make do."

"Right you are, sir," the innkeeper said, turning aside to pull out his neat, well-kept ledger for Angus to sign.

"Come along, Flowers," Angus called over his shoulder to Blanche as he followed the obliging man out of the inn back to the stables again.

Never, never had she felt like clobbering a fellow being, Blanche thought to herself as she trailed along, her fists clenched at her sides. Did her companion have not even a fleeting acquaintance with decorum? Last night had been an aberration—there were exceptional circumstances that had forced them to share a room. She had excused herself with a clear conscience—she had been too ill to abide by the strict rules of propriety. But sharing only one room *now* was certainly improper, and *would* put her in a compromising situation.

If it weren't for the fact that she was almost out on her feet, she was so tired, Blanche would have dug in her heels and demanded that they try another inn. She feared the world would consider her ruined, if it learned that she had shared a room with a man— and undoubtedly the fact that he was such a wild, devilish-looking adventurer, would see her doubly condemned. No matter that *she* was an unattractive, too-old spinster.

However, *she* would know that she had done nothing to merit such censure. She would strive to maintain her dignity, her poise, and not let Angus see just how much he ruffled her composure. *Ah, well,* she shrugged her shoulders, *what does it matter? I will never marry.*

She decided that the best policy was to conceal her feelings about the matter from Dalglish. If she were any judge, the man was entirely too sure of himself, as it was. He already seemed to be enjoying himself at her expense. Blanche decided not to give him the satisfaction of seeing how his continuing close proximity was beginning to make her uneasy.

And that was odd, she mused. Now she was coming to know him better, she would have expected to feel more relaxed in his presence. She had not been much disturbed when he suddenly appeared in her room, after all. But the longer she was with him, the more unsettled she felt.

As soon as the innkeeper left them alone in the room at the back of the stables, she turned and said with a note of ironic congratulation in her voice, "You have managed marvelously well, Dalglish, in obtaining these well-appointed accommodations for us.''

Blanche looked around at the almost bare room and was relieved to note that there were *two* narrow bunks shoved against opposite walls in the small room. ''How can I thank you?''

''Don't bother trying to wrack your brain for a suitable paean of praise, my dear. I could not have pressed the innkeeper for two rooms. You know we haven't a penny between the two of us. As I see it, we had no other choice. We are lucky to have this.'' Angus spread his arms wide and gestured at the room. ''And we're doubly fortunate that the fellow didn't demand payment beforehand.''

He stretched his arms above his head. ''I'm too fagged, in any event, to travel any farther tonight. . . . You must have a constitution of solid iron, if you can contemplate going on somewhere else after the journey today on top of what you went through last night.''

''After last night's invasion of my room and this—improper arrangement—I can only conclude you know nothing of propriety.'' She turned a cold shoulder on him.

Angus clamped his lips shut on a hot rejoinder at her cold ingratitude. ''I recommend you change into those new togs while I'm away, since you're so fond of your privacy. Such an 'arrangement' should suit your notions of propriety.''

''Where are you going?'' Blanche turned to ask with a composure she was far from feeling.

"To see if I can find anyone who remembers seeing your precious cousin and her beau in the stables here. This place is too small to support more than one inn, but perhaps there are one or two livery stables where they could have found a team of fresh horses for hire. After all, this town is on the main road to Scotland and, from all we could learn on our way here, your cousin and her companions haven't changed their cattle since they set out from Skipton. I'll make inquiries. And I'll try to order up some victuals for us on tick," he said over his shoulder as he quit the room, slamming the door behind him in his irritation at her and unknowingly knocking the door askew on its hinges and dislodging the flimsy lock.

Angus rubbed his chin as he left her. "The devil!" he muttered as he stomped away. "That female is getting under my skin! I've no time for such nonsense!"

Blanche sank down on the bed to rest her exhausted limbs, shaking her head over the situation she found herself in. She couldn't really blame Dalglish. It had been at her suggestion that he had agreed to accompany her, after all. She fell back on the bed exhausted and slept soundly while Angus was gone. She awoke over two hours later, stiff but surprisingly refreshed, and too keyed up to sleep more.

Despite her knowledge that it was far from proper, this adventure she found herself in the midst of was sending the blood surging through her veins and making her heart beat with excitement. Angus Dalglish was an exciting man. And despite the pricking of her conscience that told her it was far from wise, she determined to put her scruples aside. To be in the company of such a man was a once-in-a-lifetime experience.

With nothing to do but wait for Angus to return, Blanche's curiosity prompted her to investigate the clothes he had bought for her so impetuously. She unwrapped the bundle he had carelessly tossed onto his bed and when she took the new white lawn shirt, buff kerseymere pantaloons and jacket of blue superfine out of their wrappings and shook them out, she decided to change into them. They were not in the height of fashion, such as similar garments made by a London tailor would have been, but they were new and clean and a distinct improvement over those she wore; Blanche excused herself, admitting how much she was enjoying this unusual adventure.

Well, she may as well derive some pleasure from it, she told herself, for there was no doubt that she would ever experience the like again. Too bad there hadn't been time—or the money—for Angus to buy her a pair of boots that fit, she thought as she admired her new garb in the cracked pier glass set beside a rickety old table in one corner of the room.

Under all her calm, cool exterior and unruffled composure, Blanche hid a romantic soul. It was quite a turn around for someone of her staid disposition to disguise herself in such a way, she thought with a laugh. And it *was* practical to travel dressed thus, as her companion had pointed out.

When Angus walked into the room, Blanche was surprised that she could have forgotten how tall and dark he was, after being in his company all day. She schooled her features to show none of the agitation she was feeling in his presence.

Angus reported that they were not far behind the eloping couple. He had learned from one of the grooms that travelers fitting the descriptions of Prudie, Waddle, and the maid remarkably well, changed not only their horses, but their carriage as well, at the Golden Crown not five hours previously. The carriage the young runaways had arrived in had had a loose wheel and it seemed that the only vehicle available for hire at that time was a rickety old gig with two bone-knockers to pull it.

"Your Prudie made quite an impression on the stable lads," Angus told her with a dry look. She stared at him, appalled at his words, imagining the scene that Prudie was capable of creating.

"What did she do this time?" Blanche asked warily.

"Appears she kicked up quite a screech when she saw the gig, but there was naught she could do about it. . . . Seems the youngsters are managing to bungle it, as I expected. We should easily catch up to them tomorrow. I told you we would make faster time by riding horseback."

"Well, you've certainly proved right thus far," Blanche said, giving him a warm look. She was impressed with Angus's astute prediction and hoped that he was correct in assuming that Prudie and her companion would muff their elopement.

Angus was pleased, and his earlier ruffled temper soothed, when he saw that Blanche had changed into the clothes he had bought. "A fine young buck you make, Flowers," he complimented her on the new outfit. He bade her walk around the room so he could see that new suit of clothes fit correctly—or so he said.

Blanche's spirits were buoyed by the news of Prudie he brought. She was more in charity with him after her rest, and was resigned to sharing the same room now. So it was a companionable duo who sat down in their shirtsleeves to enjoy a large dinner of chops cut from the rack of lamb that had been roasted in the Crown's kitchens to feed the hoard gathered for the prize fight. As well as the lamb chops, they had been served stewed chicken, turbot in wine sauce, a pigeon pie, roasted potatoes and a variety of vegetables and greens, and an apple tart covered with fresh, thick cream to finish off the lavish dinner.

"An excellent meal," Angus remarked as they polished off the food in mutual good humor. "I'll have to remember this place, if I ever pass this way again." For once Blanche was too hungry to criticize Angus for wolfing down his food, although he ate three times the amount she did in half the time.

When he was finally sated, Angus sat back in his

chair, lifted his feet to the low table he sat in front of, crossed his boots at the ankles, and sipped at the tankard of ale that had been brought with the meal. He grinned at his companion. Blanche arched a well-defined black brow at him, then lifted her long legs, now encased in the buff pantaloons, and rested her boots on the table in imitation of his casual manner. She smiled at him somewhat cockily.

"You know, you're a fast learner, Flowers. If you were wearing your wig and cap, anyone would take you for a man right now."

"Why, thank you, Dalglish," Blanche replied dryly, folding her arms across her chest and giving him a gimlet stare.

Angus laughed at her look. "I thought I ordered a bottle of claret to go with this meal. Ah, well," he said, finishing off his tankard of ale. He eased himself up from his comfortable position, stretched his tired arms and back, then picked up his new jacket of bottle green superfine and shrugged it over his broad shoulders. "I must be off, Fleur. Try to rest while I'm gone, for tomorrow we must ride hard and fast and we'll catch up to that prize pair of greenheads before they know it."

"You're off to play cards?"

"Needs must, as you know only too well. We must eat tomorrow, too." He grinned. "Are you uncomfortable being left on your own out here? I noticed just now that the door doesn't close properly and the lock doesn't seem to work, but you can prop it with a chair after I'm gone. I don't think the stable lads will bother you.'' He hesitated, seeing the look of doubt on her face. "I could leave you my pistol.''

"That won't be necessary," Blanche said with more confidence than she felt. "But thank you for the offer, Dalglish.''

"Angus, Fleur, Angus.''

"Angus, then. Thank you, Angus, but you can never tell when you'll need the pistol for, ah, 'emergencies,' as I believe you phrased it," she said with a touch of humor.

He looked at her again, thinking that she was a lady of remarkable stamina. She seemed to be completely recovered from their exhausting ride, not to mention the lingering effects of her ordeal at the hands of the toothdrawer the previous night. She stood before him now, straight and tall and graceful with her long silver hair falling back over her shoulders. He noticed that she met his gaze calmly, looking at him out of those remarkable silvery eyes of hers. He felt a strange tightening in his throat as he held her eyes.

"How can you be certain that you will win?'' she asked, her eyes not wavering from his intent stare. "Perhaps you'll lose, and be unable to pay the shot here. Then where will we be?''

"Not I, my dear," he answered, mentally shaking off the strange breathless feeling she had provoked. "You'll have to trust to my skill to bring us off safely. I always quit when I'm ahead.''

"You won't play too deep, will you, Angus?''

He gave her an ironical bow. "I will try to follow

your advice, my dear. Your superior experience perhaps makes you an expert?''

"You're so impetuous. I don't know how you keep a cool enough head for gambling.''

He grinned. "Would you like to watch for a while?''

"How could I? Surely it is considered improper for ladies to observe such play.''

He cocked a black brow at her. "Ah, but you aren't a lady.''

At her look of blank astonishment, Angus reminded her, "You're a boy—and a most handsome one.''

He looked her over critically as she stood before him clad in the new male attire. "You'll be closely observed. We must make sure your disguise is impenetrable,'' Angus insisted. "The candlelight will undoubtedly be low. That will be to our advantage.''

He eyed her appreciatively, his eyes lingering at the curve of her hip, outlined in the form-fitting pantaloons.

"Well, the innkeeper certainly gave no sign that he took me for a woman, earlier,'' Blanche reminded him, but Angus was paying no attention.

Blanche reached up to adjust the cravat at her neck, pulling her shirt tightly across her breasts as she did so.

"Hmm. I wonder . . .'' he murmured. Impulsively, he moved round in front of her, reached one hand around her, and gathered her loose shirt tightly behind her back. "You're not as unendowed as I

thought. I would advise you to keep this shirt loose.''
He loosened his hold on the material and reached to adjust the shirt so that it did not stretch so revealingly over her feminine curves.

The devil, he said to himself, the girl's figure is not so straight and narrow or lacking in curves as I thought. Properly coiffed and gowned, she would attract a good deal of attention and pique the interest of any number of men. He realized he hadn't fully appreciated her until now.

''My endowments, or lack thereof, are no concern of yours, Mister Dalglish,'' Blanche said stiffly. Seeing the blazing light in his dark eyes as he gazed down at her, she quickly pulled back out of his reach. ''Kindly keep your hands to yourself!''

She had always thought it a silly, overly romantic expression, but if eyes could be said to flash, his certainly did at that moment!

Blanche swallowed uneasily.

Angus had a sudden, almost overwhelming desire to reach out and grab her by the shoulders. He didn't know if he wanted to shake her, or pull her fully against himself and kiss her soundly. Mastering his impulse with an effort, he put his hands up in mock surrender. He folded his arms across his chest, crossed his booted feet as he leaned against the large, oak wardrobe, and watched with a sardonic smile as she hastily backed away from him, her eyes wide and opaque with the alarm she was trying to control.

Well, he knew she was a spinster, probably without

any previous physical contact with a man, so what else could he expect, he mocked himself.

Blanche turned away without a word of protest at his actions and walked to the other side of the room where she picked up the wig, then set it down again. She reached for her brush that was resting on the dressing table, anxious to busy herself doing something that would take her mind off her companion's provocative behavior. She lifted her arms to brush the tangles out of her long, gleaming hair before she pinned it up under the wig once more.

Angus couldn't help himself when he saw the silver waterfall of her hair falling over her hand as she leaned to one side to brush it. The tight rein he had imposed on himself a moment before snapped. Impulsively, he walked over to her, reached out and took the brush from her hands.

Blanche almost jumped at his touch. "I thought you were going."

"Yes—in a moment. . . . 'Tis a pity to cover it," he said softly as he let his long fingers run through her hair. He captured a strand between thumb and forefinger. "Your hair is like strands of shimmering silver moonlight," he murmured as he continued brushing.

"My hair is gray, prematurely gray, as my mother's was," Blanche said firmly, holding herself still at his touch, refusing to let him see how much he disturbed her.

"*Silver*, not gray." He stopped brushing and

97

touched one of her brows. "Wings of darkest midnight."

"Eyebrows—dark gray."

"Over eyes like pools of liquid silver—a man could drown in them." He held the brush suspended in midair.

"They're gray, too. A man would be an idiot to do anything so foolish."

"Lips like dew-kissed cherries," he continued, running the pad of his thumb over her full lower lip. "Stained a deep, ripe red."

"Flesh-colored." Her voice had become slightly husky, she noted with dismay.

"Ears like pink shells."

"The ordinary kind—a matching pair. . . . Are you always so nonsensical?" Blanche was trying desperately to maintain her poise, but her heart was hammering in her breast and she found it difficult to breathe normally.

"Umm," Angus murmured, running a long finger lightly over her soft cheek and staring at her lips. She could feel his warm breath fanning her face. She was aware of a tingling warmth deep within, all the way down to her toes.

He lowered his head.

Blanche's breath caught in her throat. She couldn't look away from his mesmerizing gaze.

"Mister Dalglish!" There was a shout and a loud knocking at the door to their room. The unlocked door swung open as the servant hammered on it.

"What the devil do you want?" Angus shouted

back angrily, furiously irritated at the interruption. He released his hold on her and stepped back.

Blanche hastily took up the black wig and fitted it over her hair.

A servant entered, rather tardily, with the bottle of wine Angus had ordered for dinner. "I—I've brought the bottle of claret you ordered, sir." The servant looked extremely startled to see the well-set-up gent embracing the young man.

Chapter 6

Blanche was sleepy. Her eyelids were beginning to droop over her eyes. Her feet hurt in the uncomfortable boots and she was overwarm in the new wool jacket she wore, but she could not remove it, of course. Her masquerade would be over in the bat of an eye, if she were to shed the concealing jacket.

It was hot, loud, and smoky in the taproom where she sat on a stool watching Angus play cards with four other men at a table set back in an alcove to one side of the huge inglenook fireplace. She wished she had resisted the temptation to accompany him here. There were two other tables of card players and quite a few onlookers crowded into the L-shaped room. Raucous laughter and loud chatter filled the air as the spectators for tomorrow's pugilistic contest argued their favorite's strong points and drank long and deep in the congested room.

Several of the men were smoking cheroots or pipes and the smoke from their tobacco mingled with the smoke from the wood fire in the cavernous hearth, that must have been used in medieval times to roast oxen whole, to make the place seem like an illustration from Dante's *Inferno* come to life. The place was a real den of vice, albeit a genial and homey one, Blanche thought.

There were female servants in the room, of course, fetching food and drinks for the revelers but Blanche distinctly remembered Dalglish teasing her, saying that *ladies* did not frequent common taprooms. Well, he was wrong, she thought, looking around at the number of other women in the room. But—no, she decided, as she looked more closely at the painted faces, garish, low-cut gowns, and brightly colored hair of these women. The other females present weren't *ladies* precisely. Their dress seemed to proclaim them women of doubtful virtue. Dalglish had been right again, to her annoyance.

Blanche wanted her bed. Yet she couldn't make herself get up and leave until Angus was ready to go, too. There was something about his presence that drew her. Some magnetism that kept her from straying far from his side. She could not explain to herself why she had agreed to accompany Angus to the taproom. She really had no interest in gaming of any kind. Nor, she tried to assure herself, in this chance-met stranger whom she trusted would help her recover Prudie, and then disappear from her life forever. Perhaps she did fear to be left on her own out in the cold, drafty room in the stables, with no other female remotely within calling distance.

Yes, that was it. She had come in here to get warm near the blazing fire, not because she felt warm and safe in the presence of her hired companion.

She watched him play from her perch on the uncomfortable stool. Her eyes were drawn, again and again, to his long, slim fingers as they deftly dealt the cards or simply held them. He would play each card by putting a finger on the top of it and holding it there for a moment before revealing it to the other players, thus achieving maximum dramatic effect. She couldn't tear her eyes away from his hands.

Dalglish had slowly accumulated a few pounds in winnings over the past hour, cannily prevailing in each round by just a slim margin. The other poor souls were being fleeced, was Blanche's first thought. But, no, again. Dalglish was doing nothing but playing with consummate skill and crafty betting. He played fairly. There was no deception in his play at all that she could see.

It seemed to her that Angus was consuming an amazing quantity of wine, though. As were the others, she had to admit. Drinking deep seemed to be part and parcel of the gaming. And the more wine the men consumed, the more wreckless were the wagers. Except on Dalglish's part, of course. He watched and waited for an opportunity to take the largest pots, often throwing in his cards when the pot was small.

Was he foxed, or wasn't he? Blanche opened her drooping eyelids and looked at Angus more closely. He certainly seemed to be in control, but was there not a certain glitter in his eyes and languidness to his movements?

One of the garishly dressed females in attendance was hanging over the arm of his chair, displaying her ample charms. And those charms were quite blatantly revealed by her low-cut blouse, to Angus's considerable delight, if the slow, appreciative smile that spread over his face when he directed his gaze to somewhere below the level of the girl's neck was anything to go by.

Blanche came fully awake again when she saw the girl plunk herself down on his knee and nuzzle his ear when there was a break in the game while a fresh bottle of wine was served round. How disgusting! she thought, feeling all the warmer and more uncomfortable. And Dalglish didn't exactly push the girl away, either, she saw. Though he did disengage himself so that he could pick up the hand that had been dealt him. Blanche gritted her teeth at the sight.

She sat up straighter on her stool and motioned for a young serving wench to bring her a glass of something wet and cooling. Not only was she hot and thirsty, but she needed something to soothe her nerves. Blanche smiled at the mobcapped girl when she handed her the glass of wine. She was considerably taken aback when the girl lingered next to her stool. The girl rested her hand on Blanche's knee, and smiled up at her in a flirtatious way, mistaking Blanche for the young gentleman she was pretending to be.

The girl began to speak, batting her lashes in an

absurd manner. "Me moniker's Molly. Wot's yers?" When Blanche didn't answer, Molly said, "Wot curly black 'air ye 'ave, luv." And she lifted her hand and tried to touch Blanche's wig.

Blanche straightened her back and pulled her head up, out of the girl's reach.

Angus grinned hugely as he saw Blanche trying to fight off the amorous barmaid. "Oh my God, we're in the suds now!" he murmured, trying to stifle his laughter. Blanche succeeded in removing the wench's hand from the wig before she could do any damage or discover the deception.

"Ye's jist a lad, but ye's so 'andsome. Come on and give us a kiss," Molly said.

"I *beg* your pardon," Blanche said sternly, lowering her voice by several registers and looking daggers at the forward, mistaken hussy.

" 'Ow's about it, luv. Molly won't charge ye no bees 'n honey."

Blanche stood up hastily, caught Angus's glance and signaled to him with her eyes that she was going back to their room. He nodded and mouthed the words, "Wait for me." He rose languidly from the table where a game had just finished and picked up his winnings.

"Gentlemen. Thank you for allowing me to join you this evening. It's been a tiring day. I'm afraid I'm for bed now," he said, yawning.

"No, no," a chorus of protests rang out.

"It's early yet. You've pocketed a good deal of our blunt. Give us a chance for revenge," the heavyset man in the tweed jacket said to Angus.

"Ah, but how do you know that I won't, er, 'pocket even more of your blunt,' as you phrase it. Perhaps another time, my friends." There was grumbling and disappointment, but no one was going to make a scene, Angus saw thankfully.

He sauntered over to Blanche and detached her from the wench who seemed determined to stick like a burr to her quarry. "Who's your friend, Flowers?"

"This is Molly," Blanche said, greatly embarrassed. Angus's shoulders quivered with suppressed laughter as he took Blanche's arm firmly between his fingers.

He leaned down and pinched Molly's cheek with his other hand. "Sorry, Molly, my girl, but I can't have you corrupting young Flowers, here. He's but a lad, an unlicked cub, not ready for your sort of sport."

Molly smiled saucily. " 'Ow about ye, sir? Do ye want someone to warm yer Ned for ye ta'night?" Blanche gaped at the open proposition, forgetting again that she was supposed to be a man.

"Er, no thank you, Molly, my girl. I'm sure you could warm the cockles of any man's heart, but I'm so tired your charms would be quite wasted on an old dog like me, you see," he appeased her, slipping her a coin from his winnings as he began to guide Blanche away.

"You're just too 'handsome' for the girls to resist . . ." Angus whispered teasingly in Blanche's ear. "And for me, too," he added softly.

Blanche quelled her outrage and kept her face still.

"I'll be glad when this playacting is over," she said in a voice as devoid of emotion as she could make it.

Angus steered Blanche through the crowded room. He had a devilish smile on his face, still amused by poor Molly's mistake. Suddenly he saw three men pushing their way into the room and his expression froze. "Damn!" He stopped in his tracks and swiftly looked around the room for another exit.

"What's wrong?" Blanche asked in an undertone, feeling his tightened grip on her arm and sensing his tenseness.

"Wolverton."

"Where?"

"There." Angus tilted his head toward the door. "The burly one, with two of his men."

"What shall we do?"

"Leave. As quickly as we can. Do as I say and don't ask questions. I'm going to stagger a bit and lean against your shoulder as though I'm jug bitten. Put your arm around me and help me out. Stay to the wall on the far side of the room as much as you can. I must keep my face hidden, just in case."

Angus and Blanche were about halfway around the room to the door when a shout rang out.

"Hey! You there!" One of Wolverton's men pointed in their direction.

"Come here!"

Blanche froze. Her heart was in her mouth. She felt Angus reach for the pistol in his pocket.

"Hey, you! Barmaid!" Wolverton's man shouted again at Molly who was trailing after Blanche and

106

Angus. "A bottle for my master! And be quick about it!"

Blanche began to breathe again, though her heart was hammering against her ribs. She continued to drag Angus along until they were out the door. As soon as they were clear of the room, they stopped and looked at one another in perfect accord. Angus took his arm from around Blanche's shoulders and strode out the back door at speed with Blanche right at his side. They quickly made their way to their room in the back of the stables.

Angus slammed the door shut behind them and leaned against it for a moment. Blanche lit the lamp. She took several steadying breaths and tried to slow her fast-beating heart, and then looked at Angus, waiting for him to tell her what they were to do next to get out of this coil.

"Deuce take it! How could I have been so stupid. I should have guessed that ugly customer would be sure to turn up here for this curst boxing match tomorrow!" Angus said furiously, then moved to place one of the chairs under the door handle, cursing the broken lock. "I didn't think there was a chance in hel—er, the remotest chance they would come in this direction."

When Angus had secured the door as best he could, he turned and said, "It's doubtful he or his men would have recognized me, even if I had come face to face with them. I was quite *thoroughly* disguised last night. Undoubtedly Wolverton came for the pugilist contest, not to chase after me. Given his penchant for turning

107

up wherever there's likely to be heavy wagering, I should have been more on my guard when I learned of the match. Any chance to line his pockets, Wolverton is sure to sniff out, for he's badly dipped. He's been playing too deep for too many years and not only are his estates mortgaged to the hilt, but he's left debts of honor in his wake all over England."

He looked up at Blanche and saw that she was standing rigid, trembling ever so slightly. Her eyes looked huge in her white face as she watched him. There was only a rim of silver showing around her black irises.

"They won't think to look for me here," Angus softened his voice as he sought to calm her fears. He walked across the room to her, wanting to reassure his plucky lady and thank her. He gripped her by the shoulders. "You were admirable, as always! Any other female would have had the vapors or fainted dead away. I can't think of another woman who would have been able to carry off the game half so well."

"What good would fainting or having the vapors have done? They would have been sure to discover you then, and my deception would have been revealed for all to see. Our chances of recovering Prudie would have been nil," she said, making a little recover.

He laughed softly as he remembered the untenable position Blanche had been in before the advent of Wolverton. "That barmaid would have had you in her bed, if she could have," he said, trying to change the subject and put the recent fright from them. "Good Mistress Molly Accost."

"Hah! You can laugh. How would you feel if our positions were reversed, and a *man* had tried to take liberties with you?"

"I would have planted the fellow a facer!"

"Oh, yes, that would have answered admirably," she said dryly. "I shall be glad when I can put off this disguise. I don't want to be a man any longer!"

"Well, if you won't be a man any longer, then you could pose as my wife, as I suggested before." Angus put a hand at the back of her waist and pulled her hard against himself so that they touched at all points from chest to thigh.

Blanche went rigid in his arms, trying to resist him, but she felt the heat rise in her neck and face, a telltale sign of her agitation. With everything else that had happened that evening, and indeed since Angus Dalglish had first leapt through her bedroom window, Blanche's customary serenity had been severely tested. She wondered if she would ever be able to return to the staid, sane world that had once been hers. Her ability to remain unruffled, no matter what the provocation, had already been tried to the limits that night, and now all she wanted to do was to sag against Angus's warmth.

Angus let his long fingers trail over the smooth curve of her hip in the skin-tight pantaloons.

"What are you doing?" she whispered, her forehead almost touching his shoulder.

"Trying to throw myself at your feet."

"Feet?"

"Well," he laughed softly, his breath tickling her

ear as he buried his nose in her hair, "in a manner of speaking."

"A foolish way to speak. . . . Why bother?" She lifted her head to stare up at him. His hands continued to caress her warmly.

"To add some spice to our adventure. Why else?" He pulled her even more tightly against himself and lowered his head, gazing at her mouth. He touched his lips to hers. Feeling no softening response, he increased the pressure of his kiss, determined to melt the icy reserve of his silver lady. He wanted her warm and responsive in his arms, not stiff and resisting.

For a moment Blanche let him press his lips to hers, taking comfort from the contact, but when a delicious, treacherous shiver ran down her spine as he intensified the kiss, she pushed against his chest and shoved him away. If only he knew it, she wasn't feeling cold inside at all—she was feeling decidedly warm and was having the deuce of a time not responding to his kiss. She wished he had only continued to hold her and kiss her gently, but she could tell that he wanted more. The other was dangerous—too dangerous.

"There's enough 'spice' in this adventure to last me a lifetime. I want you to keep a cool head and save your energy to help me recover Prudie," she said, successfully disguising her inner perturbation from him.

"Oh, *kissing* doesn't deplete my energy—quite the contrary. . . . When a woman shows me a little affection, it quite makes a new man of me."

"Why waste your time on an old maid like me?"

"Oh, I *never* waste my time."

Blanche saw the strange teasing, yet intense, light in his eyes as they gleamed down at her. She made a disbelieving noise in her throat, raised one winged brow, and looked at him coolly.

"This throwing myself at your feet is proving a damnably hard task," he said. "You keep shifting your ground. How am I to know how to please you?"

"I don't want you at my feet. You can please me by helping me find my cousin."

"Oh, very well . . . for now," he said, an unspoken promise lurking in his dark eyes. "Perhaps you will reward me suitably when I've achieved this Herculean task—for I begin to believe that I will have to successfully complete twelve labors to accomplish the feat."

Chapter 7

After she had convinced Dalglish to leave off his foolishness, Blanche had gone to bed in her clothes. She fell asleep immediately and slept soundly enough in her narrow bunk, all thought of the peril surrounding them in the taproom forgotten. The presence of her companion in the room, however provoking he could be at times, was reassuring—although paradoxically it was his very proximity that brought danger nearer. However it was, she felt protected. And she would have worried about him, if he had been elsewhere. For, however illogical it might be after such a short acquaintance, she had come to fear for his safety more than for her own.

Angus was too weary to play with his sedate lady more that night. It was hard to resist trying to tease her out of her chilly aloofness, to make her show some spark of emotion. There must be *some* passion behind that damned serene facade of hers. He sighed. There would be plenty of time for his games . . . if he chose to pursue them. He didn't stop to ask himself *if* he should. Nor did he ask himself why he would do so, except for his own amusement.

With his pistol primed and ready, resting under his lumpy pillow, Angus tried to sleep with one eye open, watching the door. Despite his confident words to Blanche earlier, he was not completely convinced that his elaborately contrived disguise had proved adequate. He was fairly well known in London and someone may have tipped Wolverton the clue as to his identity.

His precautions proved to be unnecessary. As the night wore on, they were undisturbed by anything other than the occasional muffled sounds of the horses shifting about in their stalls.

Angus stared into the dark shadows of the room as he shifted his shoulders and tried to settle himself more comfortably along his narrow plank. The innkeeper had mistakenly called the narrow wooden board topped by a skimpy mattress a "bed," he decided grumpily. And the only things the blasted mattress was stuffed with was rough straw and old clothing, if the musty smell emanating from the bedding was anything to go by.

Baring these nuisances, Angus was sure he was more comfortable than his companion was on her own hard board, for he had no tight clothing to bind and chafe at him, having removed all except his breeches. Blanche had been too modest—or too prudent—to take off anything but her boots and jacket. Well, she was wise, he had to admit, for anyone could easily burst in on them through that broken door. And then where would they be?

Lord, but she was an iceberg of a woman, he thought with a sigh. And utterly desirable for all her frozen shyness. Angus turned his eyes toward the other side of the room where Blanche slept quietly, but he couldn't make out anything in the pitch darkness. His body stirred at the memory of her in those form-fitting pantaloons and loose, almost opaque shirt. And she was sleeping only a few feet away. He swallowed uneasily. If he weren't careful, he feared he would find himself honor bound to wed her.

He frowned. It was possible she was compromised beyond redemption in society's eyes, as it was. Gad, what a fix! Many might call him a ne'er-do-well, but he still had *some* claim to the name of gentleman. And he had done nothing yet to disgrace that name— save, some would say, made a profession of what most men of rank or wealth did for pleasure or sport or out of boredom.

At least gaming wasn't an obsession with him as it was for so many, to their ruin. He knew when to stop. His was a calculated approach to his chosen "calling." Angus put his arms behind his head and yawned. Perhaps the very nature of his work, temporary though it was, meant that he could leave it when he so chose. He certainly hoped so. It had been an eventful life at any rate, with much excitement along the way.

He drifted into sleep on the thought that he might well find himself a tenant for life after this particular escapade. Behind his closed eyes in the mists of his dream, he could see the shackles open and ready to clasp him about his wrists—then suddenly they disappeared, falling away as though by magic—and he saw his hand linked with Blanche's in an unbreakable clasp. Angus smiled in his sleep.

The two tired, but determined, companions in adventure set off at the crack of dawn the following morning. To Blanche's consternation, Angus insisted they stop by the haberdasher's shop where he had bought their new clothing on their way out of town. He leapt off the fresh mount he had hired and proceeded to pound on the shop door, loudly demanding admittance.

The sleepy proprietor, still wearing his nightcap, stuck his head out of his second-story bedroom window and peevishly asked what the disturbance was all about. Angus talked him into coming down and unlocking the door and, when the man had done so, he disappeared inside the shop. He came briskly out the door two minutes later, vaulted into the saddle, gave his horse a sharp kick in the side, and rode off at a fast clip, denying Blanche the chance to ask the obvious question of what he had been doing.

They rode hard through the bright red and gold November morning, not pausing to admire the beauty of the landscape they passed through. The trees in the valleys were at their peak in this late autumnal season. The reds, golds, oranges, yellows, and pale browns of the leaves formed a palette of color against some lingering green of the deciduous trees and the darker green of the evergreens. The rich colors mingled and blurred in the vision of the riders as they rode on through the morning.

They passed more slowly through a stand of twisted oaks that were beginning to drop their load of golden leaves. The wind was blowing lightly and shafts of sunlight were coming through the half-bare branches as the brightly colored leaves swirled down around their heads like so many gold coins falling to earth. In a fit of poetic whimsy, Angus turned back to Blanche who was riding a length behind him and said that he wished he could collect gold from the trees, instead of at the gaming table. Blanche replied laughingly that that was like wishing for gold at the end of the rainbow. She gave him a teasing smile from under her jauntily tipped cap. At the sight of her brilliant, warm smile, Angus experienced a sudden unfamiliar lurch in his stomach. He turned away abruptly and urged his mount to a faster pace, without pausing to analyze his reaction.

Trees became sparser when their mounts began to climb toward higher ground and the landscape gave way to scrubby bracken, broom, ferns, and prickly gorse of the open hillsides. They rode doggedly on through the rising foothills and then the mountains themselves of the Lake District until riders and horses were all four blowing hard, ready for a breather.

"We'll stop in Penrith," Angus said to Blanche as they paused to let the horses drink from a little rivulet, and he passed his flask. She was prepared for the burning sensation of the brandy this time as she took a cautious sip.

Blanche nodded her agreement. "What lake is that?" she asked, pointing to the gleaming body of water they could glimpse through the gap in the range of hills from their relatively high vantage point.

Angus turned to his left and looked in the direction Blanche pointed out. "Must be Ullswater. I hear that fellow Wordsworth resides in these parts. Are you of a poetical turn of mind, Fleur? 'Fraid we don't have time to make any social calls on this visit."

"Mister Wordsworth is a worthy gentleman, or so I've heard. I can't think he would receive such a pair of vagabonds as we are."

"Ah! Cut to the quick! You mean he wouldn't receive *me*," Angus said with a lift of one black brow. "Yet you are a worthy woman, Fleur. And you've seen fit to honor such a dastardly fellow as I with your estimable company."

"You know, I was used to thinking of you as a quick-thinking, resourceful sort of person, Dalglish. But now I see your words can be as idle as those of the foppish dandies Prudie is so fond of."

"Hit again!" Angus groaned. "Enough of our foolish banter, my Lady Moralizer. I shall henceforth take you as a model of all that is proper and correct," he said, gazing at her clothing meaningfully. "Perhaps association with you will wash my black character white."

"I fear 'tis *your* influence," she gestured at her

outfit as she sat astride her mount, "that has won out, Dalglish."

He grinned, a very knowing, white-toothed grin. "Hmm. We shall just have to see who transforms whom, shan't we, my dear."

Blanche shook her head at his foolishness.

"We've made good time this morning. See that you remember to act your part when we stop in Penrith," Angus reminded her.

The familiar glacial mask of dignity came down over Blanche's features. "You are so good at issuing orders, one has no difficulty believing you used to be an officer, Dalglish," she said. "I wonder you could bear to give up your position of authority."

"You would have made quite an imperious officer yourself, you know, Fleur. Why, if you could go amongst the *ton* with a quizzing glass stuck to your eye, you could probably best Brummell himself for cutting remarks and chilling set downs," Angus returned in a temper at her critical tone.

Less than an hour later, they rode into the small Lakelands town of Penrith and drew their horses to a halt in front of a quaint little inn called The Ship.

"A singularly unfitting name for an inn in the middle of the mountains, wouldn't you agree?" Angus said jokingly to Blanche as they dismounted in the stables and strolled toward the inn.

Blanche walked with cool nonchalance at Angus's side, her cap tilted forward to shade her feminine features. Her portrayal of a man had become increasingly convincing with practice. She now played the

118

part with unflappable assurance, assuming a look of haughty boredom that characterized a certain class of young gentleman as she sauntered along at Angus's side.

Angus pursued his inquiries and learned that travelers whose description sounded suspiciously like that of the heiress and her two companions had changed horses at The Ship less than three hours previously. Blanche wanted to hire fresh mounts and ride on immediately but was persuaded to rest at The Ship for a short time.

"I, for one, am tired of sitting my horse. We'll just stretch our legs and grab a quick bite to eat first." Angus sought to quell Blanche's impatience. "Let us refresh ourselves. We'll make better time."

"I'm sure you're right, Angus—as usual," she said equably, damping down her own impatience to be off. In truth, she welcomed the break as much as Angus— it was only her duty to Prudie which prompted her to argue against it.

Angus grinned in triumph at her easy capitulation and Blanche returned his smile in full measure. She was learning how to soothe his temper. A passerby standing in front of The Ship saw the warm look that passed between the two gentlemen and wondered at it, taking off his hat to scratch his head in puzzlement as to what the world was coming to.

Although the early November afternoon sunlight was rapidly beginning to fade, Angus and Blanche pressed on from Penrith toward Carlisle with their fresh mounts. Carlisle was the last large English town before the Scottish border, and Gretna Green was not far from there.

"We *must* overtake them before they cross into Scotland," Blanche said anxiously when they had ridden for an hour and had not yet come upon her cousin.

"There's every chance we will, Fleur," Angus assured her when they let the horses walk side by side for a break from the fast pace they had kept to since leaving Penrith.

"Their horses will be blown. Remember, a team of coach horses are pulling so much more weight than our hacks are carrying. That's why we can make better time. And I, for one, would be more than ready for a break if I had to travel cooped up so tightly inside a stuffy vehicle. I find traveling inside a coach tedious in the extreme."

"Do you?" Blanche asked with a knowing look as the wind picked up and a light drizzle began to blow in their faces and saturate their clothing. She was beginning to understand Angus very well, and of course he would be bursting with energy, not ready to sit still for any length of time, she thought with an inner smile.

"Our runaways *must* stop in Carlisle to change their team, if not their carriage, before they cross into Scotland. Remember, your cousin and her young man have no idea we're on their trail. They will stop and rest for the night with no thought of pursuit. Take my word for it, they will not attempt to reach Gretna tonight." He glanced up at the heavy rain clouds and pulled the collar of his jacket more closely around his neck as the cold breeze picked up. He reached behind his saddle where the black cloak was rolled up tightly and tied on. He untied it with one hand and tossed it over to Blanche.

"Here. Put this around your shoulders. It's getting cold."

She thanked him gratefully, for the damp chill was beginning to make her teeth chatter.

Angus had sounded so certain that they would overtake her cousin in time that Blanche was reassured. She had hoped they would have come up to Prudie on the road before now. She did not at all want to have to undertake a search for her cousin in the rather sizable town of Carlisle. But there was no sign of the eloping couple as yet.

Blanche didn't even remember how saddle sore and tired she was with the prospect of having Prudie safe in but a few hours before her. She was in high spirits and had shed some of her reserve and coolness. She was happy in the company of her companion.

They would soon be in Carlisle. Blanche felt they were almost near enough for her to reach out and grab Prudie around the next bend in the road.

"It will be growing dark soon, Angus. With these low clouds and this thickening mist, we haven't much afternoon light left to guide us. Shall we find our way?"

"Aye. This is the main road, you know. 'Twill take us right into town. And the moon is almost full. It will guide us tonight—if these clouds would just blow away. Are you warm enough? I confess, I'll be glad to find shelter in one of those friendly English inns we were discussing yesterday. I don't suppose we can expect quite the culinary expertise of the Golden Crown, though. Just so the place isn't short on spirits. A strong drink to warm my blood would not come amiss about now.''

"I'm too impatient to catch up to Prudie to know whether it's warm or cold, whether I'm tired or not,'' Blanche said spiritedly.

"Something has finally shaken you out of your tranquility. How interesting,'' Angus teased. "What would it take for you to turn giddy, I wonder?''

She ignored his mild attempt at flirtation and asked, "How much farther to Carlisle?''

"About half an hour's ride, I would judge.''

"I'd hoped we would have overtaken them by now.''

"Well, I believe we would have done so if your mare hadn't picked up that stone under her shoe ten miles back.''

"You removed it quickly enough, Angus. We can't have wasted more than twenty minutes. Are you an expert farrier, as well?''

"As well as what?'' Angus asked, turning his dark gaze on her. Blanche knew by the gleam in the depths of those black eyes that he was laughing at her. But she didn't know that he was basking in her praise, as well.

Blanche gave him a bland look and shook her head slightly, refusing to enter into his game.

Angus watched as the stiff breeze sent a shower of many-colored leaves swirling down about Blanche's head when they passed under an arcade of trees. The incongruity of her raffish cap and boyish hairstyle set against the delicate beauty of her small-boned face struck him with surprising force. One of the wet leaves drifted down and stuck to her cheek briefly. Angus wished it were his fingers that were caressing her face so lightly. He restrained the urge to reach over and brush the leaf away. He would bide his time yet awhile. But he vowed he would warm her blood for her before this adventure was over.

Angus ran his hand over his face and shook his head to clear it of these sudden uncharacteristically romantic notions. He was a man of action, impatient of nonsense, and he had best remember it before he allowed himself to get carried away. He couldn't afford to deviate from his goal for a while yet.

His objective was to restore the family fortunes, and while he was on his way to doing just that with his careful investments, he had a few years of hard work in front of him before he could hope to fully accomplish his task. He planned to give his sister Fanny a season this year. If he could persuade their Aunt Matilda to sponsor Fanny, he would call in some of his investments in order to provide the necessary funds. He had set aside a certain amount as a dowry for Fanny, too, and he hoped she would make a good match when she had the opportunity to meet some eligible men in London. He was fond of his sister and her future was of continuing concern. After he had seen to Fanny, it might take some time before he realized enough profit from his investments to be able to pay off the mortgage on the marshy acres he had inherited from his father. And then he would have to expend more money on implementing the plans he had to put in the new system of drainage he had learned about to make the acreage more productive.

Angus shook his head again. The steady clip-clop of his horse's hooves must be sending him into these idyllic reveries, he thought ruefully. Ordinarily, he was not a man who was prone to woolgathering.

He glanced about him, sharp-eyed and alert now, to see that although it had stopped drizzling, the clouds still hung oppressively low. The light of this already dull, dark afternoon had grown noticeably dimmer. The early evening air was damp and cold. He saw the black cloak Blanche wore billowing out behind her in the fresh wind. He called to her to wrap it more securely about herself.

As they rode along this dreary track, swirls of mist and fallen leaves blew out onto the road from among the trees standing in the heavily wooded land on either side of the pathway. Angus pulled the collar of his jacket up more tightly around his neck once again and felt a shiver of apprehension run down his spine as he looked out on the dreary scene.

He glanced back to see that Blanche was riding only slightly behind him with her head down, con-centrating on guiding her horse through the several

124

muddy ruts in the road. He opened his mouth to call out to her that they should spring their horses.

A shot rang out.

"What in the world—" Blanche began to say, lifting her head to look at Angus. But he was already off his horse and had his pistol out.

"Hell and the devil Get down!" he commanded.

It was too late. Two masked horsemen, their lower faces blackened and their torn, filthy clothes covered with dead leaves and other debris, emerged through the murky, smokelike mist from the trees on one side of the road. Both men aimed their long horse pistols straight at Blanche. One of the men rode forward quickly and took hold of her horse's reins. Blanche relinquished the reins without a word. In truth she was too stupified to do anything else.

"Get down, boy!" the man commanded. Blanche quickly complied. Never having faced two rough-looking masked men holding horse pistols pointed at her before, she had no thought of doing otherwise.

Angus's long, black cloak caught under her boot heel as she jumped down and sent her sprawling. She rose to her knees and the cloak fell off her shoulders to lie in the dirt and mud of the road.

The other highwayman dismounted, took hold of Blanche's arm, twisted her around in front of him, and pressed his long, heavy gun against her temple.

"Right, guv," he shouted to Angus in a rough, heavily accented, north-country voice. "Come ye out from a'hind that nag, or yer lad 'ere is for it right a'tween 'is purtty peeps."

Angus gnashed his teeth in fury at the damnable situation. He was helpless, seeing the long horse pistol held to Blanche's head. First uncocking it, he allowed his own small, silver-chased pistol to slip down inside his pocket. Then he stepped out from behind his horse with his hands held up, trying to control his raging temper for Blanche's sake.

"Let the lady—*lad* go," he said harshly to the man holding Blanche's neck cloth tightly in his closed fist and pointing the pistol to her head.

"Nay, do na get yer dander up now, guv. It be yer golden boys we be after, not yer life nor the laddie's 'ere. Jist ye 'and over the dibs and us'll be along on our way."

All Angus's hard work last night to go for nothing, was Blanche's only thought. She was in too much shock to think that the pistol at her temple might go off at any moment if Dalglish didn't comply.

Angus frowned ferociously as he reached into the inner pocket of his jacket and took out his purse with one hand, while keeping the other in the air. He bit off the curse rising in to his lips as he forcefully threw the heavily laden leather pouch on the ground. The leather drawstrings broke apart and coins flew in all directions as the pouch landed with a thud against a large stone.

The mounted highwayman jumped down and ran to collect the booty, while his partner kept the gun pointed at Blanche, holding Angus at bay. Instead of picking up the money and being on his way, the man crouched down and gathered the scattered coins into

126

a pile, than ran his hands through them with great glee.

"Cor blimey, Macheath, 'ere's enough bees 'n 'oney ta buy a parson's nose o' blue ruin," he called to his cohort, a wide smile splitting his grimy, gaptoothed face.

"Shut yer gob, Peachum," the man holding Blanche ordered. But nonetheless, he looked down with considerable interest to where his mate was running his hands through the coins. Peachum picked out one shiny sovereign and put it to his mouth to bite down on it, testing the gold.

Macheath's pistol dropped from Blanche's temple to hang loosely in his hand, pointing harmlessly at the ground. " 'Ow much did we get?" he asked with a gleam of avarice in his eyes behind the slits in his mask.

Angus saw his chance. He motioned to Blanche with his eyes, trying to communicate to her without words that he intended to challenge the bumbling thieves. He reached out with his booted foot and kicked a stone into the trees. There was a satisfyingly loud crackle as the rock landed among the crisp, fallen leaves and broken branches not far from the roadside.

The brigand called Macheath immediately dropped his hold on Blanche, turned, and fired his pistol in the direction of the noise. Blanche, taking her cue from Angus, knocked the now unloaded gun from Macheath's hand with her elbow just as Angus dove for the still-kneeling Peachum.

Chaos ensued. Angus threw a hard-fisted punch to

Peachum's jaw that landed with a crunching sound. Peachum fell to the ground face first, stunned by the force of the blow. Angus reached down and grabbed the gun away from the now insensible highwayman.

Macheath, meantime, had pushed Blanche down and now leapt at Angus to defend his fallen cohort.

A general brawl followed.

Macheath kicked the gun from Angus's hand and landed a blow to his head before Angus could turn to defend himself. The gun flew from Angus's hand and went skittering across the ground to land in the debris of dead vegetation and broken limbs at the side of the road.

Angus and Macheath traded a barrage of punches, neither one nor the other getting the upper hand.

Peachum recovered himself enough to crawl forward and retrieve the gun while Blanche sat in the middle of the road, too stunned by the unfolding events to move.

"All right, guv. The fisticuffs be over." Peachum held the gun in his right hand and with his left, fingered his bruised jaw. "That there's a right pair o' pops ye 'ave, guv. Landed me a right wisty caster, ye did." A huge grin split the now bloody and dirty, half-masked face of the highwayman.

Macheath busied himself collecting up the coins that had been scattered in the melee, then gathered the reins of all four horses while Peachum held the loaded pistol pointed at Angus. Angus had no chance to reach into his pocket and retrieve his gun. At least he wouldn't lose it to this pair of gallows birds, he told himself furiously.

"It's sorry we be that we canna leave ye the nags, guv. Me 'n Macheath needs these 'ere goldenboys more'n a smart gentry cove sich as yerself, any road. Got a parcel of bairns at 'ome, we 'as." Peachum, pausing to wipe blood from his nose and mouth on his filthy sleeve, grinned hugely as he spoke to Angus. "Find yerself a good mill, guv. We'ud wager our blunt on ye, wouldn't we, Macheath?"

Angus, bruised, dirty and seething with rage, stood glowering at the ruffian.

"Stifle it, Peachum! Cease yer runnin' at the gob, afore ye tell 'um yer life 'istory." Ye'll 'ave 'um weepin' in their 'ankies, right enough."

Angus looked to see Blanche sprawling in the dusty roadway. She had lost her hat, her wig had come off, and her silver hair had tumbled down about her shoulders. She looked slightly dazed, but otherwise unhurt. Peachum glanced around to where Angus looked.

"Ho, guv, that there's a mighty strange *boy* ye 'ave there." A great rumbling laugh shook the protruding belly of the highwayman.

"I said ta quit yer jabberin', Peachum!" Macheath shouted.

"Cast yer peepers on this 'ere *lad,* Macheath— h'it's nowt but a lass! And a fine un, too, guv! Right gradely, she be!" Peachum sniggered as he backed his way to his horse, keeping his gun trained on Angus. "Wot mischief be *ye* up ta, guv?"

The two highwaymen mounted and were off, taking Angus and Blanche's horses with them. Blanche's traveling case disappeared into the trees with them, too, for it was still strapped to the back of her mount. Angus stood in frustrated, impotent fury at his inability to act. A deep scowl marred his bruised and dirty face as he stood watching the rascals ride away, cursing softly and viciously to himself the while.

Blanche got to her feet before Angus could move to help her. She stood in the dirty roadway with her hands on her hips, watching the two bungling highwaymen ride away and disappear in the swirls of mist with the horses Angus had hired and all his winnings of the previous night.

"And as easily as these leaves blow away in this blasted wind, so does our blunt fly away with those bloody rogues," Angus said grimly as he caught one of the falling leaves in his hand and strode forward to Blanche's side.

"Well. There goes my chance to catch Prudie tonight," Blanche said with her characteristic calm. "How far from Gretna are we, anyway? I suppose we will have to walk there now," she said with resignation.

"Less than twenty miles. We'll get there tomorrow. There's a chance it may not be too late to prevent your cousin's wedding." Angus tried his best to reassure her, but he was afraid this latest twist had put paid to their hopes of preventing the marriage.

"Well," she said stoically, "I suppose there is little else I can do but try to find her. Though I fear there's little hope of finding her unwed now.''

Angus's temper gradually simmered down as Blanche continued to speak in unemotional, measured words. She saw in the fading twilight that he was looking at her with a lopsided smile on his battered and bruised face.

''Amazing! Absolutely amazing!'' he exclaimed.

She raised her brows in query.

''My dear girl, do you realize how near to being snuffed out we were just now? You've just looked into the jaws of death, yet you stand there as calm as punch and worry about that brat of a cousin of yours! I know *I* am feeling fit to do murder. *You* should be clinging to my neck and having hysterics at the very least!''

''Much good that would do us.''

''Oh, I don't know—the picture it conjures up does have a certain appeal. . . . Perhaps *I* should have hysterics and cling to *your* neck.''

She smiled at his teasing words, but only said, ''I don't feel hysterical in the least. Surely we weren't in that much danger! Those two seemed a rather foolish, bumbling pair of highwaymen to me.''

''Not bumbling enough. They got away with what they came for, didn't they?''

''Oh, your poor face!'' she said sympathetically. ''I wish we had some water to bathe it.''

Angus took out his handkerchief and began to clean his face as best he could until Blanche reached up and took the piece of linen from him.

''Here, let me.'' She did a thorough job of wiping

131

away the dirt and blood where it had congealed over the bruises. Her fingers were cool and soothing as they brushed lightly over the rugged planes of his bruised cheeks and chin.

Angus looked down, watching her with bemusement. She was totally unconscious of how provocative her gestures were, not to mention how her close proximity was beginning to heat up his blood.

He licked at a cut on his lower lip. Blanche's hand hesitated only a fraction of a second before she gently dabbed at that cut, too.

"We're extremely lucky those blackguards *didn't* murder us, you know, even if only by accident," Angus said on a sigh of breath, as much to break the tension that was building between them as anything.

"They seemed a fairly inept pair. No doubt they really did need the money," Blanche said prosaically as she gathered up her wig and hat, dusted them off, and replaced them on her head.

Angus sputtered with laughter. "Aye, no doubt they did. But where does that leave us, my dear girl?" He reached forward to tweek one of the black curls of the wig as he straightened the absurd cap for her. "We *really* need the money, too!" He smiled down at her tenderly.

"Oh, I have every confidence you'll manage something, Angus. You always do."

He shook his head, still marveling at her sangfroid. "A tender heart for a couple of bandits? My dear Fleur, you are much too forgiving."

He put his hand on her shoulder and for a fraction

132

of a second actually rocked forward, wanting to touch his lips to hers. Last night's brief touch had been altogether too fleeting for a man of his strong passions. He recollected himself in time, turned and picked up his cloak from where it had been trampled in the roadway, saying gruffly, "We'd best be off, or we'll find ourselves forced to spend the night under a pile of leaves in this outlaw-infested forest."

Chapter 8

By unspoken but mutual agreement, Angus and Blanche began the long trudge along the road to Carlisle. They fell into companionable conversation while they walked. As his face had been soothed by her gentle fingers, Angus's anger was now soothed away by Blanche's unperturbed manner in the face of adversity. Her serenity was a balm to his lacerated feelings.

Angus was not so sanguine. He hated to be put at a disadvantage. That's why he fought so hard against all the odds. Always. Even when he was outnumbered, as he had been today. But his anger and feelings of helplessness subsided as Blanche spoke on in an equitable voice, saying that it was a relief to stretch her legs after sitting on horseback for so long during the past two days, and how they would not have to worry if they were set upon again because they had nothing left for anyone to take.

Angus had an almost irresistible desire to put his

arm around Blanche's shoulders and gather her to himself, or at least to take her hand. But he was deterred by the sight of her walking beside him straight and tall in her masculine attire.

As twilight deepened, the situation took on an aura of unreality. Curls of mist blew out from the trees on either side of the road across their path, obscuring the way ahead. The wind had picked up and had blown away most of the clouds overhead so now the full moon shone down to light their way and was reflected in the patches of mist scudding across their path. But without the cover of those clouds to hold in some warmth, it was freezing.

Angus lifted his arm, intending to drape it over Blanche's shoulders to shelter her from the cold, but clenched his fist just in time and let it drop to his side. He shook out the muddied cloak, instead, and draped it over her shoulders. He was beginning to be afraid to touch her at all. Afraid that he wouldn't be able to stop at a mere touch.

Neither one of them heard the slow clip-clop of horse's hooves or the rumble of wheels approaching over the soft track of dirt road until the vehicle was quite close behind them.

They were hailed by a tall, angular gentleman driving a small pony cart pulled by a shaggy, spavin-backed horse. The man drew the cart to a halt beside them and said, "I give you good evening, my friends."

Angus and Blanche could see by the bright moonlight that the fellow wore a white dog collar that proclaimed him to be a member of the clergy.

"If you are strangers to these parts, I must warn you that it is dangerous to be out, especially on foot, once darkness begins to fall. These woods hereabouts are infested with a pair of foolish highwaymen, who pounce on unwary travelers."

"Your warning comes too late, sir. We have just this moment encountered your precious pair," Angus told the man. "They have stolen our money and our horses. Might we beg a ride into town with you? My name is Dalglish, Angus Dalglish, and this is Mis— Mister Flowers."

"Certainly, certainly, Mister Dalglish," the man said genially, introducing himself as Malachi Crane, as he reached down to shake hands with Angus. "I shall be glad to take you up, though we will be a trifle squeezed with three of us in the cart." He emitted a high-pitched whinny of a laugh.

Malachi Crane looked like a long-faced, kindly horse, Angus thought as he reached up to take the gentleman's hand, storing up the thought to share later with Blanche.

Crane cheerfully moved over to accommodate them in the small vehicle. Angus chose to sit next to their rescuer, since they were a trifle squeezed and he didn't want to chance Crane discovering Blanche's masquerade, should the fellow by chance shift an elbow and encounter one of her unmistakable, soft feminine curves during the drive.

Mr. Crane entertained them well on the ride, explaining that he was the assistant curate for the parish serving the farmers on the southern outskirts of Carlisle. He was not at all surprised to hear of his passengers' recent experiences.

"Ah, yes. Macheath and Peachum, no doubt. Our local highwaymen. They like to pretend they are the modern-day incarnations of Friar Tuck and Little John." He gave his characteristic whinny of a laugh again.

"The lads were tenant farmers hereabouts until the new landlord increased their rents fourfold. Unfortunately, those two strapping lads both have large families. There's a new baby on the way just about every year in each household. Along with most of their fellow tenants, they couldn't make enough profit from their crops to meet the rent payments and all of them were forced off their farms. It was a right shame. With no way to earn a living, I'm afraid some of the lads took to the High Toby. . . . They didn't harm you, I trust."

Angus fingered his bruised chin, but denied any hurt. He wouldn't mention the wound to his pride. He certainly didn't want to admit that this was the first time he hadn't succeeded in extracting himself unscathed from a dangerous situation. He could feel Blanche's eyes on him. He turned his head and gave her a lopsided grin, telling her with a look to keep her comments to herself. He needn't have worried; she had no intention of filling in all the details for the loquacious curate.

He gave in to his desire to hold her close, despite

137

her disguise. Of necessity, he had to keep his arm about her waist to keep her from falling out of the side of the wagon. The three of them were pressed together along the all-too-narrow bench seat, and there were no side railings for her to hold on to. She rested against his arm. Angus turned to smile down at her in the dark, pulling her firmly against his side.

"Afraid I can't convey you all the way into Carlisle. The vicarage is just beyond the next turning in the road here, on the outskirts of town. Might I suggest that you stay with me tonight, Mister Dalglish? Since our local bandits have stolen your money, I would be pleased to offer you and Mister Flowers a place to rest your heads at the monastery. Unless you have friends awaiting you in town, of course."

"The monastery?" Angus asked with surprise.

Mr. Crane gave his high-pitched laugh. "Oh yes, indeed." He went on to explain. "About a hundred years ago the monastery was used as a parish house. And a magnificent one it was, too! It was inhabited by no less a personage than the Anglican bishop himself and his court here in Carlisle. It was once part of a connecting dormitory-refectory-cloister complex adjoining one of the glorious Gothic cathedrals built by the Augustinian monks in the twelfth century, and most unfortunately partially destroyed during the Dissolution."

"And not now used by the church hierarchy any longer?" Angus questioned.

"No," Crane said, lowering his voice conspiratorially and placing a wealth of meaning on that single syllable.

"Why not?" Angus asked.

"It is reputed to be haunted by the headless monks killed by the overzealous troops sent by King Henry the Eighth to dissolve the monasteries," Crane said, in the same low voice.

"Haunted! How did a holy place achieve such a reputation?" Angus exclaimed, trying valiantly to suppress a grin.

Blanche felt him shaking where she was pressed to his side and knew he was trying not to laugh aloud.

"Soon after they took up residence, the Anglican clerics who inhabited the monastery were driven away by suspicious, unexplained sounds and reports of strange sightings of figures clad in black cassocks with white surplices, covered by hooded black cloaks. That was the traditional garb of the Austin Canons—the Augustinian monks, you know.

"The monastery has only recently been used as living quarters by the church again. Out of direst necessity, you understand. The coffers of the church in this parish have been rather sadly depleted lately, with the failure of the tenant farmers' crops and the popularity of the Nonconformists in this part of the country."

"And are you no longer bothered by these bloody monks, then, rattling their rusty chains as they traipse through the corridors of the monastery by night?"

"Times have changed," Crane said, sighing. "I do not say that we are still haunted, but whether we are, or not, we must make do with these living quarters. The church can't afford to house us elsewhere at present.''

"What form did the, ah, hauntings take?" Angus was greatly amused by this tale and decided to draw it out for all it was worth.

"The dead monks, dripping blood from the grisly wounds inflicted by the soldiers, were reported to carry their severed limbs—and in one case, head—about with them as they walked the halls and grounds of the old monastery, and were sometimes heard chanting their offices. It was said that they appeared in the bedrooms of the young Anglican priests, passing right through the heavy wooden doors, and set up such a wailing and crying out, demanding that justice be done and the place be returned to the rule of the Roman Church, that all the young men took fright and begged to be transferred elsewhere.

"One of the Archbishop of Canterbury's representatives was even called in to investigate and he concluded that the monastery had to be abandoned. This was about a hundred years ago, you understand. The grounds and buildings went to rack and ruin in the interval. The current Anglican bishop only gave permission for it to be opened again when the local vicarage for this parish burned to the ground just over two years ago.''

"Quite a tale, sir," Angus said, no longer bothering to hide his amusement. "We are in for a rare treat, you see, Flowers," he remarked to Blanche.

Crane turned down a long, winding lane that led to the partially ruined monastery.

"So you believe the place is still haunted, Mister Crane?" Blanche asked, striving to keep her voice low and masculine.

"I cannot say with any certainty."

"From ghoulies and ghosties and long-leggety beasties / And things that go bump in the night, / Good Lord, deliver us!" Angus recited the old Cornish prayer. Blanche knew he was laughing at her question and immediately put on a look of haughty dignity, which amused him even further as one of the curls of the wig had come loose and was hanging over her fair forehead in a most fetching manner, which was totally at odds with her usual neat appearance.

"Amen!" cried Malachi Crane with unexpected vigor.

"Surely you don't believe in these ghosts, Mister Crane," Angus drawled in a bored voice.

"Now, I didn't say I believed in them—and I didn't say I didn't. Some things are beyond my ken. But I recommend you don't tease the young gentleman, sir. He may have nightmares. I can assure you, that I myself have heard strange noises in the night. And I am not one given to fanciful notions," Crane said in all seriousness, nodding his long, shaggy head in energetic fashion.

"When was the last time anyone reported a sighting?" Angus egged him on.

"I don't wish to alarm you, but only last month, a visitor reported hearing noises in the night, and the next morning found what looked suspiciously like bloodstains on the door handle and on the floor outside his room,'' Crane said, bringing the cart to a halt in front of the remains of the once great church attached to the monastery. Now all that remained was a ruined shell. Moonlight gleamed through the bare ruined towers of the once magnificent cathedral, casting uneven patterns of light across the faces of three people in the pony cart.

''You terrify me, sir,'' Angus said flippantly as he jumped down, following Blanche. He turned a grinning face to Blanche, expecting her to join in his mirth as they followed the curate into the main hall. Her lips parted in only a slight smile as she looked back at him.

Angus and Blanche were invited to join the curate for an evening meal after they had a chance to refresh themselves in Malachi Crane's quarters in the still-standing Chapter House. The meal was served in the refectory, the former monks' dining hall. The long and narrow, twelfth-century refectory remained fairly well intact. Malachi was anxious to expound on the history of the monastery. He explained that it had been sturdily constructed of local stone and brick, including many bricks pilfered from the remains of the foundations of the fort built by the ancient Romans when they occupied the area. Luguvalium, the Roman name for Carlisle, had been a post guarding the northwest corner of Hadrian's Wall, and served as one of the northernmost outposts of the far-flung Roman Empire.

He told them that it was fortunate only one wall of the refectory had been damaged by King Harry's mob. Later it had been patched with some of the stones from the monastic church. The cathedral itself had been the main object of the despoilers' vengeance against rule by the Church of Rome.

Blanche listened attentively as the talkative cleric expanded his tale. She felt a pang of guilt for practicing such a deception on this convivial, clerical gentleman, but she did her best to maintain her boyish pose and kept her voice low, speaking and moving with studied nonchalance. She wisely let Angus do most of the talking, while she concentrated on sitting back, well out of the bright candlelight where Malachi might be able to get a better look at her feminine features.

Angus excused himself after the meal, requesting the loan of a horse so that he could ride into town.

"Surely you will not wish to risk a journey tonight, Mister Dalglish!" their host exclaimed.

Angus explained that he had important business that wouldn't keep until the following day. "I expect to meet some gentlemen and, er, replenish my funds, you see. You have been most generous, sir, but Flowers and I do not wish to trouble you after tonight."

"Then you are welcome to take the chestnut mare in the stables, although I fear she is old and lamentably slow nowadays."

Angus thanked him, then said to Blanche, "Flowers, I think you must to bed." He explained to Crane that his young friend was burned to the socket after a tiring day in the saddle.

Blanche did not argue with him, though she was torn. She would have preferred to accompany Angus, but she *was* bone tired.

"Take our young visitor to the guest chamber, Henley, and see that he has everything he needs," Malachi instructed his manservant after Angus departed. He told Henley to fill a bath for the young lad, who looked almost worn to a shadow.

Blanche was longing for her bed and wondered how Dalglish had the energy to go out gaming again. He must be addicted to it, she decided, dragging herself after Henley, not realizing that Angus had no choice, if they were to have the funds to continue their journey. According to her Uncle Horace, gambling fever was a common enough affliction.

Henley led the way, holding high a long taper, lighting Blanche's steps along the cold, stone passageway that led from the refectory to the wing that had housed the monastic dormitory. The light from the young servant's candle cast eerie shadows on the vaulted ceiling as they walked through the long passageway. Their footsteps echoed on the dusty stone floor. Gossamer spiders' webs were picked out in their various nooks and crannies and gleamed in the flickering candlelight.

The wind whistled through cracks in the old stones and once almost blew out the candle Henley carried. A beetle ran across the uneven flagstones, skittering and clicking over the toe of Blanche's boot. She uttered a low-pitched, muffled squeak.

"Do you sleep in this wing, Henley?" Blanche asked, feeling her skin begin to crawl.

"No, sir. I wouldn't want ta sleep over 'ere, if you'll pardon me sayin' so, sir. Folks do say spirits live in this part of the ruins. I've heard tell some of the old monks got their 'eads chopped off while they was sleepin', so's they's always wanderin' round tryin' ta find their 'eads. I 'ave a room in the Chapter House so's ta be on 'and should Mister 'Arris or Mister Crane 'ave need of me."

"Mister Harris?" Blanche asked, concealing her shudder at his gory tale.

"Mister 'Arris is the curate. He's away over ta Great Corby t'night. There be a funeral tomorra an' 'e's takin' the service."

"And there's no one else, besides you and Mister Crane in residence tonight?"

"Well, there's Mrs. Broad'ead, she be the cook, and the maidservant, Daisy, but they goes 'ome at night."

"Oh," was all Blanche could think of to say.

When the young servant had got the fire going satisfactorily in the hearth, he would have stayed to help Blanche with her bath. She flushed when she realized his intention.

"It's not—" Blanche began with a squeak. "Ah, hum," she continued, clearing her throat and lowering her voice to a masculine register. "Thank you, Henley. That will not be at all necessary."

"Very good, sir. There be a clean nightshirt on the bed." And with those words the servant took himself off, to Blanche's great relief.

She shook off the feeling of apprehension that had begun to creep up on her as she made her way through the dark passageway with Henley and luxuriated in the hot, relaxing bath, working out all the aches and pains she had acquired during the past two grueling days in the saddle. Working out all her pains except for a strange new one somewhere in the region of her heart—or was it her stomach? That organ had developed an alarming tendency to do somersaults whenever her fiery companion smiled at her or touched her. She was determined to conceal her inner turmoil from him, and hoped her features remained impassive, giving nothing away.

She had come to rely on his ingenuity and arrogant courage to help her find Prudie, but she hadn't counted on his masculine presence disturbing her so. It was just that his dark countenance was not what she was used to. She had no experience of men in a physical way. She had never even had a flirt—or even had her hand kissed before, for goodness' sake. . . . And now, not only had Angus held her tightly in his arms, but he had kissed her with an alarming intensity and let her know that she was desirable, both with words and in the heated way he had pressed his body to hers.

Blanche raised her wet hands to her face to cool her burning cheeks. Yes, she had indeed been thoroughly kissed—and she had enjoyed it and forced herself to back away from the embrace before he should find out that she was not the indifferent and passionless woman she pretended to be. He must not realize that such a pose was a masquerade, designed to protect herself from hurt.

Oh dear, she thought, as she remembered the feel of his lips covering hers, if she were not careful, she would be inviting his kisses—and his embraces. She was amazed at herself—that she would even consider for a minute inviting his amorous attentions! To show such forwardness with a man was the last thing she would have ever have expected of herself. Am I a wanton, she asked herself sternly, to be having such thoughts? No, I am only a woman—a woman with no experience of men and little chance ever to marry. But I will only be asking for heartache if I give him the least encouragement, for he will only see me as a temporary, but convenient amusement, to be enjoyed and then forgotten.

To invite his touch was to court disaster. It was difficult enough making one's way in the world alone. She must not *invite* ruin. But, oh, how he tempted her!

When she finally dressed in the clean, too-large man's nightshirt that reached almost to her ankles, she was more than ready to climb between the sheets in the high tester bed. Thoughts of visitations from the long-dead inhabitants of the hoary stone walls were dismissed from her mind as she settled herself for sleep in the solitary room. Certainly no monk had ever had a bed as soft as this one, Blanche thought drowsily as she drifted off to sleep. Her last conscious thought as she lay in the soft feather bed was of Angus. She hoped he had been given as comfortable a bed as her own.

Blanche dozed off at once and slept soundly for an hour, but then woke several times, wondering how she would know if Angus had returned safely. She didn't know where he would be sleeping and each time she woke, she fretted more, until she could no longer get back to sleep.

An owl hooted outside her window. She remembered Crane's stories and recalled that Henley said no one else was sleeping in this part of the ruins. She began to listen to the small nighttime noises that by day she would have dismissed out of hand. Blanche was not a fearful person, but the combination of the tales she had heard that night, the strange room, and her solitary presence in this area of the ruins began to disturb her. She took herself to task for being so silly, then licked her dry lips and decided she would relight her taper.

Before she could make a move, her door opened with a loud creak and someone carrying a candle entered the room. The hair rose on the back of her neck. Blanche raised herself on her elbows. "Who's there?" she called in a voice that she managed to make sound quite neutral.

"No spirit of the night to haunt you, my dear, but your cavalier returned with enough booty to last us a month."

"Angus, is that you?" she asked, recognizing his

voice with a sigh of relief. She swung her feet over the side of the bed and reached to light the candle on the table by the bed.

He laughed softly, causing her stomach to do one of those disturbing somersaults again. "Indeed, my flower, and who else would it be invading your room at this hour? Some ghostly monk? I can assure you that *I* have never been a monkish man—their pleasures are too few." There was a soft drawling note in his voice that Blanche had not heard before, not even on the night he had leapt into her bedroom at the Hen and Feathers.

He moved somewhat unsteadily toward the bed and threw a heavy leather pouch into her lap.

"To finance our campaign," was all he said as he moved to the table where he had set down his candle.

She looked down at the pouch, then lifted her head when she heard something chink. Glass against glass. She saw in the scant light of Angus's candle that he had a bottle in one hand and a glass in another and was pouring himself a drink.

"Hadn't you better go to your own room now, if you're planning to get foxed?" Blanche asked in a clipped tone, forgetting how much she had been missing him and desperately wishing for his presence only moments before.

Angus laughed. "We're sharing. Didn't you know?" He pulled off his jacket and threw it over a chair, then jerked at his neck cloth and let it fall to the floor. He was so tired he could hardly stand and here Blanche was taking him to task over the sleeping arrangements!

"Why didn't you ask for two rooms? There's certainly not a shortage of rooms here. I passed enough doors on my way to this chamber to house a dozen visitors."

"Damn it, woman, Crane thinks we're two blokes!"

Blanche could see that his mouth was drawn into a thin line—a sure indication his temper was beginning to fray. "He didn't see anything wrong with putting us in together. As a matter of fact, he mentioned that he was sure you wouldn't want to be alone in the 'haunted' wing. Why arouse his suspicions—not to mention putting him to so much extra trouble—by asking for another room? You need have no fear, this one is big enough to accommodate a small army." Angus swilled down his glass of wine, knowing that he could easily have requested two rooms. He was very much afraid that he knew the reason why he hadn't. His physical attraction to Blanche was growing by the hour.

Just a glance at her sitting on the side of the bed with her wide, magnificent eyes fixed on him and her silvery hair no longer confined under the silly wig, but falling in long waves over the front of the voluminous white nightshirt she wore, was enough to send his pulses pounding madly. Those eyes of hers were beginning to haunt him, waking and sleeping. And knowing her valiant courage in the face of the highwaymen they had faced that day, and remembering her fortitude and lack of complaint on the grueling journey they had undertaken, only added admiration and respect to his already considerable desire.

Blanche didn't like to point out that although the room was indeed cavernous, there was only the one bed. She swallowed uneasily and looked down at the leather pouch resting in her lap.

"So much misbegotten gold." She sighed, sorry that they must rely on gaming to pay their way on this journey.

"You make it sound tainted." He was hurt by her remark. "I didn't come by the money in any under-handed way or by black magic, you know. I'm not in league with the spirit world or these long-dead monks skulking around here. I'm an honest, hard-working gamester." Angus drained his glass and poured himself another, pausing before he drank it to give her a smoldering glance over the rim.

"Gaming is a devilish business, though," Blanche said firmly.

Angus was dead on his feet. His temper, already hanging by a thread anyway, flared at her criticism.

He set his glass down on the table with a bang and advanced to the bed. "If it's devilish behavior you expect of me, my dear girl, then it's devilish you'll get!"

He startled Blanche exceedingly by pulling his shirt over his head and standing before her bare-chested.

Blanche jumped to her feet. "Angus! What are you doing?"

For answer, he reached over and pulled her into his

arms, then sat down on the bed with her on his lap. He held her tightly and kissed her firmly closed lips fiercely, trying to release some of the pent-up frustration that had been building since the preceding night.

He had left a perfectly willing little wench behind him at the tavern in Carlisle where he had won over a hundred pounds at the gaming table. Just the kind of woman he liked, too—all blond curls, big blue eyes, and soft curves—cuddly and warm as a kitten. But what must he do, but come back to this staid, too-tall, *cold,* spinster, who was none of the things the tavern wench had been, but who set his blood surging through his veins as no woman had *ever* done before.

Even the sight of her in that voluminous, all-concealing man's nightshirt with her silky hair gleaming in the candlelight was enough to drive him wild. He pushed at the material of the enveloping nightshirt to no avail. The thing covered her most effectively, certainly more effectively than the revealing form-fitting trousers and shirt she had worn for the past two days.

Blanche tried to push Angus away at first, but his hold only tightened. She sat still and immobile as a marble statue and let him press his mouth to hers. She was determined to show no response to this forced lovemaking, though her mind was at war with her body—and her heart—when she felt his strong arms holding her, enfolding her in his own warmth. His warm breath caressed her face and she began to relax against him. She lifted one of her hands and placed it against his chest, but when her hand touched his bare skin, she clenched her fist and dropped it to her lap.

When he could not force a response from Blanche, Angus, his breath coming in quick bursts, drew his lips away from hers and exclaimed in frustration, "You put me in a passion with your infernal coldness. I'll heat up your blood for you yet!" he promised.

"You're much too hot for me to handle, Angus." Now that he had removed his mouth from hers, Blanche tried to pull away from him without losing her dignity. She refused to let him see that he was already a long way toward accomplishing his goal.

Angus laughed harshly, but loosened his grip on her. Blanche stood up and moved out of his reach.

"What! Where's your ambition, woman? Don't you have the universal female desire to tame a rake?" he asked on a lighter note as he regained a measure of control.

"I'd sooner tame a lion!"

He smiled in genuine amusement. "But what about the excitement. You wouldn't want to miss the excitement, would you?"

"I prefer a quiet life."

"What! After the last few exciting days! I can hardly believe it of you."

Angus rose from the bed and walked over to her. He put his knuckle to her chin and rubbed gently as he smiled into her eyes. "I'm sorry, my dear, but I want you to admit that you like me—just a little bit," he said in a soft voice, giving her a beseeching look.

Blanche felt again, stronger than before, that treacherous tingling warmth invading her limbs. One more minute and she was afraid that she would surrender to his gentle pleading as she had not to his fierce passion.

Angus leaned nearer.

A disembodied, hollow laugh rang out, echoing around the stone walls of their chamber. Angus and Blanche sprang apart.

"What—?" Blanche began to say, looking adorably vulnerable for once to Angus's eyes.

"Well, now." Angus grinned. "Seems we have an interesting situation here. Prepare yourself for visitors, my dear."

Her eyes were open to their fullest extent, only a tiny rim of silver gray visible around the irises, and a pulse was beating furiously in her throat. Blanche wanted nothing so much as to throw her arms up about Angus's neck and bury her face against his shoulder, but as ever, she was able to restrain herself and let none of these emotions show on her still face.

She took a deep, calming breath and said, "Give them my regards, will you, Angus? I'm for bed." And she deliberately climbed back into the high bed and turned her back to the door.

A wide grin split his face as he stood marveling at the sangfroid of his unflappable lady. He wondered what she would do if he announced that he would join her.

There was a rattle of the doorknob as well as a loud clanging of some heavy object just outside the

154

bedroom door. He hastily reached over and drew the bed covers over Blanche's revealing silver tresses as he saw the doorknob begin to turn. He had locked it after himself when he came in, but he didn't doubt that, whoever these tricksters were, they had a key.

"Come in," Angus called. "Come in, my brothers. Join me in a drink. For I've just now pilfered this fine claret from your cellars."

The doorknob ceased to rattle and there was a muffled whispering from beyond the locked door.

"Ah, you can't decide whether to take up my invitation or not? Well, let us see if I can persuade you." With these words Angus walked toward the door, deliberately treading heavily in his leather boots as he walked over the stone floor of the bedchamber toward the door.

He was not at all surprised when he heard the footsteps on the other side of the door hastily scramble away down the hall as he approached. He gave a full-bodied laugh as he unlocked the door, and peered out into the hall, holding his candle high and shining it in one direction, then the other.

"They're gone, Flowers. I doubt they will disturb us further this night," he called out loudly, "for they know I'll be ready for them, if they make so bold!" He closed the door and locked it.

"Did you see anything?" Blanche asked curiously, as she pushed the covers down and folded her arms calmly over the bedclothes.

Angus debated with himself whether or not to tease

her about having seen a headless monk, but suddenly he was too tired for further play that night.

"No. I'm convinced it was only the young servants or some local children trying to play off their tricks." He made a dismissive gesture with his hand.

He took a blanket from Blanche's bed and walked over to the hard wooden chair set against the wall by the hearth. "Good night, Fleur," he called as he blew out his candle and settled himself for the night. "You've naught to fear from our tricksters—or from me. Sleep well."

"Angus?"

"What?"

"I will change places, if you like. After all, I am relying on you to help me rescue Prudie and you must have some decent rest."

For answer Angus just snorted, "Go to sleep."

"Good night, Angus," Blanche answered in a voice that communicated none of the guilt she was feeling for depriving him of a comfortable bed. "And, thank you."

Chapter 9

"Where to now, Angus?" Blanche asked, drawing in a long breath of air as she pulled her heavily panting horse to a halt alongside her companion's lathered mount on the outskirts of Gretna Green.

"Your guess is as good as mine, Fleur," Angus answered, reaching forward to pat his horse's neck. "It may surprise you to hear that I've never been to Gretna before. I'm afraid I don't make a habit of rushing here, chasing after eloping couples."

They had ridden hard on the fresh mounts Angus had hired in Carlisle with his winnings of the previous night and had made fast time over the less than twenty miles to the Scottish border town, leaving the monastery at first light as they had.

Blanche ignored his teasing. She glanced up at the gulls wheeling and crying shrilly overhead and sniffed the air. She was surprised that it smelled of the sea. "Are we near the sea, then?"

"Yes, indeed. Had you not realized that Gretna is only about four miles from the Solway Firth?"

"No, I had no idea—geography is not my strong point, I fear . . . Angus, if the innkeeper you spoke to in Carlisle was right, and Prudie and Waddle *were* the couple who hired a carriage from him, then they could not possibly have arrived here until after nightfall. And I take it they could not have had the wedding ceremony performed last night, but would have had to wait until this morning?"

"So I was told. We can only hope that the sketchy information I received was correct."

"Shouldn't we check all the blacksmiths' quarters first? Is that not where the ceremonies are conducted?"

"It's not only blacksmiths who perform these border marriages over the anvil in their forges, you know. A variety of hedge priests operate out of inns and small chapels, and all manner of fly-by-night establishments, too," Angus told her, resting his hands tiredly on the pommel of his saddle as he spoke.

"How can such marriages be legal?" Blanche asked, noticing the weary note in her companion's voice this morning. He looked distinctly haggard, too, and no wonder, after his uncomfortable night—several uncomfortable nights, she amended, with a pang of sympathy.

"As long as the ceremony is witnessed and registered by one of the motley collection of these so-called 'border priests' who have set up shop here to circumvent the laws in England, the marriage is con-

158

sidered to be legally binding. I have heard that one of the more enterprising of these fellows has even built an inn on the English side of the border.''

''Why would he go to so much expense?'' Blanche asked, mystified.

''It's a common belief that a wedding held in Scotland should be consummated on English soil—to make the marriage valid, you understand.''

Angus noted Blanche's flush as he added, ''I have no idea how many such disreputable parsons there may be here in Gretna. We shall have to check as many likely places as we can.''

''Where do we start?'' Blanche asked in a level voice, concealing the impatience and anxiety she was feeling.

''This place is smaller than I imagined. I suppose the size of the town becomes exaggerated in one's imagination with all the talk about runaway marriages taking place here. . . . Perhaps we should check the blacksmith forges first. If your cousin isn't there, then we'll try the inns and boardinghouses. Are you comfortable enough with your disguise to make some inquiries on your own, while I check elsewhere? We would save time that way.''

''What *is* the time, Angus?''

Angus pulled out his heavy gold watch he had redeemed from the haberdasher's shop and squinted down at the dial. The watch was emblazoned with a crest that Blanche had not seen before, but her keen eyes noticed it now and she looked at it curiously. It was on the tip of her tongue to ask Angus where he had obtained such a thing.

"Quarter to eight." He whistled through his teeth. "We *did* make fast time from Carlisle. Has anyone ever told you that you're a bruising rider, Flowers, my lad?"

Blanche ignored his compliment. "It is not yet eight, you say?" She frowned pensively. "Prudie is not an early riser. She has trouble getting up before nine o'clock, so perhaps we have some little time. And, yes, I believe I can pull off this disguise after two days of playing at being a man." She gave him a cool smile but her eyes sparkled with humor as she added, "I must say, men have a much freer time of it than we women do."

"Indeed! I hope you don't intend to make your disguise permanent. It would be *such* a sad waste, ma'am," Angus said, trying to disconcert her. They stared at one another for a long moment before Blanche looked away.

Angus lifted his hand to rub at his tired eyes. "I'm starved! I wish we could eat first," he said wistfully, looking all around at the small shops just beginning to come to life even as they road slowly into the town.

"You're always hungry. Yet you're not at all fat," Blanche said with a twinkle in her eyes.

"Thank you, ma'am." Angus drawled. His lips twitched at the backhanded compliment.

"I don't know where you put so much food."

"I burn it up keeping up with *you,* I imagine. How can you expect me to gallivant all over the country

160

with you on this hair-raising adventure with no sustenance? I can't eat like a bird the way you do." He glinted down at her. "Where do you get the energy?"

She shrugged. "Perhaps you could leave me outside one of the blacksmith's premises and bring back a picnic? We could eat while we watched the area."

He shook his head. "No. They might not choose to have the dire deed done for them at the location you choose. Then where would we be? There are too many places to watch. We will have to inquire at the inns first, and see if we can locate them before they set out."

As they planned their course of action, they walked their horses slowly through the small town—it was hardly more than a village, really. Angus opened his mouth to suggest that he would take the rougher-looking places, while Blanche could check at the more genteel-looking inns, when Blanche turned her head sharply and cried out. "Prudie! Stop! Prudence Wilmont, do you hear me?"

She jumped off her horse, flinging the reins to Angus, and raced after her cousin who was on the arm of a rather short young man dressed in an ill-fitting, nondescript overcoat. Waddle, without a doubt, Angus decided, as he leapt down in a powerful movement and quickly tethered the two horses.

After one glance of openmouthed surprise in Blanche's direction, Prudie and Bartie took to their heels and scurried around the corner before Blanche could come up to them. Prudie knew it was Blanche's voice all right, but the words seemed to be issuing from the mouth of a black-haired youth sitting astride a piebald horse. She didn't want to stay around, though, to solve the mystery.

Angus ran after Blanche, following her down a narrow passageway between two sets of terraced houses and shops. He came up to join her as she stood with her hands on her lean hips, looking up and down the street one over from where they had left their horses.

"Now, where can Prudie have disappeared to?" she asked breathlessly.

"You didn't see which way they went, then?" Angus asked.

"No. I've lost them for the moment," Blanche answered when she got her breath back. "At least we know they are here, though. Perhaps they haven't tied the knot yet, if they felt it was necessary to run away. Did you get a good look at them, Angus? Would you know her—them—again, if we spread out to look?"

He shook his head. "I didn't see her face, but I would recognize her hat and pelisse and her small stature. She must be several inches shorter than you," he said, looking at Blanche in her men's garb. "Waddle was rather nondescript, except for that outsized overcoat. The young gudgeon doesn't have much fashion sense, does he?

"Fleur," he added with a worried frown. "It occurs to me—if your cousin won't heed you, we might not be able to stop them."

"Oh, no!" Blanche turned wide eyes on him. Angus felt a distinct jolt in his midsection at the unspoken plea in her eyes. He was undone by a show of so much uncharacteristic emotion from his capable lady. Blanche expected him to know what to do to save her cousin. He *had* to come up with a quick plan of action. He couldn't let her down, now that they'd come this far.

"Let me think." His black brows drew together in concentration. "We have to find them . . . follow them, find out where they plan to be wed—then rush in and put an impediment in the way of their being married."

"But what? Put that quick-witted acuity of yours to use now, please, Angus!"

"I'll think of something," he said with more confidence than he felt. "I'll carry her away kicking and screaming, if needs be," he promised.

They hurried in the direction Blanche thought her cousin had gone and checked two large boarding-houses in the area, but had no success.

"Lookin' for a runaway couple, are ye, laddies?" a passerby asked them with a grin wrapped round his broad Scot's accent. The two "gentlemen" had the worried air a local came to know well.

Angus acknowledged that such was the case.

"Mostly folks do na op'n so early, ye ken—they find the bridal couples prefer ta spend the mornin' in the inns—puttin' the cart before the horse, so ta speak. But there's a noo boardin'house at t'other end of the Green been trying' to compete for business lately. Op'n for weddin's at all hours, they are," the grinning stranger told them.

Angus and Blanche looked at one another. "It's worth a try," Blanche decided and Angus promptly asked the friendly Scot for the direction of this new inn.

They walked quickly, taking one wrong turn, so that it was several minutes before they reached the place the passerby had described. They were at the other end of the street when they saw Prudie and Bartholomew rushing in the door of the rather rundown guest house, whose front gate was hanging askew from its hinges and whose shutters were in dire need of a new coat of paint. Prudie's maid, Sukey, disappeared into the house behind them.

"Thank heavens Prudie has Sukey with her, at least," Blanche muttered, consoling herself with the thought that if the maid had shared Prudie's room during their three nights on the road, then perhaps her cousin hadn't been fully compromised, after all. The thought did not once enter Blanche's head that *she* had had no maid to give her countenance under similar circumstances. She held onto her cap, pressing the wig in place against her head, and started to run, following Angus who had sprinted ahead.

Angus thrust open the door to the inn with a bang. Blanche was hard on his heels. They entered a large, rather dingy, two-story hallway with several doors leading off it. They tried first one, then another of the doors, and found all of them locked. Angus put his ear to one of the doors and motioned for Blanche to do the same along the other side of the long hallway.

At the door farthest from the entryway, Angus heard a voice droning on. He put his shoulder to the door, heaved twice, and burst through to see a large but rather shabby parlor that someone had decorated with oddments of old lace and fresh greenery to make it look festive enough for a wedding.

There was an old, wooden lectern set in front of the windows. Prudie and Waddle stood in front of the lectern. Prudie's maid Sukey stood behind them along with another witness, a stooped, toothless, old man leaning on a cane. To the side stood a heavyset, dour-looking woman with wiry, grizzled red hair, who waited at the ready with a feathered quill and the register for the bridal couple to sign when the short ceremony was completed. A little terrier dog with a white satin bow tied round its neck sat on a tartan cushion, its ears pricked to the alert.

A rather seedy individual with a shiny bald head stood behind the lectern holding a grubby piece of paper in his hand. His reading glasses had slipped halfway down his nose as he read the words on the paper in front of him. A bent ear trumpet rested beside the lectern.

"Do ye, Miss Prudence Wilmont take this gentleman, Mister—Bartholomew Waddle, for yer wedded husband?" the man read from a paper he was holding up to the light.

"No, she doesn't!" Blanche cried as Angus rushed forward.

"Stop the proceedings!" Angus commanded in a voice resonate with military authority.

"Och, laddie! Jus' what do ye think ye're a doin'?" the heavyset woman shouted, waving her laden arms as though to drive Angus and Blanche back out the door.

Prudie and young Waddle turned at the same time. "They can't stop me! I don't even know these people!" Prudie cried out, while Bartie looked frightened as he gazed at the two "men" bearing down on them. One looked no older than he, but the other gentleman had an air of authority that boded ill for his plans to wed the heiress.

When the balding man droned on, seeming not to hear the cacophony around him, Angus stepped round the lectern impatiently and grabbed the fellow by his jacket lapels. "Are you deaf? I ordered you to stop this ceremony immediately."

At this, the man did indeed halt and glanced up in surprise. Angus looked like a devil with a black scowl marring his handsome face.

"Aye, me son-in-law Urquart be deaf as a post," the toothless old codger informed Angus with a satisfied cackle of mirth.

"You have no business marrying these two children, here," Angus shouted at the man who was standing bewildered behind the lectern.

"Wheesht, these be yer children here, ye say?" the balding Mr. Urquart asked, staring at Angus in confusion. He recognized that the tall, fierce fellow gripping him tightly by the lapels was a man to be

166

reckoned with, but he was struggling to understand just what it was the angry, muscular gentleman wanted done.

"My children!" Angus exclaimed, staggered by such an idea. "Not on your life!" He released his hold on Urquart's jacket and stepped back.

"Do na let him chouse ye outta yer fee, Urquart!" Mrs. Urquart waved her feathered quill in the air like a sword, looking as though she would like to smite them all.

"I demand that you go on with the ceremony, Mister Urquart," Prudie screeched.

"Miss Wilmont," pleaded young Bartie in a voice no one heeded, "perhaps we *should* wait and speak to your father."

The little terrier began to yap furiously as everyone tried to have their say. It seemed to Blanche that everyone spoke at once. There was such a clamor in the room that no one could hear themselves think, much less speak.

"Not yer child but yer wife, ye say?" Urquart asked as he squinted at Angus.

"No! She's not my wife!"

"Who be ye, then?"

"Angus Dalglish!" Angus told the man. He continued to speak in a loud, threatening voice as the deaf man questioned him, while Prudie and the quill-waving Mrs. Urquart screeched and shouted, and the little dog howled.

"I demand that you cease this ceremony at once!" Angus ordered.

"Reet ye are, sir . . ." Urquart, thoroughly confused but anxious to comply with whatever the fierce gentleman wanted, misheard the words as to " '*complete*' this ceremony at once." And so he looked down and continued to read in a droning voice from his paper. His words were drowned out by the mingled shouts and cries of Prudie and the enraged Mrs. Urquart, not to mention the chorus of barking dog and cackling old man.

"Then if ye, sir, be content ta take this woman for yer wedded wife—" Urquart read on, looking at Prudie.

"No! This girl is not to be married, I tell you! Flowers, er—Miss Charolais here is the girl's guardian. You must listen to her!" Angus, beside himself with anger as the farce continued, pulled Blanche forward by the wrist. "This is the lady you must heed."

Prudie continued her high-pitched protests, making so much noise that she didn't hear Angus pronounce her cousin's name. Poor Sukey had already succumbed to the vapors and was leaning against the old man, who balanced himself on his stick with one hand and held the comely little maid tightly about the waist with the other, while he cackled with mirth throughout.

"So, ye, Angus Dalglish," Urquart said confusedly, "and Miss Charlotte—"

"Charolais! Miss Blanche *Charolais!*" Angus shouted.

"And Miss Blanche Charolais agree that ye will take—"

Prudie was screaming at Bartie, insisting that he *do* something.

"Yes! We've agreed to take her away," Angus interrupted over Urquart's mumbled words "one another in legal wedlock."

"Haven't we?" Angus looked to Blanche who nodded and mouthed "yes."

Mrs. Urquart was urging her husband to hurry before they lost their fee and the toothless old man was smiling widely and nodding vigorously as he held on to Sukey.

"Then I pronounce ye man and wife," Urquart completed, looking at Angus and *Prudie*. "Ye may kiss the bride, sir."

"No, no!" shouted Prudie hysterically, clenching her fists and drumming her feet on the floor.

Blanche and Angus looked at one another thunderstruck.

"He doesn't mean he's married us, does he?" Blanche exclaimed faintly.

"What's the meaning of this? Carry on with *my* marriage ceremony, Mister Urquart!" Prudie demanded in a high-pitched squeal.

"There ye be, Maggie," Urquart turned to his harridan of a wife, beaming proudly. "Ye see, I dinna allow the Sassenach to chouse me outta me fee. Buckled the lad and lassie up all reet. Tight as houses they be joined noo! Ye an' yer da be witnesses, Maggie."

Urquart, thinking he had married Angus and Prudie, reached to shake Angus by the hand, and beamed at Prudie. Angus saw in a flash that perhaps this mis-

169

taken "marriage" might be just the thing to get them some way out of the difficulties they were in. He put his arm around Blanche's superfine-clad shoulders and bent to kiss her briefly on the lips. Urquart's glasses fell from their precarious perch on his nose and his jaw almost dropped to the floor in his astonishment at the sight.

"Och! Lads canna marry lads!" Urquart uttered in a shocked voice as he stood looking at what he thought were two gentlemen. "Never heerd o' sich irregular carryin's on!"

Angus flushed to the tips of his ears. He turned quickly to an equally embarrassed Blanche and snatched off her hat and wig. Blanche shook out her long, silver tresses, concealing her embarrassment—and her anger at Angus for acting as though they had just been truly married—behind the fall of her hair.

The old man cackled louder than ever in glee.

The yapping dog danced round their heels in a frenzy.

"Cousin Blanche!" Prudie screamed in shock. "How—? What are you doing here, dressed like that?"

"I've come to take you home to Uncle Wilmont," Blanche answered, trying to impose some order on the wild scene. She would sort out this bogus marriage with Angus later.

"No! You have no authority over me. I shan't go with you!" Prudie shouted petulantly, almost beside herself at having her plans thwarted at the last minute.

"Oh, yes, you will, young lady, for I am your

cousin now, too—by marriage. And I insist that you obey my wife.'' Angus's harsh voice brooked no gainsaying.

"That wasn't a proper ceremony. My cousin can't be married to this—this monstrously overbearing stranger!" Prudie cried, pointing to Angus as she turned to the other people in the room, looking for support.

Mrs. Urquart loudly insisted that the ceremony was legal and that Urquart had earned his fee. "One 'o ye lassies be married ta this greet, glowerin' laddie here!"

"You must marry Bartie and me now, Mister Urquart!" Prudie began to screech and drum her heels on the floor.

Bartholomew put his arm about Prudie's shoulders, trying to calm her, and desperately wondering what they could do to retrieve the situation. He was quite taken aback to witness the transformation of his beautiful, high-spirited heiress into a screaming harridan before his very eyes. "I'm sure that ceremony wasn't legal!" Prudie yelled again.

Mrs. Urquart bent her threatening gaze on the young lady. "Aye, they is buckled. Ye heard them, dinna ye, da?" She turned to the old man who nodded vigorously and said, "Aye, daughter. They is. I be a witness. I will sweer in a court o' law—"

"Ye see, me da will sweer in a court o' law," Mrs. Urquart said with grim satisfaction, allowing no further argument. The toothless old man continued to nod his head vigorously.

171

"I—we shall just go to the blacksmith's shop and get married, if you won't perform the ceremony here," Prudie declared loudly with a stamp of her dainty foot. She was cross as two sticks to have her will thwarted so, not to mention having her romantic elopement spoiled at the last second.

"Your father is going to cut you off without a penny, if you do any such thing," Blanche warned her cousin.

"He can't do that!" Prudie insisted, lifting her chin and glaring at Blanche.

"Ah, but he can. He has complete control over your funds," Blanche said calmly, looking at her cousin out of a face that had gone as pale and still as marble.

Young Waddle was ashen. "Perhaps we should wait until your father comes round to view our marriage with favor," he suggested to Prudie.

"You don't know him. He never will! If you're such a coward, Bartie Waddle, then I won't marry you after all!" Prudie stamped her foot again.

Prudie was a fickle young girl and she had begun to have doubts about actually carrying through with the impulsive scheme. It was only the exhilaration and romance of such an adventure—and the thought of defying her father and fooling Blanche, her always sensible, hard-to-shock, older cousin—that had made the idea of an elopement so appealing in the first place. Prudie had not considered that she would have to live forever as "Mrs. Waddle." This unappetizing thought occurred to her now and gave her pause.

172

"Good!" said Blanche. "I will take you home, then."

"I don't want to go with *you*," Prudie said rudely, a frown pulling down her bow-shaped mouth unattractively.

"Your father has put you in my charge and I consider myself your guardian in his absence," Blanche said, tight-lipped. After that farce of a ceremony, her own temper was in shreds.

"How can you be a proper guardian, all rigged out in those indecent clothes and running around with this odious man who I've never seen before?" Prudie asked peevishly, indicating Angus.

"Ah, but she is wed to me now, Miss Wilmont, and her authority as your guardian is shared with me," Angus insisted again.

"See here, Urquart must have his fee whether any o' ye dafties be married or nae." Mrs. Urquart shoved the register at Angus and Blanche. "Sign here. Urquart's fee be ten guineas."

Angus took the feather quill and scrawled his name, then put his hand in his pocket and pulled out the requisite ten guineas.

Blanche uttered a sound of protest and balked at signing her name on the paper she feared would legally bind her to Angus.

"You must sign the register to make the marriage ceremony valid," Angus insisted to Blanche in a low voice.

"Angus, this is madness! I won't do it!" Blanche countered in a fierce whisper.

173

"Sign it, Blanche." Angus spoke to her in a low voice. "Don't you see, it will be more prudent if we, as a proper married couple, escort your cousin back to her father. We can discuss whether to keep to the marriage later," he whispered in Blanche's ear. "A marriage so easily contrived, must be as easily ended," he said confidentially, but with no actual knowledge of the legal standing of such a union under the reformed marriage laws of 1753.

"Consider how you have been unchaperoned in my company for three days now, not to mention nights," he pointed out. "If you wish to arrive back at your uncle's with your cousin properly chaperoned, not ruined, then you had better arrive back as Mrs. Dalglish, or else all our efforts will have been wasted. I saw that last night," he urged in a whisper, trying to overcome Blanche's hesitation.

Prudie had been standing, arms akimbo, watching them with a sulky expression on her face. "My cousin Blanche is at her last prayers. She's always been afraid *I* would be married before her. But she's such an antidote no *gentleman* would ever have her," she said with childish spite.

"Meaning *I'm* no gentleman, Miss Wilmont?" Angus asked in a deceptively soft drawl. "Well, if that's what you think, brat, then that's how you will be treated!" Angus clamped a hand to Prudie's upper arm and turned her about. "Apologize to your cousin. Now!" he commanded in a voice of steel.

"I'm—I'm sorry, Blanche," she said grudgingly as Angus tightened his grip. "Ow!"

174

Prudie's insult to both herself and Angus prodded Blanche into taking up the quill and hastily signing her name in the register without further protest. Mrs. Urquart's hard mouth actually turned up a quarter of an inch in what passed for a smile as she handed Angus a copy of the marriage lines.

With an exasperated look at Prudie, Blanche said, "It's back to Heywood for you, cousin. Immediately." Now all Blanche wanted to do was to take Prudie away as fast as she could and sort out this fiasco with Angus.

Angus held Prudie by one arm and Blanche took her by the other, to lead her from the room.

Sukey followed them.

Prudie had hysterics.

Bartie hung his head.

Mr. Urquart mopped his shiny pate.

Mrs. Urquart danced a jig with her father.

And the little dog yapped to see such sport.

Chapter 10

Angus sat with his booted feet resting on the battered oak table in the private parlor he had hired at a nearby inn. He was finishing the last cup from a pot of coffee he had ordered up with the breakfast that he, Blanche, and Prudie had shared.

He had just consumed what Blanche had called an indecent amount of food. And he had to confess that he had indeed made severe inroads into the mound of shirred eggs, two slabs of ham, huge beefsteak, plate of deviled kidneys, loaf of freshly baked bread, freshly churned butter, and selection of jams and marmalade served up to them. He had wryly asserted to Blanche that, considering the amount of energy he had expended in the past four days, the "small" breakfast he had just devoured had gone only a small way to filling the hole where his stomach had once been. He had had the pleasure of forcing a smile from her with his teasing words. She had been even more reserved than usual after they had left the Urquart boarding-house that morning. He would have to talk with her later and try to bring her around to his way of thinking that the morning's farce could have unforeseen dividends.

Angus sat at his ease, but alert for any tricks, as he watched Prudie wander restlessly about the parlor. He warned the bird-witted little minx in no uncertain terms not to try to leave the room. She chattered on about how ill-done-by she was, and stopped occasionally to glance out the window facing the street to comment ill naturedly on the fashion, or lack thereof, of the passersby going to and fro.

Because Macheath and Peachum had absconded with Blanche's valise containing all her clothes, she needed to purchase a gown and other feminine accoutrements. She had gone out shopping, and had taken Sukey with her. As she was still disguised in her male attire, she was going to pretend to the shopkeepers that she was buying clothes for her ''sister'' and had brought along her sister's maid to help.

Angus had agreed with Blanche that it was time she threw off her disguise and resumed a proper lady's wardrobe, though he experienced a pang of regret that he would not be able to admire her long legs encased in those provocative pantaloons any longer. He had had the deuce of a time persuading her to take his blunt. Blanche had insisted that she would pay him back the whole sum she had borrowed. Just where she thought to get the money, Angus hadn't a clue.

As they waited for Blanche to return, Prudie alternately vexed and bored Angus with her self-centered chatter. He couldn't deny that she was easy on the eyes, though, if not on the ears—or the temper. Prudence Wilmont was indeed almost perfectly beautiful, he saw now as he watched her pace about the small room.

She had removed her bonnet and he could see that her bright golden hair caught the light and gleamed when she moved. Her complexion was that perfect blend of cream, dusted along the cheekbones with a rosy pink, that proclaimed her a true English rose. Her large cornflower blue eyes were surrounded by absurdly long, dark lashes; her nose was small but not at all snubbed, while her red rosebud of a mouth was made for kissing, Angus thought appreciatively. However, she marred all her good looks by holding that mouth in an unattractive pout much of the time.

And, if those assets were not more than should fairly be bestowed on one female, there was her figure. It was ripe—too ripe. A seventeen-year-old girl had no right to such a figure. Many gentlemen would be lost after one look at the perfect features of the young lady, Angus guessed, and their fingers would just itch to twine round that tiny waist and pull those soft, well-formed curves against themselves. Yet, he wasn't in the least stirred.

He glanced away from the girl and took a sip of his coffee. No, he did not feel one iota of desire for Miss Prudence Wilmont, despite her admitted perfections and enticements. She was too immature, too vain, too hot-at-hand. Nothing but a spoiled child, really.

And besides, he was caught in the toils of another woman. Little did she believe it, though. Never before when he had been interested in a woman did it prevent him from being attracted to another . . . or two or three—or a dozen—others.

Angus could acknowledge Miss Wilmont's attractions without feeling the least inclination to flirt with her. He smiled mockingly at himself. If anything, his feelings for the girl were strictly avuncular. His only real interest in Prudence Wilmont was to save Blanche from any anxiety or trouble over the girl's mad escapades.

He didn't need any other complications in his life just now, Angus thought, then sighed. It was too late. This growing desire he felt for Blanche was enough to keep him awake at night and on tenterhooks throughout the day. And now they were married. . . . It was beginning to dawn on him that it might be difficult to abandon the masquerade and let her go, once they had returned her cousin to her home.

Prudie got tired of passing judgment on provincial bonnets and gowns and sat down in a chair facing Angus. She took a sticky cake from the table and bit into it with relish. Her little pink tongue darted out to lick at her sticky fingers when she had finished. She slanted a glance at Angus from beneath artfully lowered lashes to see if he was watching her.

"I'm glad you sent that foolish Bartie Waddle away," she said with a simper, thinking to ingratiate herself with her captor, as she had dubbed him.

Angus laughed. "Those weren't your sentiments

179

an hour ago, Miss Wilmont. I believe, given half a chance, you would have scratched my eyes out at the time.''

"Oh, well." She giggled and batted her lashes at him. "I hadn't met *you* properly, then, Mister Dalglish." Prudie sat directly opposite and demanded Angus's whole attention.

"I'm so glad cousin Blanche met you and persuaded you to come after me. How else could you have gotten to know me so easily?" she asked pertly. "What fun to have a gentleman such as yourself along to protect me from fortune hunters. I think that's all Bartie was, despite his hints that he was heir to some obscure title or other, for he gave me up soon enough when Blanche told him I wouldn't be able to touch any of my fortune if I married him," Prudie ran on as she pouted prettily.

"Besides, he was no fun at all on the trip. Always nattering on about propriety. . . . I thought it would be such fun to pretend that we were already married, but oh no, Bartie said his papa wouldn't approve. Even after we came here, he wouldn't do it. He was always sooo careful to call me 'Miss Wilmont,' as though he hardly knew me! Why, he even insisted that my maid spend the night in my room, instead of in the servants' quarters. It was not at all what I'm used to, you know, sharing a bed with my own maid! I don't think Bartie was a grown man at all, but only a boy. Why, he was forever wanting to turn back and consult his papa—worrying over what his *papa* would think.

He seemed to think his papa would prevent *him*

from marrying *me*. *Imagine!* And he was forever looking over his shoulder, afraid that someone was coming after us. Though I assured him that my cousin was laid upon her bed with a toothache and I'd taken all the money so she couldn't follow us anyway. . . .

"But someone *was* coming after us!" Prudie put her hand up to her mouth and giggled through her fingers, marring her efforts to appear grown up with the childish gesture. "And I'm so glad it was *you,*" she said archly, leaning forward and laying her little hand on Angus's arm while she gazed soulfully into his eyes.

Now that she had had a good look at Angus Dalglish, Prudence had decided to set her cap at him. Especially since she believed it would irk her cousin Blanche if she did so. The ridiculous ceremony he had just gone through with her cousin couldn't possibly count for anything, she was sure.

The tall, devilish-looking gentleman presented a challenge she couldn't refuse. She *would* win him away from Blanche, she thought with a mental stamp of her foot. After all, she had never met a gentleman, young or old, handsome or otherwise, who could resist her. The only man she had ever failed to bring round her thumb was her father. And although Angus was older than most of the beaus she favored, and had an air of dangerous excitement about him that tingled her toes, that only added to the enticement of the challenge. Though she wasn't precisely sure what a rake was, Prudie felt certain Angus Dalglish would qualify. The thought made her little game all the more

enticing. Yes, he was a rake, if she had ever seen one.
. . . She gave him her sunniest smile.

An hour later Prudie sat in the comfortable, heavy-
sprung traveling coach and four Angus had hired to
take them back to Heywood with Sukey sitting opposite her. She was waiting for Blanche, who was
inside the inn changing her clothes, and for Angus,
who had stepped to the door of the inn for a moment
to arrange for a basket of provisions to last them some
while, should they find themselves peckish along the
way, or should they not wish to waste time by stopping for lunch. There was little enough daylight left
for travel on this November day, as it was, without
squandering any of it.

Prudie was glad to know that her bulging traveling
case had been collected from the inn where she had
stayed with Bartie and was now tied on top of the
coach. She didn't like to travel without a large number of fashionable gowns and other accessories. She
enjoyed parading around in all manner of finery to
entice all the gentlemen.

Angus kept her under surveillance, Prudie saw, as
he turned toward the coach several times to check that
she hadn't bolted. He was met each time by a wave
of her dainty little fingers and her prettiest smile, until
she noticed that he seemed to be flirting with one of
the inn's serving girls—or perhaps it was the bold
wench who was flirting with *him*. However it was,

she pouted and flounced to the opposite side of the coach.

Prudie put down the glass and rested her two arms along the window ledge with a cunning smile on her face. She gazed unseeingly out through the great double doors leading from the inn yard into the main road beyond. She couldn't wait to put her plan to capture Mr. Angus Dalglish's heart into operation. Then she would tread on it without mercy, to pay him back for the way he had treated her at Mr. Urquart's . . . or perhaps she wouldn't. She smiled smugly.

"My dearest Miss Wilmont!" Bartie popped up beside the coach and grabbed one of the hands Prudie was resting along the window ledge.

"Bartholomew Waddle! What are you doing here?"

"Miss Wilmont! I had to see you one more time! I followed you when they bore you away between them. I longed to set you free from your captors! Was one of them really Miss Charolais—your cousin— dressed as a man? What a shocking display! I hate to entrust you to a person so lacking in propriety, for you may find yourself ruined by associating with her."

"You had better take yourself off and not let Mister Dalglish see you, Bartie, for he would likely thrash you within an inch of your life!" Prudie hissed, paying no attention to Bartie's foolish rantings about "propriety."

"Aren't you glad to see me? After all we've been to one another?" He bent his head to kiss her gloved

183

fingers, but Prudie pulled her hand away from her would-be Romeo.

"Go away, Bartie!"

"But, Miss Wilmont—Prudence—my love! Can you not give me some hope that you will wait for me? If not until you are twenty-one, then until next year— eight months from now. I will come into my majority then and—"

"I'm not at all sure I wish to wait that long, Bartie. Besides, I've changed my mind." Prudence drummed her fingers along the window as she snubbed her adoring swain in best Prudie fashion. "I think I shall marry a lord, for I would prefer to be a lady when I wed," she said artlessly, opening her blue eyes wide.

"But, Prudence—you said you were perishing to marry me. You were so anxious to come here that—"

Angus's voice could be heard in the courtyard. "Mister Dalglish is coming with my cousin. Go away, Bartie, do!" Prudie recommended in an undertone.

The lovelorn young man had no choice but to take himself off without further delay.

"Well, I think we're well rid of that cowardly, sniveling ninnie, don't you? Who wanted him anyway?" Prudie asked in a carefree manner, turning her brightest smile on Angus as they sat in the hired coach on their way back to Heywood.

Angus couldn't believe his ears. He raised a brow and glanced at Blanche. The look of resignation on her face silently said, "I told you so." He saw that Prudie's words, at total variance with her previous behavior, were not at all surprising to her long-suffering cousin. He shook his head and turned back to the girl, wondering what outrageous pronouncement the little minx would come out with next. The chit was proving as much of a handful as Blanche had warned.

"I think he just wanted to marry me for my fortune, you know," Prudie confided to Angus, batting her lashes at him and trying to look demure.

"That is by no means certain, Miss Wilmont. I'm sure many a gentleman would be captivated by you at first glance," Angus said suavely, gratifying the girl exceedingly by giving her the compliment she was so obviously angling for. "You must have many suitors at home."

"I do," she announced complacently, patting her blond curls with smug satisfaction. "It's because I'm so beautiful, you see."

"That will do, Prudie," Blanche said repressively, turning to her cousin who sat along the seat from her. "Your sad want of conduct will give Mister Dalglish a disgust of your character. Try to behave with a little more modesty."

Blanche was feeling blue-deviled, when she knew that she should be feeling elated now that she had recovered her heedless little cousin unwed. And she had Angus to thank. But here she sat in the unfashionable gown of unbleached muslin she had sensibly purchased with only two of Angus's shillings that morning, with her hair scraped back under her bonnet, feeling a real dowd. And she was supposedly married to the dashing gentleman lounging at his ease opposite her. How absurd! No matter that he was a gentleman of disreputable reputation, if he were the common gamester he claimed, he was surely above her touch. After all, he had been a commissioned officer in the king's army before he turned to the gaming tables. He had even admitted that he was the grandson of a man of title and property.

Laying aside their inequality in birth, he was too wild, too impetuous, for her, whose life had been of the most mundane until this adventure. His overwhelming masculinity threatened her hard-won tranquillity. It had taken years of struggle to learn to maintain an aura of unruffled composure in the face of so many difficulties. And now, whenever he touched her, she was in danger of losing that control—in danger of losing herself. She was too proud to let him see his effect on her.

Her cousin was speaking and interrupted Blanche's thoughts. "I'm glad you came this morning, Blanche, for I'd no more money," Prudie said ingenuously. "Bartie wanted to take charge of my blunt for me, but I insisted that I would hold the purse strings."

She turned wide blue eyes on Angus. "I had no idea hiring horses and paying for meals and arranging for rooms at an inn would be so expensive. And we had separate rooms, too, you know, for I kept Sukey with me the whole time. I know how to behave with propriety, no matter what cousin Blanche may have told you.'' Thus spoke a girl who had just run away to be married in Gretna Green with no one but her young maid to lend her countenance!

"The mind boggles," Angus said in a bored voice.

Prudie appeared not to have understood his comment for she continued blithely, "Yes, and I was so brave, too. For it was a long, tedious journey and I had nothing to do but talk to Bartie. It was a good thing he had *some* money of his own, after all, for otherwise we would have been stuck forever in Carlisle. It's such a *boring* place," she said, resting one of her elbows on her knee and her dainty fist against her cheek.

"Oh, yes, it was very brave of you to snub the conventions and run away to get married with nothing but a bandbox," Angus said sarcastically, "not to mention how kind it was of you to leave your cousin behind to suffer from the toothache, with not a sou to her name to pay for medicine or a toothdrawer."

"Well, I had no money, either, after I bought this hat!" Prudie patted the large bandbox that rested beside her on the seat. "But I *had* to have it when I saw it in the window of that shop in Carlisle. The woman in the shop assured me it was a bargain, for it was only five guineas."

"Five guineas!" Blanche exclaimed faintly, but Prudie ignored her as she opened the box and took out the outrageous high-crowned confection of purple and gold ribbons with lace trim and placed it on her head. Two peacock feathers curled down around the brim and tickled one of her little ears. "It's all the crack. None of the milliners at home have anything like it in their shops.''

"I should hope not!'' Blanche said in an undertone that Angus's keen hearing picked up.

"The milliner in Carlisle was a Frenchwoman. And you know what good taste the French have.'' Prudie preened with the colorful concoction sitting at a tilt over her blond curls.

Angus's shoulders quivered as he smothered a laugh.

"Cousin Blanche always forces me to buy things that make me look like a schoolgirl, saying that I mustn't wear anything vulgar or violate propriety. Much I care for that!'' Prudie complained with a sniff, thus easily contradicting her earlier statement that she was indeed a model of propriety.

"Your cousin is a high stickler about such things?'' Angus asked, thinking that the forward little minx certainly didn't lack for brass.

"Yes, she is,'' Prudie said with a dark look at Blanche. "She never lets me have a silk gown. That was one thing Bartie promised me,'' she remembered now with an air of regret.

The coach hit a rut in the road and Angus put his booted foot on the seat opposite to brace himself. The boot rested against Blanche's thigh.

Angus thought she looked tired, and no wonder after their three hectic days on the road. She had told him earlier that she was pleased they had managed to stop Prudie from ruining her young life, no matter the cost to herself.

Angus had been somewhat taken aback by her remark. He didn't consider marriage to himself would be reckoned a high price to pay by most women. Oh, yes, the daughters of the aristocracy would undoubtedly be throwing themselves away on an impoverished gamester such as he, with no settled life, no matter how exalted his relations.

But, blast it all, Blanche Charolais wasn't a lady whose status would mean that she would have a wide choice of suitors. And with her lack of dowry and somewhat advanced age, her choices were already severely limited. She had admitted that she was pretty well on the shelf. And he wasn't an antidote, after all! At least—he didn't think he was. He had never thought of himself as less than a desirable man, no matter his lack of prospects as a provident husband. After all, many women had languished after him. Could it be that he just wasn't to her taste? He would find that difficult to accept, but he supposed, if such were the case, it would be easy enough to obtain an annulment.

He could not rid himself of a niggling worry about her future, though. From what she had told him of her Uncle Wilmont, the man was likely to cast her out, even though she had saved his silly daughter.

Perhaps they would have the marriage put aside and he would find another way to help her. Perhaps she could serve as companion to his sister, Fanny. After all, he didn't really want a wife, did he?

He considered this for all of five seconds.

Well, why not? He was almost ready to give up his

vagabond existence, anyway. His investments had prospered. Blanche objected to his gaming, he knew, but mayhap if she could tolerate it for one more year, he would have enough to pay off the mortgage on those soggy acres of his father's and he could set up as a gentleman farmer.

Blanche Charolais intrigued him in any number of ways. She had had a hard life, as had he. But she had worked diligently and triumphed, maintaining her sense of self, her dignity, as he hoped he had. She was more tolerant of the foolishness of others than he could ever be, however. Only look at the patience and tolerance she showed toward her featherheaded little cousin! He could appreciate the control she had over her temper, but could never emulate it. At times, she could soothe his own uncertain temper with just a look from those wonderful eyes of hers. He felt relaxed in her presence; she calmed his restless spirit. They complemented one another: he with his hot impetuosity, she with her cool grace.

He and Blanche Charolais should be able to make something of a life together. He felt sure she was a woman he could be true to. She was intelligent and capable and altogether lovely. If only she weren't so cold . . . but now she was his, and he fully intended to teach her to enjoy her role as his wife.

Angus slanted another sidelong look at Blanche as she sat sedately in the corner of the coach opposite him, looking the model of modest respectability. He couldn't get over how different she looked now that she was clad in women's clothing once again. Her glorious hair was all but invisible now, pulled back and hidden under her less-than-fashionable bonnet. Her modest cloak of dark wool covered an equally nondescript gown of some rough, pale fabric. She had spent a grand total of six shillings of the money he had given her that morning on the outfit and it did not suit her.

She almost faded into the background, sitting back against the padded squabs of the coach seat. But he knew what she looked like in other clothes, without those enveloping folds of material to conceal and deceive. He knew how the curves and slimness of her body were revealed in those pantaloons—and that thin lawn shirt. He couldn't help but remember how she had looked, or how she had felt when he had held her and kissed her and molded her to himself, or how soft and responsive she had been in his arms. He knew he was just beginning to awaken her womanhood, and the desire, the need, to be the one to bring it into full flower, was irresistible. . . . He vowed he *would* have her warm and passionate in his arms, if it took him the rest of his life!

Angus bit off a curse. He positively squirmed in his seat at the direction his thoughts were leading him. He shifted his position and cleared his suddenly constricted throat.

Blanche felt his intent stare. "What is it, Angus?" she asked, seeing the fire in his eyes as they were fixed on her and the high flush along the ridges of his cheekbones.

"Nothing," he said huskily, flushing more deeply. He swallowed uneasily, rested an elbow against the ledge of the window, and crossed one booted foot over his knee.

Prudie, who sat facing Sukey, and diagonally opposite from Angus, was tired of being ignored. She didn't like the way Angus and Blanche were staring at one another.

"Oh, Angus," Prudie said, daringly using his first name. "Do you plan to be in London in the spring? I'm to have my season then, you know. I think I will appoint you my official escort, for I will need protection from fortune hunters. You were *so* forceful with Mister Urquart, I just know that you would protect me," she said flirtatiously, trying to turn Angus's attention from her cousin to herself.

"A signal honor, I'm sure," Angus replied sardonically, turning his brooding regard from Blanche. " 'Twould be a treat quite above my touch, however, I do assure you, Miss Wilmont."

"A final decision has not been made on the matter of your come-out, cousin," Blanche said depressively. "When your father learns of this episode, I doubt he will trust you on the town."

"Yes, but I will tell him I will have Angus to protect me, Blanche. I won't run away from *him!*"

"I am not at all sure I will be able to accept your

offer, flatter me though you do, Miss Wilmont,'' Angus said repressively. "I believe I have an engagement in, ah, the north of Scotland for the entire season,'' he said, trying to name somewhere as far from London as possible.

Blanche bit back a smile when she saw how Prudie's invitation to be her escort had brought a curl to Angus's lip and a wary look in his eye. "You mean you don't relish being on hand to witness Prudie with the bit between her teeth, kicking up her heels and setting the *ton* on its ear? You wouldn't enjoy chasing after her when she goes haring off on another elopement or engages in some other *exciting* escapade? How very poor spirited of you, Angus!'' she quipped mockingly.

"Well, my dear, you and I will no doubt still be celebrating our honeymoon,'' Angus replied smartly, with a gleam in his eyes.

Blanche blushed rosily, and lowered her eyes. She didn't know where to look and had not another word to say.

"Oh, but you can't take cousin Blanche on a honeymoon, Angus. You're not *really* married,'' Prudie said, interrupting this byplay.

"Oh, but we *are,*'' Angus replied, sitting back and folding his arms across his chest.

"Do you think we might stop for luncheon soon? I'm *very* hungry,'' Prudie complained, winding one of her blond curls around her finger and pouting as she spoke. When no one paid the least attention to her, she exclaimed, "How boring it is just sitting here like this! I wish something exciting would happen!" She giggled. "I do hope we'll be held up by some masked men!"

Chapter 11

Angus decided to press on southward, retracing their previous journey. It had been close to midday when they left Gretna Green, but even so, he hoped to travel as far as Penrith today, before lack of light forced them to halt for the night. Despite his dislike of being cooped up inside a bouncing, airless, closed carriage, Angus had decided to accompany the ladies. For one thing, he had spent so much money on hiring the comparatively luxurious vehicle and team of four horses to pull it, that he didn't want to expend the extra funds to hire a mount for himself—particularly if he was going to curtail his gaming to please Blanche. For another, the weather was miserable, overcast and drizzly with an icy wind blowing. And, lastly, he was tired—he would welcome a chance to close his eyes, however stuffy and jolted about he would be in the lumbering vehicle.

Angus dozed, as did Blanche, both exhausted from their several days of chasing after Prudie. The sky had been overcast and a light drizzle had begun to fall when they crossed over the Scottish border back into England again, but now darker clouds hung low in the sky and it began to rain in earnest. A brisk wind had blown up and dead leaves whirled past the windows of their coach and crunched underneath its heavy wheels as it rolled on. The coachman stopped to put on his rain slicker and to have a few words with Angus about the advisability of continuing their journey in the inclement weather.

With a glance at Blanche to ascertain her wishes, Angus told the man to drive on, but to slow the horses if the ground was too muddy or the wind and rain were making it difficult for driver or horses to see the road ahead. He could perceive that Blanche wanted to get her charge home as quickly as possible. Angus wanted that, too, so that he could take Blanche away and have her all to himself and begin his campaign to convince her to keep to this marriage, despite its irregular beginning.

When they were passing through Carlisle on their return journey, Prudie pressed her nose against the glass of the coach window and gazed at the shops along the way. She even waved to a buck who ogled her. She tried to wheedle Angus into stopping at one of the inns she saw from the coach window, but he refused, saying they had to press on. They paused only long enough to take the basket of food out of the boot of the carriage so that she could eat her fill.

Despite her woeful plaints of hunger, Prudie only took a piece of bread and an apple before Angus put

196

the food back in the boot again. With four persons, and one large bandbox, occupying the two seats of the coach, there was not enough room inside to store the large basket of food. Sukey took a small portion of ham and Angus appropriated a leg of chicken to top up his earlier meal, but Blanche ate nothing, claiming she was not hungry after such a large breakfast.

The rain seemed to be letting up as they drove slowly through the city of Carlisle. Angus relaxed and fell into a doze again. But on the southern outskirts of the city, the rain picked up. The coachman slowed the horses to a crawl. Gusts of wind blew the driving rain hard against the sides of the coach, rocking it from side to side. The motion only caused Angus to fall into a deeper sleep. Three days with little or no rest had taken its toll, even on a man as rugged and vital as Angus Dalglish.

Blanche, herself heavy-eyed, watched him sleep, with his head falling to one side, almost resting on his broad shoulder. Prudie had curled up in her corner and was fast asleep, too. Blanche wasn't sure, but she thought that Sukey had nodded off, as well. The little maid's head in her heavy bonnet seemed to be drooping suspiciously low on her neck.

Blanche allowed herself a brief smile and turned her eyes back to study Angus. She was again affected by the softness that came over his face in sleep. The hard line of his mouth was relaxed and those long, midnight-black lashes of his curved down over his closed eyes and lay against his swarthy skin. An odd fluttering sensation, as though her stomach had suddenly been invaded by butterflies, surged through her. Warmth flooded her face.

And this dangerously attractive man was now her husband. She drew in a deep breath. No! She would not indulge in that dream for a moment. That had been an absurd piece of work back there in Gretna, not a real marriage by any means. It must be overturned as soon as they restored Prudie to her father.

Such a havey-cavey marriage was not for her, no matter how desperate her cousin thought she was to make a match with some man, any man. She had too much pride to trap a man in such a way. If she were ever to marry—and she had long ago given up the idea as impossible for one in her circumstances—it would be because a gentleman could not live without her, or she him.

She sighed. Such a man did not exist! Or if one did, and his name wasn't Angus Dalglish, then Blanche very much feared that she would have to decline the honor. She had to admit the truth at last—much against her better judgment, she had fallen in love with her hot-tempered, impetuous, swashbuckling cavalier.

She gazed at him as he dozed quietly and caught her lip between her teeth. It was going to be so difficult resisting him.

The coach lurched to a halt. Inside, its four occupants were jarred against one another. Angus opened his bleary eyes as he jerked forward, put his hands up and braced himself against Blanche's shoulders.

"Are you all right, my dear?" he asked with concern as he looked into Blanche's eyes inches away from his own.

They heard a commotion above the sound of the rain and wind. Angus passed a hand over his eyes, rubbing away the sleepiness he felt. It sounded as though the coachman was having some trouble on the box. Angus was instantly alert. He opened the door and leapt out, his pistol at the ready.

The report of a gunshot sent him crouching down beside the vehicle.

"Was that a shot?" Blanche asked at the same moment that Prudie squealed, "Blanche, we're going to be murdered!"

"Get down!" Angus growled. "We're being held up!" The coachman tumbled from his box, to land stunned at Angus's feet. Angus looked up to see Prudie's heavy traveling case falling toward his head from the roof of the coach. One of the highwaymen had climbed up onto the roof of the vehicle, untied the case, and was pushing it over the side of the roof at that very moment. Angus attempted to step back but he slipped in the wheel rut in the muddy roadway. The hard edge of the bulging case caught him on the side of his head.

"Bloody hell! Macheath and Peachum!" were the last words Blanche heard before Angus lapsed into unconsciousness.

When Angus awoke some time later with a pounding headache, he opened his eyes to total darkness.

199

"Damnation, they've blinded me," he groaned. At the same moment he felt that his hands were bound behind him and his feet were tied at the ankles.

"I hope they haven't damaged your vision, Angus. I believe you'll find that you can't see anything because it's pitch black in here." Blanche spoke quite close to his ear.

"Fleur! Where are we?"

"In the boot of the coach," she answered in that calm way that Angus had grown to admire so much. "Are you hurt badly?"

"Oh, I'm in prime twig, aside from this devilish pain in my head," he answered. He felt himself lying in a rather uncomfortable position, tightly cramped against Blanche.

"You are bound as well?"

"Of course. Our two friends did not leave anyone free. After they searched our pockets and reticules, and took anything of value we had about us, they tied us up."

"Your cousin and the abigail?"

"Bound together inside the coach."

"I never realized the boot of a coach was spacious enough to accommodate two people, hidden as it is behind this leather covering. Pah! The cover smells most vilely of horse and sweat in this rain. Why did they put us in here anyway?"

"They were being kind, I suppose, not wanting to leave us to freeze or to drown out in the rain."

"Kind! Oh, yes, I should have remembered—you

200

have a theory about those two rogues, don't you? I ask you, was it kind to hit me so hard?''

"I hope they did no permanent harm."

"I shouldn't think so. I've been told often enough I'm too hardheaded by half. They didn't harm any of you women?'' There was a serious note of anxiety in Angus's voice. His stomach clenched at the possibility of any man touching his Fleur.

"No." Blanche tried to shake her head, but their quarters were too cramped. "They left Prudie and Sukey tied together, back to back, and shoved the unconscious coachman into the coach after they had bound him. The girls were very frightened. Prudie thought the man was dead, you know, and set up such a screech that our friends had to gag her," Blanche said in such a matter-of-fact voice that Angus laughed.

"But you, my intrepid wife, weren't frightened?"

"No. . . . And I'm not your wife, Angus."

"Perhaps not in one sense, but legally you most certainly *are*. Why are you not in the coach with your cousin and her maid?"

"Because I insisted on seeing that you were not badly injured. And because our two friends thought it a great joke to bind us in here together. They remembered us from before, you see, when I was, er, garbed somewhat differently.''

"They would! The blood-blasted scoundrels. I suppose they searched my pockets and took my money again.''

"Of course. And all four coach horses. At least they left Prudie her hat. She told them she would see

201

them hang if they laid one of their grubby paws on her new bonnet.''

Angus guffawed. ''Ouch,'' he said, trying to control his laughter. ''It hurts to laugh.''

''I imagine it might. Prudie's traveling case must weigh ten stone.''

''Is that what they hit me with? Guess they didn't want any more of the home-brewed I served up to them last time.''

''Oh, I don't think they intended to knock you out. Peachum could not have known you would choose just that moment to leap out of the coach. They did rifle through Prudie's case, though, and took most of her things, saying that their Gussie and Mabs at home would like some pretty new frocks.''

''Lord! I suppose that means the little minx is beside herself at having a few froufrous stolen.''

''She's already beside herself at the treatment she's been subjected to.''

''I don't suppose it would do any good to point out to her that if she hadn't run away, none of this would have happened in the first place, and she would not have lost her precious frippery.''

''No, not a particle of good. And now she will demand to go shopping so that she can replenish her wardrobe, once we are rescued.''

''After I replenish our funds again, you mean?''

''Of course.'' Blanche bit her lip, remembering how she had upbraided him for gaming and taken him to task over the evils of his ''profession.'' ''I'm sorry

202

I ripped up at you before about—about your gaming . . . Angus?''

"Umm?'' His head had drooped against her shoulder.

"Do you think we might try twisting around so that we can attempt to untie one another's hands?''

"We could . . . let me just come fully to my senses, first. That was quite a blow I took. I'm enjoying just resting here for the moment.'' And his head sank lower onto her soft bosom, where he nestled quite comfortably. Blanche would have suspected him of shamming it, if the situation had been somewhat other than it was.

"Does your head ache very badly, Angus?''

"Yes, abominably.''

"I'm sorry. I wish I could help you.''

He laughed softly. "Oh, you can.''

"Tell me what I can do.''

"Kiss me. That will take my mind off the *excruciating* pain.''

"Will you be serious?'' She tsked, ignoring his baiting. "We'll be stuck here all night, if we don't make some effort. My hands and feet are already going numb. Use that keen wit you boast of to get us out of this predicament.''

"Alas! I fear my wits are scrambled at the moment.''

"Angus, please be sensible.''

"Never fret, my dear. Some passerby will come upon us sooner or later. Sooner, I hope. It's cold.

Sounds as though that rain is turning into ice now, too. And I'm fair to perishing with hunger.''

"You're always famished!"

"I'm so hungry, I swear I can *smell* food."

"I imagine that would be because the basket of food you procured at the inn is just beyond your left shoulder."

"You don't say so? Why didn't you remind me straightaway? At least we won't starve. Do you think we might manage to use our chins to shift it between us?"

Blanche gave a low laugh, sending a wave of desire rippling through Angus, pressed so tightly against her as he was.

"And then what? Open the basket with our teeth?" Blanche asked.

Angus's laugh rumbled against her.

"Angus, if I didn't know you better, I would think you were enjoying this interlude."

"Umm. But you *do* know me better, as you say. And I am a man of action, as you know so well . . . I think *action* is what's called for right now."

"Wha—?" Blanche began to say, thinking he really did mean to try and shift the basket of food between them, before she felt Angus shift his head and bring his mouth against hers. He covered her mouth with his own, blocking her protest. His mouth moved over hers, slowly, tenderly, until he felt her lips soften and she began to kiss him back.

He exalted at eliciting a response from her at last.

Finally the ice was beginning to melt! She must feel the same as he did, then. He knew she did!

"Umm. Why didn't I think of this before?" he said unevenly, moving his mouth away from hers a fraction of an inch.

"Angus, I—we—You can't be kissing me now!" she whispered against his lips, unable to move back from him, bound as she was. "This isn't the proper time or place—" She was completely breathless and flustered.

"Oh? You admit there will be a *proper* time and place, then?" he teased in a raspy voice as he feathered tiny kisses across her cheek. "I'm open to any suggestions."

He closed the minute space between them and began kissing her again. The slow, tender kiss of a moment before became deeper and infinitely more pleasurable. He opened his mouth over hers, invading her soft mouth with his tongue.

Blanche couldn't help but be aware of the hard male body pressing so intimately against her own, nor could she mistake the kindling of his body as sensation engulfed her. She allowed his tongue to invade her mouth and moaned softly, responding to his kiss with a stirring of her senses that was so new to her, it was frightening. Somewhere in the back of her mind a tiny voice warned that she should resist this treacherous reaction, but she did not want to resist at all. She wanted to surrender to the feeling of yearning and tenderness that was overwhelming her. She twisted her hands against the ropes binding them so tightly. If only their hands were free . . .

The sound of a horse's galloping hoofbeats drawing nearer and nearer brought them to their senses. The hoofbeats stopped right outside the coach. They could hear a rider dismounting from a heavily blowing horse.

"Halloo? Is anyone there?" a voice called. A voice strangely familiar to the ears of several of the prisoners in the coach.

Angus and Blanche were chagrined to discover that their rescuer was none other than Bartholomew Waddle, who looked rather like a drowned rat when he answered Angus's shout and lifted the leather covering of the boot. They both rendered the young man their thanks with a good grace once he had opened the boot and untied them.

Young Waddle explained that he had followed them from Gretna, belatedly realizing that his honor as a gentleman behooved him to call on Sir Horace Wilmont. He was prepared to render his deepest apologies for his misjudgment in eloping with Sir Horace's daughter and placing her in a compromising position. He would acknowledge his fault and offer to make whatever recompense Sir Horace decreed, even should it come to pistols at dawn.

"You needn't worry, Mrs. Dalglish," he said to Blanche in his high, boyish voice. "I won't try to abduct Miss Wilmont this time. It's not what my father would expect of me." And he had drawn himself upright and looked almost manly, Blanche thought, when he said this.

They found that the coachman had recovered consciousness in the coach, and Prudie and Sukey were unhurt but very frightened when they were released from their bonds. Prudie screeched loud and long on learning that the contents of her traveling case had been pilfered. Angus remarked *sotto voce* to Blanche that it was a shame they couldn't leave the girl tied and gagged until they returned her to her father.

Prudie showed remarkable restraint in greeting her savior, however. She exhibited not the smallest inclination to throw herself on Bartie's neck, as Blanche half expected her to do. It seemed that she took it entirely as her due that he had followed her.

All Prudie had said was, "Bartie! Imagine you riding out in all this rain and dirt. I thought you were afraid to get your coat wet for fear of catching a chill."

"Now, Miss Wilmont, you malign me, you know you do. I said I was weak-chested as a boy. It has been several years since I've been recovered."

"What are you doing on a horse, anyway, Bartie? I thought you said riding wasn't one of your favorite pastimes."

"Yes, well," the young man admitted, while a flush crept up from his neck to suffuse his face. "You were the one who said you weren't overfond of riding, and I didn't want you to think I was criticiz—"

"I never said any such thing! Why, how else could

I show off my blue velvet habit, if I didn't go out for a ride?'' Prudie interrupted Bartie's explanation.

"Cease your brangling, infants," Angus said in a harsh voice. "We must seek shelter for we're, none of us, going to get any drier or warmer sitting here *reminiscing* all night. The rain has turned to sleet and soon the roadway will be iced over."

He turned to Blanche. "You realize, my dear, that we had only just passed the gates of the monastery when Peachum and Macheath stopped us again. We have no choice but to beg Crane's hospitality once more."

"Oh, Mister Dalglish, I—I have some money. Since you were robbed, I shall be glad to pay for a night's accommodation for everyone," Bartie stammered.

Angus raised his brows, concealing the awkwardness of his predicament. He did not relish being placed in the position of having to accept money from the young man whose elopement he had just foiled. "Save your blunt, you young gudgeon," he said casually, waving away Bartie's stammering offer, then cuffed the boy lightly on the arm in a friendly manner.

"Mrs. Dalglish and I know the assistant curate who resides nearby. He will put all of us up for the night. Do you dare risk yourself overnight in a haunted ruin for the second night in succession, my dear?" Angus turned to ask Blanche with a glint of humor in his eyes.

Blanche, feeling slightly flustered to meet Angus's

208

eye, made a motion toward Prudie, trying to discourage him from referring to the purported "ghosts" at the monastery in her cousin's hearing. Angus just smiled at her. His words had been quite deliberate, calculated to give the little minx a fright. He was hoping to discourage Prudie from wandering about the place, causing mischief, or attempting to escape.

And so it was that Angus took Bartie's horse, having no fear that the young man could abscond with Prudie with no transportation in a sleet storm, and rode to the ruined monastery to seek shelter once more. The gregarious curate was surprised, but not displeased, to see Angus again. He apologized because Mr. Harris had not yet returned from Great Corby with the closed carriage and explained that he could only lend Angus the pony cart and some oilskins to provide protection from the rain. He was afraid that Angus would have to make two trips to convey the four persons waiting in the horseless coach, since, in addition to the two ladies and their maid, the coachman would also have to be carted to the monastery. At least the other young man had a horse he could ride.

"Oh! I've never seen you wearing such a smart outfit before. Why, it's all the crack!" Prudie exclaimed to Bartie as they sat in the stranded carriage, waiting for Angus to return. She had noticed for the first time that Bartie had changed his clothes from the rather drab checked woollen overcoat he had worn over gray woollen trousers on their journey from

Skipton to Gretna to a more dashing outfit of a many-caped greatcoat over buckskin riding breeches, black Hessian boots with golden tassels, and a tall curly brimmed beaver hat, slightly damp from its office of providing Bartie with some protection from the elements as he rode to their rescue.

"Yes, well, you left me rather in the lurch back there in Gretna, Miss Wilmont. I didn't know what to do next. I thought of riding home to consult Papa, but then I remembered I didn't have any riding clothes with me. And besides, I knew what Papa would advise anyway. . . . So I went out and purchased some appropriate togs and hired a hack to come after you, instead."

"And what would your papa have advised?" Blanche asked, when Prudie showed no interest in the senior Mr. Waddle's advice, but only wanted to talk about Bartie's stylish new clothes.

"Well, Miss Charolais—I mean, Mrs. Dalglish," Bartie continued with an embarrassed flush on his cheeks, "Papa has brought me up to know the right and wrong of a situation. When we were in Harrogate, I asked Miss Wilmont if I could approach her father, but she seemed to think that my case would be hopeless. She seemed so set on an elopement. She persuaded me—ah, that is, I mean, I knew better than to run off to Gretna Green with her."

Blanche saw that Bartie was not such a nodcock after all. Indeed, she herself knew how hard it was to resist Prudie's determination to have her own way.

How much more difficult it would be for a young man who fancied himself head over heels in love with her lovely cousin to resist Prudie's whims and wheedles.

Chapter 12

Blanche had just had a hot bath. She was having difficulty fastening the tiny row of buttons on the cuff of her sleeve when there was a preemptory knock on the door of the chamber she had been shown to so that she could take off her wet cloak and freshen up. She was thankful the room was in the Chapter House and not in the dormitory wing where she and Angus had been disturbed by the tricksters the previous night. Before she could call out "Who is it?" Angus entered the room.

"Ah, you've finished. Good. You look a deal more comfortable now than you did when we first arrived. I hoped Crane's servant would build up the fire so that you could dry your garments properly and I see he made a good job of it," Angus remarked, walking over to the hearth where Blanche stood and holding his hands out to the blaze. "I daresay we all looked like a pack of drowned rats when we arrived."

"You might have waited for a proper invitation to

enter, Angus. What if I had still been in the bath?'' Blanche asked. She was glad that her gown had indeed dried quickly in front of the fire burning brightly in the hearth, otherwise her companion would have found her in considerable dishabille, wrapped only in a towel, for she had no dressing gown and her woollen cloak was still quite wet.

"Ah, then you could have made use of me. I suppose it would have been my husbandly duty to scrub your back for you,'' Angus said with a straight face and a gleam in his eye. He slipped off his damp jacket and hung it over the back of the chair Blanche had placed in front of the fire to hold her wet clothing.

Blanche ignored his comment, refusing to be drawn, although she felt herself flushing under his steady regard.

"I'm glad to see you are feeling better, Angus. I was afraid the blow to your head had seriously distorted your senses,'' she said.

"Oh, the knock on my head wasn't what made me so light-headed in the boot of that coach,'' he murmured. He noticed her difficulty with her sleeve buttons and held out a preemptory hand. "Here. Let me,'' he said, taking her arm. He easily did up the tiny buttons.

"Thank you,'' she said, reclaiming her arm and taking up a comb, still avoiding his gaze. She began to work it through her still damp hair. "Was it really necessary to tell Mister Crane that I was your wife?''

"Well, when he noticed what a remarkable resemblance you bore to young Flowers, excepting only the

213

color of your hair, what else could you expect me to do? I hoped that you would congratulate me for my quick thinking in saying that your brother had accompanied me to your uncle's home where he was to meet some friends, while I was to escort you and your niece back to our own home.''

''Oh, Angus,'' Blanche said in exasperation, stopping in the motion of combing out her hair. ''With your facile tongue, I expect you could have come up with something else. You could easily have said that I was Flowers's sister without saying that I was your wife and that Flowers was your brother-in-law.''

''Yes, but, Fleur, you *are* my wife.''

''Do not be foolish! You know that was all a ridiculous mistake this morning.''

''And was that episode in the boot of the coach all a 'ridiculous mistake'?'' he asked in a low voice, beginning to feel irritation with her for not admitting that she wanted him as much as he wanted her.

But Blanche was speaking and didn't hear the question. ''You know we must have this so-called marriage overturned.''

''I think we should seriously consider keeping to this 'accidental' marriage—'' Angus began to argue before they were interrupted by Henley, Crane's servant, saying he had brought the extra can of hot water Mr. Dalglish had ordered for the bath.

Clouds of steam rose as Henley poured the boiling hot water from the large brass bucket into the tin hip bath set behind a painted screen in one corner of the room.

"Will ye be needin' another bucketful, sir?" Henley questioned Angus as he completed his task.

"No, thank you. That will do nicely," Angus answered, drawing his neck cloth from round his neck.

"Very good, sir." Henley bowed himself out, with a sideways glance at Blanche as he went.

"What are you doing, Angus?" Blanche asked, startled, as Angus began to untie the ribbons that pulled the neck of his shirt closed.

"Preparing to take a bath. Did you think I had something else in mind?" he asked provocatively as he slipped his waistcoat over his arms and bent to remove his boots.

"I'll be out of your way, then." Blanche turned hastily to gather up her hairpins and prepared to leave—quickly.

"That's not at all necessary, *wife.*" Angus pulled his shirt over his head and stood before her in nothing but his breeches.

"But if I see you, er, unclothed, won't that jeopardize the chances for an annulment?" Heat suffused her cheeks as she gazed at the thick mat of dark hair curling across his broad chest, tapering to a vee above the waistband of his breeches.

"*Looking* won't compromise you, my dear girl, or jeopardize anything . . . unless—who knows—you might like what you see!" Angus said with a wolfish grin as his hands went to the buttons of his breeches. "Seeing me in my, ah, natural state is not consummating the marriage, you know!"

Blanche heard him break into a low laugh as she

whisked herself out the door. She knew this was definitely *not* the time to discuss separate sleeping arrangements. Her cheeks positively burned as she thought that she must insist that they have separate apartments. . . . And not because she didn't trust Angus—but because she didn't trust herself!

An hour later Blanche faced her freshly scrubbed and shaved husband across the scuffed and gnarled wooden table in the old monks' dining hall where they all gathered for dinner. Thoughts of her earlier encounter with Angus still plagued her and left a faint trace of color across her high cheekbones. She tried to distract herself as she gazed about at the ancient room.

Only a section of the original hundred-foot-long refectory remained after Henry VIII's men had demolished one side of the cloisters adjacent to it. The beams of the room had been charred in the fire started in the refectory to burn some of the artifacts considered too "popish" to be of use to the new Church of England headed by King Harry, though Malachi Crane assured his guests that they were in no danger from the roof collapsing onto their heads. Though six-centuries old, the beams were sturdy enough to hold up three roofs, he told them proudly, explaining that the beams had been hewn from the nearly indestructible wood of oak trees that grew thickly thereabouts.

At one end of the refectory, the remains of a once

brightly colored wall painting were faintly visible on the original twelfth-century stone wall. At the other end, the damaged wall had been repaired higgledy-piggledy with stones gathered from the cathedral itself that had been the main focus of the soldiers' destructive spree.

A petulant Prudie sat beside Angus squabbling with Bartie, who was placed across the table from her next to Blanche. They were not the only guests the good curate entertained to dinner this night. He sponsored a young people's evening once a month and this happened to be the November convocation. It was not unusual for more than two dozen of his young parishoners to attend the gathering. Little did he know it, but they came not because of his excellent religious instruction, but because it was a fine way to meet those members of the opposite sex who might prove potential mates. But there were only eight youngsters in attendance tonight because the weather was too poor to allow those from outlying farms to make their way to the monastery.

Several robust lads and buxom lasses, children of the local farmers, sat down at the far end of the table, laughing and talking among themselves and trying to engage Bartie and Prudie, whom they judged to be about the same age as themselves, in conversation. One raven-haired young woman sat next to Bartie and did her best to draw his attention to herself from time to time.

Two able-bodied brothers, Ned and Ted Cunningham, both took a fancy to Prudie. Always ready to bask in male admiration, Prudie was nothing loath to flirt with them to the top of her bent. Blanche judged that her cousin was trying to make someone jealous, and that *someone* was probably Bartie, although Prudie had been making sheep's eyes at Angus since they had set out from Gretna Green. Blanche didn't put it past her to try to arouse his interest with just such obvious stratagems as she was engaged in now. Blanche clenched her hands in her lap, hoping that she would not have to deal with such an unwelcome complication.

The table was laden with the bountiful plenty of the season's recent harvest. A robust Scotch barley broth, followed by boiled mutton and a haunch of venison roasted to a turn, were supplemented by a large roast goose, a dressed partridge, a couple of brace of grouse, a number of pigeon pies, and a jugged hare. Vegetables of every variety (turnips, potatoes, carrots, cabbage, onions, and parsnips among them) were served—boiled, basted, baked, or sauced. A selection of breads (both sweet and savory, plain and ornately shaped), cheeses, fruit pies, puddings (custard, bread and suet, including a spotted Dick), iced cakes and all manner of desserts and sweetmeats covered almost every spare inch of space on the long, rough table.

With wry amusement, Angus concluded that the veritable banquet of food sent along by the mothers of the youngsters for the impromptu meal was the impetus behind the idea for such a gathering. The underfed curate would dine on the leftovers until the next monthly meeting, Angus judged.

"Remarkable resemblance you bear to your brother, Mrs. Dalglish. Remarkable," Malachi Crane observed to Blanche, who was placed to his left as he presided at the head of the table.

"Yes, we could be taken for twins, were it not for the difference in our ages. He is several years my junior, you see." Blanche was sorry she had to sit at such close quarters to the man. Angus sat across from her, to Crane's right, and was deriving considerable amusement from her predicament, Blanche guessed, if the wide grin decorating his face was anything to go by.

"Yes, I thought he must be a youngster," Malachi said, looking at Blanche's silver hair in puzzlement. Mrs. Dalglish was surely under thirty, yet her gray hair made her appear a much older lady. "Was your hair the same jet black as your brother's when you were his age?" he asked curiously, if not very diplomatically.

Blanche gave him an imperturbable look. "No. I was born gray, though my hair was a lighter shade than this when I was a girl."

Angus bit back his grin at her dilemma. Though she looked completely at ease and dignified, Angus was beginning to read the feelings behind that mask of cool, self-composure well enough to know just how uncomfortable she was with Crane's comments and questions. He opened his mouth, intending to draw Crane's questions to himself, but Prudie pulled on his sleeve and he had perforce to turn his attention to her for the moment.

"How long have you and Mister Dalglish been wed?" Malachi asked Blanche.

She blushed and said in a strangled voice, "Not very long."

"Ah, I thought not. You have the look of newlyweds. And besides, there's been no mention of any young Dalglishes. You have no children as yet?"

"No. My cousin is the only 'youngster' I have responsibility for just at present."

Malachi reached over to pat Blanche's arm. "Don't fret, my dear. It's early days yet."

Blanche almost choked on the sip of wine she had just taken to calm her nerves at his persistent questioning.

Angus eventually came to her rescue, drawing off Crane's attention, asking when the headless monks had last been heard from.

This question prompted much guffawing and a certain amount of young male braggadocio among the local lads who began to boast of the times they had confronted those phosphorescent phantasms. The two strapping, red-faced Cunningham brothers boasted that they had stood up to a whole band of the black-robed, headless ghosts and sent them packing, with their gory tonsured heads held under their arms. The story elicited frightened squeals and admiring looks from all the girls, for the brothers were great favorites and much sought after by the local maids.

"Those two lads are stout enough to frighten *me*,"

Angus remarked in an undertone to Blanche at the conclusion of this absurd story.

Crane and the local youngsters began to trade stories of reported encounters with the ghostly monks. This seemed to be the central activity of the meeting, rather than religious discussions and sermons, as might have been expected. The boys egged Malachi on, then topped his stories with yarns they had been hearing from their births, long before he appeared on the scene. The colorful elaborations and inventive embroidery of these terrifying fables afforded Angus much amusement. He judged that the boys were just trying to frighten the girls, as well as impress them with their own bravery in facing the specters.

In an effort to reclaim his standing with the young people, Malachi Crane hoped to impress them and to change the tenor of the recent conversation by reciting a dramatic passage from one of his favorite plays. He stood up, called for quiet, placed his hand over his heart in a theatrical gesture, and declaimed, "Act five, scene three, lines nine to nineteen from *The Duchess of Malfi*, by John Webster. Ah, hem:"

I do love these ancient ruins.
We never tread upon them but we set
Our foot upon some reverend history:
And questionless, here in this open court,
Which now lies naked to the injuries
Of stormy weather, some men lie interred
Loved the church so well, and gave so largely to 't,

They thought it should have canopied their bones
Till doomsday; but all things have their end:
Churches and cities, which have diseases like to
men,
Must have like death that we have.

His recitation was met by catcalls from the local
boys, while the girls hid their giggles as best they
could. Angus raised a brow and looked at Blanche,
inviting her comment. No visible reaction passed over
her face, but she politely clapped her hands, Angus
joined her, and everyone else followed suit.

Prudie stared round-eyed at all the tall tales and
Mr. Crane's recitation. She was as affrighted, if not
more so, than any of the local girls. The local lasses
had the advantage over the newcomer—they had been
hearing such fantastic fabrications all their lives.

Prudie clung tightly to Angus's sleeve as he es-
corted her to her room after the dinner wound down
to its conclusion, and prattled on about what a horrid
place they had come to, what with bloody, headless
ghosts just waiting to jump out and terrify her.

Blanche preceded them up the crumbling staircase
with a lighted taper in her hand that cast its flickering
shadow on the hoary stone walls and ceiling.

"Ah, but I thought you liked adventure, Miss Wilmont," Angus said, patting her hand. "Why, if you
were intrepid enough to run away with no one but
your maid and young Waddle to protect you, then I

think you can brave one night in these haunted ruins.''

Prudie glanced up at him wide-eyed and said flirtatiously, ''Oh, I shan't be afraid now I have *you* to protect me.'' But she shivered nonetheless and drew even closer to Angus's side as she saw the dancing shadows cast on the walls by the flame of Blanche's candle as it lighted them on their way up the bare and uneven stone steps.

Prudie shivered again. ''It's cold,'' she said in a small voice.

''Aye, cold as death,'' Angus echoed in a deep, portentous voice. ''We mustn't forget what Propertius said: 'Sunt aliquid Manes: letum non omnia finit, / luridaque euictos effugit umbra rogos.' ''

''Wh-what d-does th-that m-m-mean?'' Prudie asked in a quavering voice.

'' 'There is something beyond the grave; death does not end all, and the pale ghost escapes from the vanquished pyre.' ''

''Angus . . . please,'' Blanche admonished him. ''Must you?''

Angus laughed and desisted, paying no further heed to Prudie's burgeoning fear or to her attempts to flirt with him. He was silently cursing the inclement weather that made it impossible for him to venture out to a friendly tavern where he could engage in a hand or two of cards to replenish his pockets. He certainly didn't want to borrow money from young Waddle and the only money left he had was the ten guineas he had stashed in his boot for safekeeping

223

after the previous encounter with the two highwaymen.

Angus's hopes had been dashed when he had begged a ride into town from the farmer who owned the land not a quarter of a mile beyond the monastery gates. The farmer had arrived just as they had finished dinner to take some of the young folks home in his sturdy wagon, but he told Angus that his farm was in the opposite direction from Carlisle. And besides, he had said to Malachi Crane, it had begun to sleet so heavily and the wind howled so fiercely that it was "fit to wake those dead monks of yourn."

Angus then asked Malachi if he could borrow the chestnut nag for the purpose of riding into Carlisle. The curate had given him a friendly smile, but had declined to risk his ancient beast on such a night. "Should the weather prove more clement tomorrow, I shall gladly lend you the horse or give you a lift into town myself."

It was decided that the farmer would take his daughter and the other girls to his large, rambling farmhouse, since it would be difficult for the other girls to make their way home on such a night, and it would not be proper to leave so many unmarried young ladies at the monastery with only one married lady to chaperone the lot of them. Blanche had blushed at the man's words, taking her for a proper married lady as he had. His own sons and the other boys stayed behind. The lads all relished the chance to stay overnight in the haunted monastery.

* * *

"No harm will come to you, Miss Wilmont," Angus said now, "if you do not venture to walk abroad during the night." Angus stood with Prudie at the door to her room where she continued to wail loudly about how frightened she was. "For that *would* be unsafe—and we don't want anything untoward to happen to you. I will personally lock the door to your room and keep the key. No one will be able to get in except your cousin or myself—and you will have your maid to bear you company. We will be in the room directly across the hall from you. You will be perfectly safe."

Blanche gave Angus a wry half smile from under lowered brows, knowing that he was trying to alarm Prudie just enough to keep the girl from even *thinking* of setting her toe outside her room during the night. Blanche had warned Angus that she didn't trust Prudie not to try to run away again. She had even taken charge of Prudie's outrageous hat as insurance. Knowing her featherheaded cousin as she did, Blanche felt sure that Prudie would not leave without her coveted headgear.

Blanche felt more confident of Bartie's pledge to elope no more, but she was not at all sure that Prudie would not try to persuade him to take her away, despite renouncing her engagement to him.

She smiled as she recalled the scene at the dinner table—Prudie, turning up her nose at Bartie's attempts at possessiveness, flirting with the local farm

225

lads—then Prudie, angry as a wet hen when Bartie gave up and turned his attentions to the smiling, flirtatious, dark-haired local girl at his side. Blanche suspected that Prudie wasn't so much jealous of Bartholomew's attention, as she was peeved that she had lost the interest of *her* admirer to another young female. Will do her good to realize she's not the only girl who can pique the interest of a young man, Blanche thought with her characteristic sense of fairness.

"I'm sorry, Mrs. Dalglish, I'm afraid that I will have to put all the boys in the west dormitory wing where your brother stayed with your husband," Malachi had apologized to Blanche when she had inquired about changing her room before they left the refectory.

"The boys must all spend the night here, with this foul weather upon us—not to mention the possibility of their being set upon by Peachum and Macheath. Though, if you were to ask me, I think the local lads are sometimes in league with those two rascals." He had winked at Blanche and put his finger beside his long nose.

"You and Mister Dalglish will be quite comfortable in the east wing, I hope. As you will wish to keep your cousin well chaperoned, the chamber I've put you in has the advantage of a small dressing room across the hall where Miss Wilmont and her maid can sleep.

"I hope you will take the opportunity to study the chamber for I believe it served as the monastic library. And the dressing room was, in all likelihood, the bishop's inner sanctum, where he prepared his learned sermons," Crane digressed, always ready to expound on the history of the monastery.

"You seem to be very knowledgeable about the history of the various buildings here, Mister Crane," Blanche said, gratifying him exceedingly by remarking on his learning.

"Yes, I have made a thorough study of these old ruins and have uncovered some interesting new information about the placement of various outbuildings and such," he said importantly. "Perhaps you and Mister Dalglish would like to see the plan I've drawn up of how the entire monastery complex was laid out before the Dissolution. Such a shame that the soldiers got so carried away as to destroy the cathedral itself and half the other buildings. It was a true medieval work of art. Quite a treasure trove it was. Why, the stained-glass windows alone took more than fifty years to complete. Alas, now the cathedral and all its beautiful artwork is lost forever. Such a sad waste," he rambled on. "All that remains besides the shell are a few broken shards that I pick up from time to time as I wander through the old ruins," he concluded sadly.

"Where is Mister Waddle to stay?" Blanche asked, calling him back from his reverie. She was anxious to know Bartie's proximity to her cousin, should Prudie try to speak with him during the night.

"Oh, don't worry your head about the young man, Mrs. Dalglish," Crane answered. "He can rack up over in the Chapter House where I have my rooms. Our dear vicar, Mister Harris, is still away and there is an extra bed for Mister Waddle. At least you and Mister Dalglish will be perfectly comfortable—and the library is one of the more interesting rooms in the monastery.'' He began to tell her the tale of a long-lost manuscript found behind one of the secret panels in the room, unfortunately not by him, but by one of his predecessors.

Thus Blanche found that she had no alternative but to share a room with her temporary husband.

''But you surely agree with me that we should seek an annulment as soon as possible!'' Blanche said to her glowering companion behind the closed door of their cavernous bedchamber. He had returned at an advanced hour of the night from his sojourn in the vaulted rooms under the dormitory where he and Malachi Crane had made considerable inroads into the store of excellent wine left behind by the Anglican bishop. Malachi had opened first one bottle, then another, heartily encouraging Angus to sample them all. And he had.

''I will never agree to anything so foolish! Why would I want to shed my new bride? I'm a happy bridegroom, content with my lot.''

''How can you be any such thing?'' Blanche asked disbelievingly.

He walked over and drew Blanche into his arms,

raised her chin with one long finger and kissed her briefly on the lips.

"Would you be so faithless as to kiss me and leave me? Would you be so cruel as to abandon your waiting groom and leave him in misery, Fleur? I would take to haunting you like one of these damned specters here, wailing and gnashing my teeth, if you were to do anything so cruel."

Her heart began to beat faster at his touch. With an effort, she managed to still her instant response. "You've been imbibing over much again, Dalglish!" she accused when she detected the combination of alcoholic fumes on his breath as she tried to disengage herself from his arms.

He did not deny it, but only increased his hold on her.

"Let me go—else I *will* demand that this mock marriage of ours be irrevocable."

"Good. I have been doing my best to persuade you to accept that idea."

"What? Why, you've given me to believe you prefer a bachelor's existence and the freedom it brings. You can't persuade me that you *truly* wish to remain married to me!"

"I'm beginning to think that I would like nothing better than to remain married to you!"

"But why?" Blanche asked, truly baffled. She had thought to cool his ardor with the mention of a permanent marriage, certain that the purpose of his honeyed words and persistent attempts at lovemaking was to persuade her to agree to a brief liaison. He made these romantic overtures because he was tempted by her proximity, that was all—not because he truly desired her as a wife, or a lover even. No man could, Blanche was convinced, with her lack of dowry, undistinguished birth, and obvious imperfections. She knew also that she was too pale, too tall, too thin— and too old.

"Why not? Look at yourself in the glass." Angus drew her over to the long cheval glass standing to one side of the oaken dressing table. His long fingers tangled in her gleaming, silver tresses while his other hand skimmed lightly over her bodice as he held her back against himself, forcing her to look at herself in the glass.

"You see. You are beautiful . . . so beautiful," he whispered huskily as he showed her her attractions . . . her eyes, her hair, her face, her figure.

A warm lassitude spread from her throat down through her womb and into her legs as his hands worked their magic over her body. He was slowly melting her reserve but her pride and doubts about his sincerity forced her to resist him and, almost against her will, she was compelled to say, "You might condescend to remain married to me, but I could *never* consent to remain married to *you!* A hardened gamester! An inveterate adventurer! You would leave me within a fortnight! Even though I am at my last prayers, it would be better for me if you would agree to have this union put aside." She uttered the wounding words, knowing that she did not mean them, but she was afraid that he was just play-

230

ing with her, and that as soon as they returned Prudie to Heywood, he would not be so eager to continue with the mistaken marriage.

Angus growled deep in his throat, turned her about, and put his slender fingers on either side of her face to gaze deeply into her eyes.

"Never say never, my dear Fleur," he told her with a look of determination flashing in his eyes.

"Oh, Angus, don't you see—we're too unlike to suit," she whispered as she put her hands against his chest and rested her head on his shoulder. She was trying one last time to convince him to let her go before she lost the last vestiges of control.

"I see nothing of the kind—"

He sat down abruptly in the large overstuffed chair on one side of the dressing table and jerked Blanche down with him, imprisoning her in his arms. One hand went up to hold her behind her head. His mouth took hers roughly at first, then softened when he felt her returning his kiss, while his other hand moved from his tight hold on her waist to skim over her bodice with those featherlike touches that caused her breasts to swell and strain against his caressing hand.

He lifted his mouth away to set it at her neck and press soft kisses there, while his thumb brushed gently over her lips. He returned his mouth to hers, touching her lips lightly with his tongue, seeking entrance. Blanche wound her arms around his neck and made a small noise in the back of her throat as she allowed him to take her mouth deeply. His rapid breathing fanned her face when she felt him lift her slightly as he shifted his legs under her.

"Fleur, Fleur . . . my beautiful girl." Now he was murmuring in her ear . . . words of endearment, words of persuasion . . . words of almost boyish passion and desire.

"Oh, Angus, don't—no," Blanche murmured breathlessly, moving on his lap as he unbuttoned her gown and pushed it aside to caress her flesh.

"It's all right. We're married now. . . . Beautiful, beautiful, Fleur . . ." he breathed raggedly. "Sit still, darling. If you continue to move like that, I can't guarantee I'll make it to the bed."

"Oh, my dearest," Blanche murmured on a sighing breath, on the verge of surrendering to his hot passion, not knowing if she wished to urge him to stop or to make her his without further delay.

"It's our wedding night, my love," he whispered. "I would be much more comfortable on the bed, wouldn't you?" he said, as he put his arms under her legs, preparing to pick her up and carry her there.

"Bla-a-a-an-che!" A bloodcurdling scream rent the air. Blanche jumped and Angus loosened his grip on her as he looked up, listening, trying to right his reeling senses.

"Bla-an-che!" the scream came again. "He-ee-lp!"

Prudie's voice!

"Blanche! Come quickly! There's a ghost trying to break down my door!"

"I must go to her!" Blanche broke out of his embrace and jumped up. She took the key from the dressing table where Angus had left it, threw her cloak about her shoulders, and ran from the room.

"*Damn* the girl!" Angus swore, grinding his teeth in frustration. Just when he no longer needed to practice that restraint that had almost killed him the past three days, that little minx ruined things! He laughed harshly. They were even *married* now, for God's sake.

Angus grabbed up a candle and stormed out into the hall in Blanche's wake, caught the flicker of movement down the passageway and ran to catch the tricksters, nearly tripping over the tangled length of rusty chain they had left behind in their haste to get away. With his temper hot and his frustration soaring to the heights, Angus needed some action to relieve his pent-up feelings. Anger spurred him on and he took the stairs at a dangerous run, leaping down three or four steps at a time, and was just in time to catch two of the local lads, dressed in old black monks' robes with their faces dusted with flour and streaked with some sort of red paste.

He caught the "ghosts" by the peaks of their hoods and yanked off the musty old robes with force, taking some of the lads' hair along with the cloth covering their heads. With no Blanche there to restrain his fiery rage and frustration at having their lovemaking interrupted at such a crucial moment, Angus gave both tricksters a thorough shaking.

"I ought to pound you both to a pulp, you half-witted clothheads!" Though he badly needed to pound his fists into something or some*one,* Angus settled for relieving his pent-up feelings verbally, cursing the boys loud and long for their demented, adolescent, thoughtless, harebrained masquerade. Not having to restrain his language, as no delicate female ears could hear him and the hearers be put to the blush, he felt free to use words the two lads had never heard before, but whose meaning was crystal clear, nonetheless.

Chapter 13

"Oh, I am quite determined to make Papa take me to London for the new season in the spring. I'm sure the *ton* will like me. Do you think they will say I'm an incomparable, Mister Dalglish?" Prudie looked up archly at Angus. "I only encouraged Bartie because he's not old and decrepit like that Jebediah Lodestone at home . . . Papa wanted me to marry him just because his estate marches with ours, you see," Prudie confided with the air of a tragedy queen. "But I refused!"

Angus sat with her as she lingered over her breakfast, cutting her toast into minute pieces and batting her lashes at him. Prudie prattled on while he brooded. He was not in the best of humors this morning, still feeling aggrieved over the events of last night. He could cheerfully strangle the girl sitting beside him for her part in ruining his evening.

* * *

Precisely one hour ago in the refectory, Angus had set eyes on his "wife" for the first time since she had run from their bedchamber the night before. Blanche had met his fiery gaze with her chin up and an icy look. She had looked as composed as ever, as though nothing of import had taken place between them only a few hours previously. She had evidently spent the remainder of the night in Prudie's room and looked rather heavy-eyed this morning. And he thought he could detect a faint tinge of color under her normally clear alabaster skin.

In a brisk tone, she had requested that he keep watch over her cousin for a short time while she gratified Malachi Crane's insistent request that she accompany him on a short tour of the ruins so that he could explain his recent discoveries. She told Angus she didn't know what to expect from Prudie today— except more tiresome, mischievous behavior—so he was to keep his guard up, should her cousin take it into her head to try to run away again. "Don't let Prudie out of your sight," were her exact words, he recalled with a pained expression.

He had earlier borrowed Crane's broken-down nag and had ridden into Carlisle where he had arranged to hire a team of coach horses to replace the ones the highwaymen had stolen yesterday. When he told Blanche that they could leave as soon as she was ready, she had looked surprised. She had wondered where he had gotten the money to hire a team. She had seen Peachum take the wad of bills from the inside pocket of his jacket yesterday. Surely he couldn't

236

possibly have found a card game *that* early in the morning, could he?

He had maintained an air of mystery, preferring not to tell her that he always had his boots made specially so that he could use the heel as the repository for extra cash, when the need arose. After their first encounter with the two highwaymen, he had taken the precaution of stashing some of his winnings in that hiding place yesterday morning.

Blanche would not stay to discuss with him why she had not returned last night. A shuttered look had come over her face when he had attempted to open the subject. She had stepped back, raised her hand, palm up, and said in a freezing voice, "No. I would prefer not to discuss that."

"What, *never?*" he had exclaimed heatedly, his nostrils flaring with temper.

She had turned to leave, adjuring him to keep an eagle eye on Prudie as she walked from the room.

So it was no wonder he was like a bear with a sore head now, after the frustrations of last night and this morning. The lingering effects of the spirits he had consoled himself with, when it became clear Blanche would not be returning to the bedchamber, didn't help matters, either.

After he had released the two boys last night, with no more than a shake and a cuff to their already burning ears, Angus had gone back to the bedchamber, to await Blanche's return. He had paced about for some time, rehearsing a speech to convince her that he was serious about their marriage.

Angus knew Blanche objected to his gaming. He debated how he was to reconcile such a profession with his desire to have her as his wife. She did not consider it a respectable way of life—and no more was it, he had to admit. But he didn't feel it made him quite the unsavory character she had branded him. Well, he had already decided to give up his gaming career, knowing how much she disliked it. He had hidden away those ten guineas in his boot. If she didn't want him to gamble again, it would just have to serve to see the four of them to Heywood. He had no objection to young Waddle paying his own way, of course, if the young man was determined to accompany them.

He was going to fold, to throw in his last hand, call it a day, and live off those investments he had made when he got home, anyway . . . when he took his *bride* home, he amended deliberately. He had already planned to hire a house in town and give Fanny her season in the spring. He hoped Blanche would like that. She would be the perfect chaperone for his sprightly sister.

Those thoughts had kept him occupied for some time, but when Blanche did not come back, Angus had made his way down to the vaults again and appropriated two bottles of claret. He had consoled himself with the excellent wine of the long-departed bishop for the remainder of the night. Now this morning he was feeling distinctly the worse for wear. Prudie's incessant self-centered chatter was only making his headache worse.

For her part, Prudie was "coquetting" her hardest, trying to capture the interest of the intriguing gentleman whose black good looks and impressive physique were almost *too* overpowering, even for one of her naive but overweening vanity. He was so tall, dark, and formidable looking she was the tiniest bit intimidated by him. It was a good thing her cousin Blanche had somehow persuaded Angus Dalglish to come after her, Prudie thought, having not the least idea how her reserved and always correct cousin had achieved such a thing. If she had had a scintilla of sense, Prudie might have been frightened by such a man, but as she remained unencumbered by that commodity, she remained blithely unaware that she was playing with fire.

For Prudie, there was no doubt that Angus Dalglish would soon be smitten by her charms, if she called attention to how young and attractive she was often enough. That had always worked for her in the past. At home her posturing and references to her own beauty had never failed to call forth admiration from the men she met. Though her experience heretofore had been confined to her narrow country neighborhood—farm lads, local gentry, the curate of the local parish—and to the somewhat broader assortment of unlicked cubs, widowers on the lookout for mothers for their children, fortune hunters and a few hardened, down-at-the-heel rakes, and elderly roués she had encountered in Harrogate, nothing in her short, relatively sheltered life had prepared her for a gentleman of Angus Dalglish's ilk.

She had praised him as her hero and thanked him gushingly for chasing away those ''horrid ghosts'' after he had produced the two Cunningham brothers, the mischief-makers who had pretended to be the murdered monks, to make their apologies. The brothers had presented themselves that morning to humbly beg Miss Wilmont's pardon for frightening her out of her wits during the night. Prudie had given the boys a simpering smile, captivating them forever, and told them, without a blink at the patent falsehood, that she had known it was a joke all along. And what a good joke it was, too, she had congratulated them and laughed.

Angus did not feel so charitable toward the pair whose antics had interrupted a crucial moment for him. Scowling heavily, he had dismissed them when their apology was made with a grunt and a warning not to try such a stunt again. He had dragged the information from them that Henley, the curate's young servant, had provided them with the robes and other paraphernalia. He was not surprised; it must have been Henley who had tried much the same trick the first night he and Blanche had stayed at the monastery. He had reported the two incidents to Crane and left him to deal with his servant.

* * *

"If I don't find an eligible *parti* soon, I will be too old and ugly and will never be wed. Then I will be on the shelf just like cousin Blanche," Prudie complained with a little moue pulling down the corners of her mouth as she finished her last crumb of toast. She gazed at Angus soulfully as he helped her rise from her chair.

Angus had a hard time controlling the urge to give the little baggage a set down for casting such ill-natured aspersions on her cousin. No matter how provoking the chit was, though, he felt he must keep her sweet-tempered and compliant for Blanche's sake.

And so, feigning shock, he exclaimed, "You! Old and ugly? Never!" If the girl sought flattery, he would oblige. She would be easier for them to handle, he reasoned, if he could curb her tantrums and keep her mind off other tricks by bringing her round his thumb with a few empty compliments. Maybe if Blanche weren't so worried about the willful little baggage, she would pay more attention to his attempts to woo her.

"You're beautiful enough to be a duchess!" Angus exclaimed, realizing that wasn't so far from the truth. The girl was *awfully* lovely. Most men would be tempted when she batted those big blue eyes at them. Too bad she was such a spoiled little piece of mischief.

He put his long fingers under the girl's chin and lifted her face up so that she gazed into his black eyes. It was wicked of him to tease her so, but he was caught up in the playacting he had started. "You

241

don't want to throw yourself away on the Bartholomew Waddles of this world," he said at his most urbane.

Prudie licked her full red lips with a little pink tongue. The look of invitation on her face was so ludicrous that Angus was hard put to it not to laugh. Neither of them was aware that they were being observed.

Blanche came up behind Bartholomew who was standing in the doorway to the refectory, looking thunderstruck as he watched the tableau unfold before his shocked eyes. Blanche gazed at the young man's parchment white face, saw the hurt expression in his eyes, and looked to see the cause. She beheld Prudie swaying toward a besotted-looking Angus who looked as though he was about to kiss her.

Blanche walked briskly into the room. "Are you ready to leave, Angus? The coachman has returned from hitching up the team of horses you hired to the coach where we left it along the road last night," she said in a businesslike voice as she interrupted them. They jumped apart.

Angus looked up guiltily.

Though she spoke in a matter-of-fact voice, Blanche felt a sharp pain in the region of her heart for a moment before a cold anger swept through her. She managed to maintain her dignity, though it cost her more than a little effort to do so. So, Angus is captivated by Prudie, she thought. Well, what man would not be!

Prudie preened, patting her blond curls into place.

She hooked her arm through Angus's and turned to look at Blanche. "We're just coming, Cousin Blanche. Aren't we, *Angus?*" she purred sweetly, deliberately using his first name. She looked like a cat who had just discovered the creampot.

Angus saw the withdrawn expression on Blanche's face, and felt irritated and a little hurt. You've put me in an impossible position, you know. You asked me to watch her and I was only trying to turn the little minx up sweet to help *you!* he wanted to shout. But he remained tight-lipped, not uttering a word.

It was a good thing she had been too embarrassed to return to their room after she had calmed Prudie down last night, Blanche decided, for her embarrassment then would have been as nothing to the chagrin she would have felt this morning coming upon such a scene.

Blanche castigated herself for a prize idiot. She must have been a fool to have allowed herself to act like a besotted pea goose over the man. To have believed for one minute that he was in earnest . . . to have been *almost* persuaded by the angry protestations, honeyed words, and hot embraces of a rogue like Angus Dalglish! Well, the bards said love was blind. Now she knew what they meant!

If he had been so prompt to aid her in order to collect the thousand pounds she had foolishly promised him, why wouldn't he just sweep Prudie off her feet instead, and possess himself of her cousin's entire fortune? Blanche asked herself. He was, after all, a gambler and an adventurer and now he had an heiress in his grasp—a pigeon ripe for the plucking.

There was only the small matter of the annulment of this absurd marriage to see to. A man who had no compunction about jumping into a stranger's room in the middle of the night would not stop at compromising a young girl.

And poor Bartie. The young man looked as though he had been poleaxed. Blanche had completely revised her opinion of the boy. He was just a sweet-tempered, innocent victim of her cousin's machinations to defy her father. She was sorry young Waddle had succumbed to Prudie's lovely face and been caught in her claws—for her cousin played with him much as a cat toys with its prey before dispatching it.

"It's not your headstrong hoyden of a cousin who needs protection, but young Waddle! I shall take it upon myself to save the young greenhead from a fate worse than death!" Angus had declared earlier, suddenly becoming Bartie's champion. Blanche had silently agreed, but the thought occurred now that perhaps Angus just wanted to save Prudie for himself.

"You compare marriage to death? It's a wonder, then, that you haven't run a mile from this mock marriage of ours," she had said, giving him a sharp look.

"Marriage to your *cousin,* I'm speaking of," Angus had answered with a tightening of his jaw.

"Casting out lures to your cousin's husband is the outside of enough!"

244

"Well! How dare you speak to me like that, Bartie Waddle!" Prudie said furiously as she waited under the towers of the ruined cathedral to climb into the waiting coach. Bartie had caught her by the elbow to bid her farewell. "Anyway, they don't have a real marriage, you know. Blanche doesn't want him . . . and Angus certainly doesn't want *her!*"

"I'm only telling you for your own good. If you want to flirt with every man who comes along, then you're a heartless jilt and I will ask you to release me from our engagement," Bartie said manfully.

"Our engagement, indeed! If you had to marry me so badly, you should have spoken up and forced that Mister Urquart to perform the ceremony!" Prudie felt angry enough to scratch his eyes out. How dared Bartie Waddle treat her this way! He couldn't jilt *her!* She was the one who had the right to call off any engagement.

"I see now that I was sadly mistaken in you, Miss Wilmont. I should have followed the dictates of my conscience and written home to Papa. I bid you a safe return to your home," Bartie added with boyish dignity before he turned to mount his horse.

Tears of anger and frustration stood in Prudie's eyes as she saw Bartie ride away. Blanche came round the ruined building to see her cousin standing with her gloved hands clenched and her lower lip protruding. She sighed. Prudie was in a high miff. There was no telling what mischief she would plunge into now.

Prudie recovered her spirits in short order when she recalled that Angus would be accompanying her. Certainly he was a gentleman worthy of her mettle. She was the only smiling member of the coach party as they set off.

Angus kept his pistol primed and poised at the ready as they passed by the infamous spot where they had been held up twice. Prudie squealed when she saw the small, silver-chased firearm.

"Third time lucky," Angus said when they were several miles past the area where the dense shelter of trees had provided cover for the highwaymen, ". . . for us, that is." He put the gun away, feeling the danger was past.

They traveled through more open land for quite some time. It was a raw, gray November day and soon they were climbing through the windswept hills of the Lake District. The magnificent scenery offered some solace for Blanche when she gazed out at the beauty of majestic mountains, green fells, sparkling lakes, and the crisscross of small streams set in such ancient solitary splendor. A shaft of sunlight pierced the dark clouds and spread out like a fan of many-colored light, extending its benediction out over the hard outline of the hills, lending a magic to the rugged landscape. She wished they could stop so that she could indulge in a walk to restore her tranquility, but of course there was no time.

Angus was unmoved by nature's beauties. He did not look out at the passing scene but instead clenched his teeth in anger and frustration as he watched

Blanche who sat opposite, avoiding both his gaze and all conversation with him. He had put his hand on her arm just before she mounted into the coach, and attempted to explain the earlier scene with her cousin, but she had shaken him off and refused to listen.

Every time he tried to engage her in conversation, she responded in polite monosyllables, accompanied by one of her patented regal looks, guaranteed to freeze the recipient. His mood became blacker by the minute. He began to deliberately encourage Prudie, trying to provoke some response from Blanche, daring her to call him to book for his behavior. He wanted to test her, to see if she cared at all.

Prudie, still feeling aggrieved at Bartie, was more than willing to make do with Angus. To have him as an admirer made her smile contentedly. She flirted with him to the top of her bent. His answers were set downs more often than not, but Prudie either didn't understand him or thought he was just teasing her.

"Well, Miss Wilmont, let me see your profile again. No, no—the right side this time. Ah, yes. Exquisite. Quite exquisite. Your profile puts me in mind of the portrait painted of the young Lady Georgiana Spencer. She's the Duchess of Devonshire now, you know, and quite one of the most beautiful ladies in the *ton*."

The more he flirted with Prudie, the stiffer Blanche's spine became. The longer she refrained from comment, refusing to intervene or even to take any notice of his behavior, the more outrageous Angus became. He wanted her to rip up at him, show some anger, some emotion—anything but present him with that glacial mask of icy politeness.

"Do you think I will take the *ton* by storm next spring?" Prudie asked, giggling with delight.

"Oh, without a doubt, my dear. Without a doubt. . . . You will be besieged with admirers. You must remember to save some time for an old friend, my dear Prudence, when he asks you to 'come out to play.' " He was watching Blanche out of the corner of his eye for her reaction. He saw that she had her head turned away from them and was sitting as still as a statue.

"Oh, Angus," Prudie simpered and leaned diagonally across the carriage to lay her little hand on his arm, "I will always have time for *you.*"

Angus abruptly tired of his game. "Enough infant!" he said curtly, disengaging her hand and sitting back in his seat.

He saw that all his impetuosity was achieving nothing. Slouching in his seat, he buried his nose in the paper he had picked up in Carlisle that morning. After a time, he suddenly sat up straight and exclaimed, "Good God!" then muttered a string of curses under his breath.

"Bad news?" Blanche asked, finally breaking her silence. "Has one of your 'investments' failed?"

He scowled. "No, no, nothing like that. There's a report here of the death of my—my cousin and another relative."

"Oh, I'm so sorry, Angus. Did you know them well?" Blanche asked sympathetically.

"Er, no, I didn't," he said with finality. He turned to look out the window, closing the subject, but

Blanche could see by the clenching of his jaw and the way he drummed his fingers on his knee that the news had in some measure upset him.

Prudie, miffed at Angus's dismissal, paid no attention to the conversation. She had taken her prized hat out of its box and was fitting it over her curls with Sukey's help.

Her companions were both on edge when they stopped in a sizable town for a midday meal, but Prudie was in high gig when she saw the fashionable inn Angus had selected. When Angus and Blanche finished their meal, there was a misunderstanding about which of them would stay with Prudie while the other went to take care of some minor business.

Angus stepped down to the kitchen to ask for a basket of provisions. Blanche went out briefly to purchase a nightrail and a simple day gown for Prudie. The previous evening Prudie had slept in her shift because the highwaymen had taken her night things, along with all her fine gowns and undergarments, whereas the small paper-wrapped parcel, containing a simple, muslin nightgown and a few necessities Blanche had purchased for herself in Gretna Green, had lain unnoticed in the coach amid all the excitement.

Blanche had been forced to ask Angus to advance her a small sum to make the purchases for Prudie. "I'm sorry, Angus, but Prudie must have something else to wear." She had made the request in a stilted manner, trying to conceal her embarrassment at having to ask him for money again. "Uncle Horace will pay you back, with interest, I'm sure."

"Why?" he asked with an angry glint in his eye—that she should finally speak to him and it had to be about that ninnyhammer of a cousin of hers exasperated him, kindling a spark of anger. "She's got a gown and a cloak to keep her warm—just as you do."

"But she's never worn the same gown for more than a day at a time. Actually, she's accustomed to changing her attire two or three times a day at home."

"Spoiled baggage. It won't hurt her to slum it for a day or two before we get her home. It's the price she must pay for her foolishness in running away. Tell her it's part of the adventure—she likes to see herself as a heroine." He grumbled, but handed over a golden boy that he could not very well spare. He had hired a team that morning and would have to hire another tomorrow. In addition there were meals to pay for, not to mention the major expense of accommodations for them all that evening. At this rate, he would have to break his self-imposed ban and find a card game that night.

Blanche was glad to see that Angus had assessed her cousin correctly, but knowing that he had to live with such a spoiled creature wouldn't deter a man who was determined to gain a fortune for himself, would it? She acknowledged the unpalatable truth philosophically. And now that Bartie had taken himself out of the running, Angus's way was clear.

She didn't dare tell her cousin she was going out

to a shop, for fear Prudie would want to accompany her—and then they would soon be without a feather to fly with, for her cousin could never resist buying anything that took her fancy.

Angus thought Blanche would take Prudie with her, whereas Blanche did not realize Angus meant to step out of the private parlor he had hired and leave Prudie on her own. And so, as soon as her feuding guardians were gone, Prudie, feeling bored, stepped out of the inn with Sukey at her heels. She immediately spied a peddler with his wares set out for sale on the back of his wagon just down the street. She quickened her footsteps toward his wagon and "ohhed and ahhed" over his gaily colored collection of goods.

Angus and Blanche nearly collided as they met at the door to the inn and simultaneously saw Prudie down the street, chatting animatedly with the Gypsy.

"You tolerate this sort of forward, ill-bred behavior?" Angus asked Blanche, turning to her with a tightening of his lips that she knew betokened a flaring of his temper.

"What choice do you think I have? I assumed you were watching her!" Blanche exclaimed.

"I thought you were!" Angus said.

They glared at one another, then turned and hurried down the street after Prudie.

Blanche thought Angus was blaming her for the incident, criticizing her for not taking better care of his precious Prudie. Why did he think she had asked him to help her in the first place, if it were not to rescue Prudie from the consequences of her "forward, provocative, ill-bred behavior?'' she had to prevent herself from asking ill-humoredly.

Angus, his black brows lowered dangerously, was mumbling curses under his breath. His anger was directed at himself. He wanted to ingratiate himself with Blanche, not criticize her. He would have to be more careful to help her watch the girl, though it would be a sad trial, else she would blame him if the feather-brained little pea hen ran away again. He would never be able to persuade Blanche to remain his wife if he lost the damned silly chit. He was feeling hard-pressed not to take the minx by the shoulders and give her a good shaking.

Two well-dressed bucks passing by the peddler's cart were not slow to saunter over and join the unaccompanied beauty.

''Those gents will take her for a lightskirt, you know,'' Angus said to Blanche as they walked quickly down the street.

''What's a little doe like you doing out on your own?'' the tall, saturnine gentleman asked Prudie as he came up to her.

Prudie turned obligingly and began to exhibit all the more outrageous tricks in her coquette's arsenal—smiling flirtatiously, simpering, glancing up from under her lashes, laughing loudly, and pointing to the things she liked, trying to get the men to buy them for her.

Angus came up behind her and abruptly put an end to the show. ''Come along, Mis—er, my dear,'' he said in a harsh voice, recollecting just in time that it would be unwise to reveal her name to the bystanders. He grasped her elbow in a proprietary fashion and began to pull her away from the goods wagon.

"Ah. It would appear the little lady is spoken for, Soames," said the taller of the two gentlemen to his friend in a rather bored fashion. He spoke in cultivated accents as he surveyed them all through half-closed eyelids. He casually took out his snuffbox, opened it with one hand, and offered his companion a pinch.

Angus turned with a pugnacious grimace on his dark face. "I suggest you take yourselves off," he said with a hard, challenging look at the two men.

"But he's promised me a treat, Angus," Prudie said, happy to be the center of attention. It would be ever so exciting, she thought, if she could provoke the men into fighting over her.

"Well, well. Perhaps we should ask the little lady if *she* wishes me to leave. We had just been discussing this little, ah, feathered object—a budgerigar, I collect—the lady has expressed an overwhelming passion to possess. . . . A little yellow bird for a little lady bird, eh," the gentleman said sardonically. He put his quizzing glass to his eye and looked defiantly at Angus.

Angus clenched his jaw in anger and turned to the man, the light of battle burning fiercely in his dark eyes. The two men loomed over her but, nonetheless, Blanche quickly stepped between them and put a hand on Angus's arm to constrain him. "Rescue her from them and buy her a trinket and she will come away happy," she said to Angus in a low voice. Her reasonable words uttered in her inimitable manner had an immediate calming effect on his temper.

"Won't you buy this sweet little bird for me, Angus? Look! It's such a lovely yellow color. Why, its little feathers are almost the same color as my hair," Prudie remarked fatuously.

Angus turned to the peddler and parted with three of his precious few shillings to buy the brightly colored bird in its gilded straw cage. He presented it to Prudie and she began to coo and poke at it. The two bucks, seeing no more sport to be had, sauntered away, swinging their canes.

Though she had suggested his course of action, Blanche was none too happy when she saw Angus give in to Prudie's childish pleading and buy her the foolish, extravagant present. It was yet another example of how he, like any other man, could not resist her beautiful cousin's blandishments, she thought. Well, she couldn't blame him if he was not immune to Prudie's undeniable physical charms. But she wondered again why in the world he had bothered to make up to a gray-haired, old maid like herself.

Chapter 14

"Three rooms, innkeeper!" Angus demanded at the first decent inn they came to when fast-falling darkness made it difficult to continue their journey that day.

His temper was in shreds and he forgot to be ingratiating to the innkeeper. He had been working hard, trying to show Blanche he was willing to perform the service of keeping Prudie in order by distracting the chit. But all he had gotten for his efforts was a snub. Blanche had ignored his hand when he tried to help her from the coach a moment ago.

What with Prudie's vapid chatter, languishing looks, and provocative behavior, things had gotten out of hand, Angus admitted. Several times the girl had puckered up her lips and made little kissing sounds to the bird he had bought for her, and once had even gone so far as to lift her skirt several inches, complaining that her foot hurt, giving him a good look at her well-turned ankle as she leaned down to rub it. Now he was reaping a harvest of stiff looks from one of the ladies, and a surfeit of sugary smiles from the other.

"Why, Angus dear, don't you mean two?" Prudie asked mischievously, "Oh, I forgot! Blanche doesn't want to share with you, even though she is supposedly your wife," she cooed, giggling through her fingers. "You and Blanche *did* say you would be getting an annulment as soon as may be, didn't you? Didn't they, Goldy?" she said inanely to the little bird whose gilded cage she held in her other hand.

"Stifle it!" Angus said harshly to Prudie, no longer caring if he upset the girl. He was unwilling to stand by and let the silly chit embarrass them all with her improper remarks. "Three rooms, innkeeper, if you please," he repeated more politely.

"Sorry, sir," the innkeeper said, agog with the liveliest curiosity as to what the little beauty on the gentleman's arm could mean. He glanced up to see a tall, pale lady in a nondescript dark cloak standing just behind the man's shoulder, with what must be her maid beside her, holding a large bandbox.

"I have but two rooms available," the man said apologetically. "I would like to have your custom, sir. Perhaps the ladies would not object to sharing. Otherwise," he shrugged his shoulders, "I'm afraid you must try elsewhere. And I'm much afraid that would mean you traveling on another ten miles or so, for we're the only inn hereabouts that caters to the gentry," he said with a measure of pride. And indeed his establishment did look warm and welcoming, Angus noted as he glanced about him.

"We will take the two rooms," Angus said decisively, with nary a glance at Prudie *or* Blanche.

"Very good, sir. One is in the front over the taproom, but I'm sure you'll find that it's quite a comfortable room, nonetheless. The other is set in the back, away from the inn yard. It's very quiet, isolated as it is at the back of the house."

"I shall have to share with my cousin," Blanche said to Angus in a low voice as they made their way up the stairs in the landlord's wake. Prudie pranced ahead with her maid.

Angus took her by the elbow and brought them both to a halt on the stairs. "Fleur, you are my wife. There is nothing improper in us sharing a room."

"Your temporary wife—only until we deliver Prudie safely to Uncle Horace."

"We'll see about that," Angus promised, letting her break free from his hold for the moment and hurry after Prudie.

Dinner in the private parlor Angus had engaged was an uncomfortable affair for two of the three persons at the table.

Angus's frustrations were running high. The more Blanche opposed their marriage and resisted his attempts to validate it, the more determined he was that she *would* accept him as her husband. Yes, and by God, she would enjoy doing so, too. He was resolved on that. How to go about bringing her to that point, however, was something he had not quite worked out.

Blanche was ashamed to admit that her irritation with Angus stemmed from jealousy of his attentions to Prudie. The more Angus had humored the girl, the more upset she had become. She was afraid she would make a dreadful fool of herself if she were forced to share a room with him tonight. Just a glance from those flashing black eyes of his, staring at her over the rim of his wineglass as he was doing now, caused her to feel flustered. And his briefest touch sent a spiral of warmth flooding through her, churning up her insides. He had worn down her defenses, whether she would or no. And now that his interest in her seemed to have cooled, Blanche admitted just how much she wanted that interest to continue.

Prudie had been chattering away, taking no notice of the silence of her companions.

"Quiet, brat," Angus said. "You're giving me a headache. Your cousin and I want to enjoy at least a few moments of peace and quiet on our honeymoon."

"Oh, but you're not *really* married," Prudie insisted pertly, giving them a knowing look.

Angus sent Blanche a smoldering glance over the rim of his glass as though it were she who had spoken, rather than Prudie. Blanche flushed and looked away.

"How old did you say this chit was, my dear?" Angus asked Blanche. He was tired of Prudie's childish behavior and her interference in his attempts to win Blanche. "Shouldn't we send her off to bed now?"

"Why, I'm seventeen! All grown up," Prudie answered him smartly. "And I can stay up as long as I like!"

"Really? I would have taken you for a child of twelve, not yet accustomed to *polite* society." He intended to set her down for her lack of manners, but Prudie was too full of her own consequence to understand that he had insulted her and interpreted his remark in another way.

"Oh! That's because you've only seen me wearing these unfashionable clothes my Aunt Lottie and Blanche made me wear in Harrogate." She turned to her cousin and said, "Blanche, you will have to press the red velvet gown I found in the wardrobe upstairs before tomorrow morning, for I want to wear it then. That white muslin you bought for me won't do at all— it's for a little girl. I know that the gentlemen always appreciate it when I wear something more fashionable, something that becomes me," Prudie said, fluttering her lashes in Angus's direction. "Such a coincidence, that gown fitting me so perfectly. I can't imagine why anyone would leave behind such a gorgeous creation. Why don't you go and press it now?" she asked Blanche in a voice dripping with sugar, while it was apparent that she meant her suggestion as an order. "Go and ask the landlady for an iron."

"Your cousin will do no such thing! She's not your slave, brat," Angus said with a heavy scowl. He was determined to take the girl to task over her continual incivility to Blanche. He wouldn't have the bossy little minx ordering Blanche about as though she were some slave. He was reminded again that the lot of poor relations was not a happy one, and filed the thought away to use the next time he set about convincing Blanche that she must remain as his wife.

"She's employed by my father to look after me, you know." Prudie, not used to having her will thwarted quite so emphatically, said angrily and unwisely.

"Don't think to impress me with your hoity-toity airs, you spoiled, ill-bred little chit." Angus's hair-trigger temper exploded. "Your cousin is *my* wife now. She no longer owes you any consideration and I won't tolerate your impertinence to her. I suggest that if your overweening vanity requires you to wear a different dress—and the one you 'found' sounds to me like some lightskirt's castoff—then have your maid iron it. Or better still, do it yourself. It would be the first useful thing I've ever heard of you doing," he blistered her with his tongue.

Prudie burst into noisy tears and drummed her feet on the floor. "No one—*no one* has ever spoken to me in such a way. Tell him he can't speak to me that way, Blanche!"

"You must learn to mind your manners, or the gentlemen will take you in dislike, as I've tried to warn you before," Blanche said in those modulated tones that made Angus want to shake some emotion into her. He wondered how she could restrain herself from boxing the girl's ears or giving her a good shake, as he was tempted to do himself.

A silent "Oh" of astonishment curved Prudie's lips and her eyes were like saucers as she realized Blanche wasn't going to protect her from Angus's tongue-lashing. She jumped up from her chair, lifted her skirts so that she could run, and flew from the room in a rage.

Blanche started to follow her. "Leave her for now, my dear. She can't run away in the middle of the night with no money," Angus said, putting out a restraining hand. "Let her sulk in her room. Mayhap it will improve her temper."

"You talking about learning to improve one's temper, Angus?" Blanche's eyes sparked as she gave him an ironic smile. "Talk about the pot calling the kettle black!"

But Prudie didn't make it to her room. She got no farther than the foot of the stairs where she literally ran headlong into a gentleman just coming down.

"Whoa there, miss," the lanky, garishly dressed man said, putting his hands out to steady Prudie's shoulders. "What's got you in such a pelter?" he asked, seeing the tears staining her reddened cheeks and the clenched fists at her side.

"Oh, sir!" Prudie intoned melodramatically, not noticing the fellow's vulgar dress and coarse manner. "My guardian is the greatest beast alive. I *hate* he—him!" She cast a wrathful look over her shoulder, not thinking about the consequences of striking up such an improper conversation with a stranger.

"Strong words, missy," the man said cunningly. "What's your name, my little beauty?"

"I'm Prudie . . . Miss Prudence Wilmont, that is," she simpered. Seeing a youngish man dressed in an extravagant style, Prudie peeped up at him from under her long, long lashes. "Would you help me, Mister—?" She didn't notice his oily hair, thin shanks, buckram-padded shoulders and calves, and shabby clothes that proclaimed him a hedgebird of the first order.

"Finch. P'haps I *can* help you." The man stroked his long, lean chin consideringly. "What manner of man is your guardian?"

"Beastly!" Prudie repeated, thinking her listener lacking in wits.

"Yes, but is he, er, warm in the pocket?"

"No! He's only a common gamester and his pockets are to let much of the time. I think he's after my fortune," she confided unwisely. "He shan't have any of my money after this, though!"

"You have a fortune?" Finch's little beady eyes gleamed at this information.

"Yes! Well . . .. I will have when I come into my majority."

"Ah. And when will that be?"

"Four more years."

"Oh," he said with a disappointed air. " 'Fraid I can't help you, then, miss."

"Oh, please!" Prudie reached up and grabbed him

262

by his wide lapels. "Just take me and my maid to the next town."

"How much money do you have with you?"

"Well, I've spent all *my* money. Why do you think I'm asking you to help me?"

He detached himself from her gripping hands. "Hiring horses and a carriage costs a bundle. If you ain't got the wherewithal—"

"I'll get it," she hissed. "Meet me here an hour before dawn, Mister Finch, and—" she paused as the door opened behind her.

"What in Hades are you about now, you little fool!" Angus growled, coming up to Prudie and grabbing her elbow roughly to swing her away from the man she had accosted. He had been on his way to the taproom to order a pot of coffee for Blanche and a brandy for himself, hoping to put her in a better mood so that he could talk her around to accepting their marriage.

At the sight of the tall, powerfully built gentleman coming toward Prudie with a black look on his face, Finch quickly backed away and retreated into the taproom.

Prudie kicked Angus's shin when he grabbed her. "Let me go."

"Ouch! Stop that, you little hellcat!" Angus commanded as Prudie tried to tear herself out of his grip. He picked her up, pinning her arms against her sides. He had to do something, or he would have given in to the urge to shake her until her teeth rattled.

"Stop your screeching! If you won't be still, you

little she-cat, you'll give all the Peeping Toms in the vicinity a fine view of not only your ankles, but your legs as well!'' Angus warned harshly as Prudie flailed about, trying to break out of his hold. She only succeeded in flipping her skirt up almost to her knees, revealing her full, lacy petticoats underneath.

Prudie ceased her fighting and wiggling, feeling Angus's strong arms pinioning her to his chest. She tried pouting but when he only glowered down at her, she peeped up at him from under her lashes—an artifice that had always been successful in the past in persuading a man to do whatever she wanted.

"Please, Angus. You're hurting me," she said in a small voice, then allowed her lips to tremble appealingly and managed to squeeze a tear from her eye.

He grimaced at her request, but loosened his arms, knowing it was not his business to physically discipline the girl, however much he was tempted.

Prudie's first thought was to deal him a stinging slap across the cheek, but over Angus's shoulder she caught sight of Blanche just emerging from the private parlor down the hall. Angus had his back to the hallway and could not see Blanche approaching. With a flash of feminine intuition, Prudie knew that Blanche was displeased to see Angus holding her so. Now was her chance to divide them. She put her arms round his neck and smiled sweetly up at him. If her "gaolers" were at odds, it would be easier to shab off on them, she reasoned. Divide and conquer, she had often heard her papa say.

Blanche had come out of the room to see what all the commotion was about.

"Well, I see you and Prudie have settled your differences," she said blandly, but her heart had sunk to her shoes at the sight of Angus holding Prudie in his arms. And after his strongly worded set down of her cousin, too! It just went to show that a man had trouble resisting a girl with such a lovely face.

The look on Angus's face was ludicrous as he realized how it must look to Blanche. He set Prudie down but she still clung to his neck and leaned against his chest for a moment, pretending to have difficulty getting her balance.

"I found your cousin, making up to a dam—dashed hedgebird out here, right under our noses," he said defensively, seeking to excuse himself. He pushed Prudie's hands away. He could see the accusation in Blanche's eyes—and something more. Her face was still, but he could read hurt in her eyes.

"Did you?" Blanche asked in a voice heavy with irony. "I suppose you came to the rescue, substituting one fortune-hunting 'hedgebird' for another."

"Now, Fleur—" Angus stretched his hand toward her, seeking to explain.

"Come along, Prudie. I can't have you fraternizing with any more *hedgebirds* at this time of night," Blanche turned her back on Angus and took her cousin's arm, ready to lead her upstairs. "This inn seems to attract them," she murmured under her breath.

Prudie went along with a little glance back at Angus. "Good night, *Angus.*" She smiled triumphantly to see her strategem work so well and waggled her fingers at him.

He passed a weary hand over his face and turned to go into the taproom.

Angus opened one eye.

"What the devil do you think you're doing?" His hand snaked out from under the bedclothes and captured Prudie's wrist in a viselike grip. She was reaching toward his jacket that was hanging over the chair by the bed.

"Oh! You startled me," Prudie exclaimed, dripping hot candle wax on his hand so that he released her with a muttered oath.

"How did you get in here, girl?" he asked.

"Oh, Angus, you must come quickly!" she said, sounding frightened. "Blanche is not feeling at all the thing. I don't know what's wrong with her. But she's asking for you."

"What!" Angus exclaimed, sitting bolt upright and letting the coverlet fall off his bare chest. He started to throw the bedclothes off, but remembered just in time that he wasn't wearing a nightshirt. He pulled the sheet back up to cover himself from Prudie's interested gaze. "Hand me my clothes. Quickly."

"Here's your jacket, but where are the rest of your things?" Prudie pretended to look all around, lifting her candle high to highlight the room.

"Hell! Where are my breeches? I swear I left them right here, draped over this chair."

"I don't see any other clothes," Prudie said innocently. "Hurry, Angus, there's no time. I'm frightened for her."

"Hand me my cloak, then. It's hanging on the back of the door," he said impatiently, anxious to get to Blanche and find out what was wrong.

Prudie did as requested.

"Is your maid not with her, then?"

"No. I sent her to rouse the landlady. To ask her to brew a posset."

"Quickly, run back to your room. I will follow you. We shouldn't leave your cousin alone for long!"

Prudie left, lighting Angus's candle for him before she went. Angus threw off the bedclothes and jumped up. He had one last hurried look about for his clothes, but he couldn't locate anything but his jacket. He even bent down and shone his candlelight under the bed, but all he saw there was the dust the housemaid had neglected to sweep away. He hurriedly wrapped the rather dusty long, black cloak about himself to cover his nakedness as well as he could, and raced out the door. Fleur needed him. Time was of the essence. Hell, no one could see anything in the dark, anyway, he reasoned as he ran down the hall in his bare feet.

Prudie greeted Angus as he rushed up to the door of the room she was sharing with Blanche. "Shh!" she cautioned him, finger to lips. "She's finally fallen asleep, thank goodness. She's been so restless. Don't wake her!"

Angus walked quietly to the bed and knelt down, reaching for Blanche's hand. She appeared to be sleeping peacefully. He stayed motionless for a short time, not hearing the soft click of the door behind him.

He leaned over carefully and gently kissed her forehead to find it cool, not fevered as he had expected.

Blanche opened her eyes and stared up blankly for a moment. She lifted her hand and laid it against his unshaven cheek. She had been dreaming of him. "Angus? What are you doing here?"

"Prudie, she came to get me—she said . . . Fleur, you're not ill are you?"

"No. Of course not."

Angus jumped to his feet and looked around at the empty room swearing, "Why, the lying little jade!" He strode barefoot to the door and tried the handle.

"Locked! Just as I thought!"

"What do you mean?" Blanche asked, confused and still groggy from sleep.

"Your precious Prudie has pitched me a tale of gammon and, like a greenhead, I fell for it, hook, line, and sinker. She's given us the slip, played us like a fish on a line."

"Prudie gone? But, where—? How?"

"I'll lay you any odds you care to name, the hedgebird in the hallway."

"You mean there really was someone she was speaking to out there."

"Of course there was. And trying all her wiles to wheedle him into running away with her, or I miss my bet."

"Oh."

"You didn't think I was physically restraining her for the pleasure of holding a kicking, screeching little brat in my arms, did you?"

Even in the faint light given off by his candle, Angus could see that Blanche blushed.

"Fleur, Fleur . . . when are you going to learn to trust me? I would have to be a mooncalf to be interested in your ninnyhammer of a cousin—beautiful though she is. She will make some poor soul a fine harridan of a wife someday."

"What are we to do, Angus?"

"Shout the house down, I suppose," he said, suiting action to words by banging on the door with his closed fist and yelling, "Innkeeper, innkeeper! I say there, innkeeper! Fire! Fire! In the back!"

His cloak flew open as he vigorously pounded on the door and Blanche emitted a faint shriek before she could help herself. Angus looked over at her averted profile and realized his state of dishabille. He pulled the cloak round himself again.

"This was the only thing to hand when your cousin came rushing in to tell me you were deathly ill. By God, *she* hid my clothes! And I wager she searched through all my pockets for my money, as well. Yes, and devil take it, by now she will have searched my room and found all the blunt, except the stash hidden in my boot, and fleeced me, too. Damnation! How did such a little pea goose with more hair than wit come to be so cunning?" He began to shout for the innkeeper again but Blanche stopped him.

"But, Angus, if you call the innkeeper and they

find us in here together and you—ah, not quite properly dressed, what will they think?''

"Ah. Not so calm and collected now, madam wife?'' He turned and actually grinned at her. ''Why, they will think nothing of a man and his wife together behind a locked door. What say you we leave your cousin to her fate and make the most of this opportunity? Just one kiss and I'll try to rouse the innkeeper again,'' he said, coming toward her purposefully. ''Unless you change your mind and agree with me that we should forget the chit and enjoy this interlude.''

"If we lose our heads, Angus, you'll lose your chance at the reward.''

"Ah, you admit you are capable of losing your head, then.''

"Angus, please. We're losing valuable time.''

He laughed. ''Well, would you prefer I try to break the door down? Hmm. It's more usually the *lady* who tries to break the door down, or so I understand. I wouldn't want to give anyone the impression that I was running away in fright,'' he joked.

"She will be miles away by now, while you stand there teasing me.''

"Yes, but how can you expect me to go after her when we have no money and I have no idea where my clothes are. She may have taken them with her, for all I know. Summoning the innkeeper will do no good whatsoever under the circumstances.'' He folded his arms under the cloak and grinned at her.

Blanche tried to retain her composure but her very

effort to look unconcerned told Angus that she was struggling. He laughed devilishly, then took pity and shouted for the innkeeper again.

By the time the innkeeper heard the racket at the rear of the house and found an extra key to the door, the sky was lighting a new day. It took Angus some while to locate his clothes. Eventually he found them behind the clothespress where Prudie had wedged them. He discovered that he was right when he checked under his pillow and found his money—and his pistol—gone.

He and Blanche were at the top of the staircase about to descend, when they heard a familiar voice insisting petulantly, "I won't say I'm sorry, Bartholomew Waddle. I won't! I won't! I *won't!* . . . And you can't make me!"

"Why, it's Bartie! I thought you said it was some hedgebird she ran off with," Blanche said to Angus as they stood at the top of the stairs and gazed down at the commotion below.

"It was," Angus insisted.

"I don't care if you found me in a ditch!" Prudie was standing below, arguing with Bartie. She looked very wet and bedraggled in the red velvet gown she wore. The feathers in her prized hat were drooping and dripping water on the floor. "It was all that nasty Mister Finch's fault! There was never such a take in! He promised to convey me to London where I could stay with great Aunt Tabitha, but it was all a hum,"

271

she complained to Bartie, shaking the poor budgerigar about from side to side as she gestured with the hand that held its cage.

"Hardly chastened behavior," Angus said in a low voice.

"Well, what can you expect? She's nothing if not imprudent," Blanche murmured back.

"After he took all my money, he forced me and Sukey to get down and he drove off just like that in the carriage *I* had hired!" Prudie snapped her fingers in Bartie's face.

"*Your* money? You spent all your money on our way to Gretna Green. Where did you get this money?" Bartie asked suspiciously. "I hope you didn't steal it."

Prudie looked down guiltily and began to poke at the budgie through the bars of its cage, trying to encourage it to sit on its little perch instead of on the floor where it had sought refuge.

"You'll pay back every penny of it, if you have," Bartie promised firmly, putting his hand under Prudie's chin and forcing her to meet his eyes.

Angus turned to look at Blanche with raised brows. Young Bartie's voice was resonant with authority. He was ringing a peal over her.

"Why, he's scolding her!" Blanche said to Angus with surprise and just a hint of laughter.

Angus grinned. "I didn't think the boy had it in him. Just goes to show that even the mildest mannered of men can be provoked by such a little bundle of duplicity as your Prudie. She will be extremely lucky if she gets off with only a thundering scold when I get hold of her, however. You'll have to use all of your considerable talent at softening me up and calming me down to prevent me from strangling her," Angus said to Blanche as they stood watching the play from above.

Over a large breakfast and a steaming pot of coffee the story was told. Prudie cleared up the mystery of how she had been able to get into Angus's room. She had sent Sukey to ask the landlord for a spare key. "Say it's for *Mrs.* Dalglish, Sukey," she had commanded her maid in a whisper behind Blanche's back while she pretended to send the girl on some other errand.

"Why would you do such a thing, Prudence Wilmont?" Blanche asked.

"I wanted to pay him back—he was so mean to me!" Prudie said sulkily. She was not loathe to tell the whole story, seeing herself as a famous heroine in a melodrama.

She had been so excited, it was easy to pretend to sleep until she was sure Blanche was asleep. Then she had gotten up, dressed and packed her things, awakened Sukey, and tiptoed down the hall to Angus's room. She had let herself in with no difficulty and left Sukey guarding the door. She had searched through his clothing, but when she couldn't find his money, she had had a brilliant idea. She would hide his clothes and pretend Blanche was ill. When he went to check on her cousin, she would lock them in together.

After this part of her plan had been accomplished with not the slightest hitch, she had returned to Angus's room and found the money under his pillow. She had taken his pistol for good measure, but Mr. Finch had filched it from her.

"Why, you little thief! I think I'll have you prosecuted!" Angus said, when he heard Prudie confess that she had taken his money and his weapon.

"And I'll have you prosecuted if you don't live up to your marriage vows with my cousin!" Prudie retorted.

Angus opened his mouth to say that he was more than willing to do so, but the pressure on his arm from Blanche's hand restrained him from trading insults with the girl.

Prudie was reminded of her grievances against that lying knave Finch and this led to a retelling of how he had abandoned her beside a large stack of wood ready to be lit up on Bonfire Night the next evening. A sinister-looking, stuffed effigy of Guy Fawkes had been placed atop the pile, and it was staring down straight at her, or so she believed. She had been very frightened, afraid that the crude but remarkably lifelike effigy would come alive and pull her onto the pyre with him, she told her listeners with a shiver of fright.

"Remember, remember, the Fifth of November, / Gunpowder treason and plot. / I see no reason why

'*Prudie's*' treason / Should ever be forgot,'' Angus re-cited in a menacing manner.

Prudie ignored his mocking words and said how glad she was to see none other than "my Bartie" riding up on a strawberry roan horse to the rescue.

Bartie took up the tale now. He explained how he had found Prudie and Sukey beside a large gulley near the bonfire just on the edge of town. Prudie was standing in a puddle and crying. She had been abandoned by her hedgebird and the red velvet dress she wore was wet to the knees, but at least she was still wearing her prize hat, he told them in all seriousness.

"A good thing, too, as it was probably the only thing that kept the rain off her," Angus said in an aside to Blanche. He sat with one leg hooked over his chair while his other booted foot rested on the fender in front of the hearth and listened to the explanation with a sardonic look on his face. He glanced at his boots with disgust. The Spanish leather had been nicked and scuffed by the rough treatment the boots had received when Prudie pushed them behind the large piece of furniture.

"And I had my dear little budgie to bear me company," Prudie added, poking at the unfortunate bird again.

"But not a ha'penny of Angus's money was left," Bartie continued. Of course, Finch had taken that when he had demanded payment for services rendered.

Bartie had lectured Prudie severely on the perils of her action, trying to explain to her the risk she had run, and telling her she was lucky that she had been abandoned before more serious harm could be done to her.

"How did you come to be in the area to rescue her in the first place, Bartholomew?" Blanche asked, after she had thanked him for his action. "I thought you had decided to return home."

Bartie explained that he had ridden away the previous day in a miff, intending to ride ahead of the coach party to make his call on Sir Horace alone, and tender his apologies before Prudie arrived home. But he had changed his mind and come after them, knowing that Prudie was not very good at looking after herself, and likely to give anyone who was not sympathetic to her a certain amount of trouble.

He begged Angus and Blanche to be allowed to finance the rest of the journey, since, he said, it was his fault for agreeing to run off with Prudie in the first place that they were all in the suds. He manfully took full blame upon himself for all of Prudie's indiscretions.

"How do you come to have any money, Bartie?" Prudie asked suspiciously. "I thought you wanted to marry me because I'm an heiress."

"I recommend you watch your pockets, Waddle, else this little brat here will be filching all your money, too," Angus admonished Bartie.

Bartie blushed as he said, "I never did say I hadn't any money, Miss Wilmont. My father is rather plump in the pocket, and he doesn't stint me. I'm afraid you rather jumped to a false conclusion when I requested that you hand over your money to me for safekeeping in Skipton. I thought I could look after it better than you. I'm sorry, Mrs. Dalglish, I didn't know that she had taken all of your money, as well, and left you in such dire straits," he apologized to Blanche, with an earnest sincerity.

As they had no choice, other than for Angus to try to find a card game in this out-of-the-way place, Angus and Blanche had to accept Bartie's offer as graciously as they could.

Chapter 15

The dusty coach crunched over the graveled drive and rumbled up to the front of the ivy-covered portico of the new Georgian-style manor house of Sir Horace Wilmont late that afternoon. The occupants of the coach were cold, tired, and excessively relieved to reach the end of their journey, albeit each for a different reason. Even the budgie seemed a bit downpin, sitting drowsily on the floor of its cage, looking much the worse for wear.

Blanche had convinced Bartie to remain at a nearby inn while she smoothed the way for him with her uncle. It would be better if she prepared Uncle Horace, she had said. As she said a temporary farewell to the young man, Blanche reflected that Bartie had changed out of all recognition from the callow youth she had known in Harrogate. As she had gotten to know him better, she had come to see him in a better light. Not only had his appearance improved, but his character was better understood on closer acquain-

278

tance. He certainly seemed to have grown up in the past week, which was more than could be said for her cousin.

Blanche had tried to convince Angus to remain at the inn, too. But he would have none of it. She had only succeeded in aggravating his temper.

"What kind of man do you think I am, to let my wife face a possibly hostile employer without me there to protect her? And if your uncle hears from me, man to man, about young Waddle's heroics, possibly he won't horsewhip the boy for running off with his daughter in the first place."

"Horsewhip? Uncle Horace? I don't think he would ever do such a thing!"

"Well, I should be tempted, if any young weasel ever tried to run off with a daughter of mine. A daughter of *ours,*" Angus amended, looking at Blanche with a light gleaming in his eye.

A faint flush mounted in her cheeks at his words, but she didn't respond.

The butler had seen the approach of the strange coach and had sent a footman down to the gravel drive to open the door for the arriving passengers. Before Angus could climb down to assist the ladies out of the vehicle, Prudie, in her haste to get out, knocked him in the head, first with the bird cage, then with the bandbox containing her now ruined hat, stepped on his toes, and tumbled out. She was saved from a fall by the waiting footman who exclaimed, "Miss Wilmont! Sir Horace has been worried. We expected you home several days ago."

"Never mind, Watkins. I'm here now and I've had such an adventure. Where is my papa?"

"In his study, miss, as he always is at this hour." And Prudie rushed off, running up the steps and shouting, "Papa, Papa, I'm home!" as she disappeared into the house. No matter how much they argued, no one spoiled Prudie like Sir Horace, Blanche thought with a resigned smile.

Angus jumped out and gave Blanche a rueful grin as he turned to assist her out of the coach.

"Well, my cousin is a scatterbrain. What else could you expect?" She smiled into his eyes as she put her hands on his shoulders and he lifted her down. He set her on her feet and extended his arm to her while the footman stared at them curiously. "Miss Charolais! Sir Horace has been wondering what has been keeping you. He sent his agent to intercept you on the journey," the footman told her.

"Yes, well, unfortunately our coach broke down outside Skipton and we were forced to spend a few extra nights on the road," Blanche said. "This gentleman, Mister Dalglish, has been so good as to escort us home. Could you ask Potter to prepare a room for him, Watkins?"

"Very good, miss." Watkins bowed and turned to see to the luggage, such as it was.

Angus looked at Blanche, placed his free hand over hers where it rested along his sleeve and squeezed it as he said, "As my wife, we should share your room, you know."

"No more of this nonsense. We are not properly married, Angus."

"We are *legally* man and wife, Fleur. You *do* want to convince your uncle that all has been aboveboard on this mad journey, don't you?"

"Of course!"

"Well, then—"

Blanche bit her lip. This did present a problem, but she was unwilling to continue the argument with Angus in the middle of the drive. She went with him up the steps into the house.

Sir Horace was embracing his daughter when Blanche and Angus entered the hallway. He let Prudie go when he glimpsed his niece. "Blanche, I can't make heads or tails of Puss's tale of why you were delayed on the road for four extra days. And why, in heaven's name, have you allowed her to purchase a blasted budgerigar?

"What—? Who—?" Sir Horace sputtered as he spied Angus over Prudie's golden head. He lowered his brows. He was instantly suspicious that the tall, dark stranger had come with some mercenary intention toward his daughter. He frowned as he took the stranger's measure. Sir Horace didn't like the look of the unknown gentleman—such a formidable man might challenge his own authority. "And who are you, sir?"

"Oh, Papa, this is Angus Dalglish," Prudie said offhandedly. She gave Angus a dark look. She had not forgiven him for taking her to task over her various sins—saying he would have her prosecuted as a thief, indeed! She looked down her little nose and glowered at him.

"Ah, Dalglish, is it? And how came you to escort the ladies home, sir?"

"I believe it would be better, Sir Horace, if I spoke to you in private where we would not be interrupted" Angus began, trying to restrain his temper and placate the blustering gentleman, however much he longed to let the man know how his "precious" daughter had placed herself and her cousin in several awkward, compromising situations.

Prudie spoke up, cutting Angus off. "Oh, Papa, Angus is a gamester. He paid our way home by gambling."

Sir Horace lowered his bushy brows. "Paid your way home? A gamester?" he sputtered. "What happened to the money I sent to Blanche? And what is this fellow to you, miss?" he asked suspiciously, jumping to his own conclusions. Humph! This stranger was certain to be a rogue and a fortune hunter, if he knew anything, and Sir Horace, never backward in thinking himself a downy one, up to all the rigs, fancied that he knew quite a bit.

"Oh, Papa, he's nothing to me," Prudie said with a sniff. "Well, actually, I suppose he's a kind of cousin."

"A cousin? What do you mean?"

"Well, he's married to cousin Blanche so—"

"Married to Blanche? When? How?" Sir Horace shouted.

Angus arched a brow at Blanche and she looked

282

back resigned. She knew it was useless trying to explain the circumstances to her uncle now. Trust Prudie to let the cat out of the bag in such a negligent way.

Prudie compounded Blanche's problems when she went on to reveal how Blanche had traveled with Angus disguised as a young man, and how they had been wed by mistake.

"Oh, the wretched girl. We're truly in the basket now," Blanche whispered to Angus. He put his arm around her waist protectively and gave her a reassuring hug.

"Now, see here, niece! How dare you corrupt my daughter by exposing her to such goings-on! I demand an explanation of such a scandalous report!" Sir Horace began, sputtering and fuming.

Angus's jaw hardened and he glared menacingly as he took a step toward Sir Horace. "You will apologize to my wife, sir—"

Blanche felt the tightening of the muscles in his arm that was clasping her. She put her hand over the fist clenched at her waist to stay him. His anger at her uncle's rudeness to her would serve no good purpose.

She moved forward gracefully, folded her hands in front of her, and said with a regal air, "Unfair, Uncle! You must listen to the correct version of events before you make a judgment. You know how careless Prudie is. . . . She has not explained the whole story to you, the circumstances—and her part in it. It was all a mistake, you see, and—"

"A mistake? How can you be married by mistake?'' he roared. After a moment's reflection, Sir Horace saw that it was not in his best interests to object to any marriage his niece made, no matter how havey-cavey the circumstances. He had lately been wondering what he would do with his penniless niece, once Prudie was fired off. This marriage would be a most effective way to rid himself of a dependent relative.

He looked at Angus consideringly and decided that the man with his good looks and powerful build could well take the fancy of his flighty daughter. It was much better to have him buckled to her cousin—unless the fellow turned out to be a duke or something equally unlikely. After a few ''ahems,'' he turned to Blanche. ''You admit you are married to this fellow, niece?''

''Well . . . I suppose that is the case, though the particulars surrounding the ceremony were, er, unusual.''

Well, Blanche's future was settled, then, he thought. His relief was evident on his face. ''That's all right and tight, then,'' he said, going forward with his hand outstretched. ''Welcome to the family, Dalglish. I'm sure you will make Blanche an exemplary husband.''

''Sir Horace, if I might explain,'' Angus interjected. ''Fleu—ah, Miss Charolais and I were married in Gretna Green as we attempted—''

''Gretna Green! What in heaven's name were you doing there? And where was Prudie all this while? You had no business taking her to such a notorious

284

place, Blanche. Why, some fortune hunter might have attempted to force her into one of those havey-cavey marriages over the anvil. It was your responsibility to keep her safe, niece!'' he lectured Blanche severely.

Angus was indignant at Sir Horace's treatment of Blanche. He decided it was time for some plain speaking. He would not have his Fleur criticized and castigated by this father who had neglected to do his duty by guarding his headstrong daughter himself, and who had placed his own niece in such compromising circumstances that she was left alone and penniless while in a great deal of pain.

Light blazed in his eyes as he spoke to Sir Horace. ''Miss Wilmont abandoned her cousin, who was ill at the time, in Skipton, took all the money you had sent them for the journey, and eloped with a young man she had met in Harrogate. Through a fortuitous meeting, I came to Miss Charolais's assistance. Solely through her determination and unflagging energy during two days of almost nonstop riding when she had just recovered from a painful tooth extraction, we followed Miss Wilmont to Gretna Green and were just in time to prevent your daughter from being joined in wedlock to Mister Bartholomew Waddle.

''You niece is a heroine, sir, and I won't have you casting any aspersions on her character or her motives. Both were, and are, beyond reproach! You should be proud to be related to such a sensible and selfless lady. I know that I am bursting with pride to call her wife!''

"Heh?" Sir Horace roared. *"Prudie* eloped, you say!" He had gone very red in the face.

Prudie, with her hands behind her back and an innocent look on her face like a child caught out in some mischief, had tiptoed backward toward the door that led down to the kitchens.

"Prudence Wilmont, you minx! How dare you defy me in such a way! Come here this instant!" Sir Horace was beside himself. He looked to be on the verge of an apoplectic fit.

Father and daughter began arguing loudly with one another before Angus could finish his catalogue of Blanche's virtues. He turned to Blanche and they spoke in an undertone.

She was flushed with pleasure at Angus's unexpected and extravagant praise and she smiled up at him warmly, her silver eyes sparkling. She was not afraid, for once, to let her admiration of him show in her expression. She leaned against his arm that had come round to encircle her waist possessively and felt a warm glow melting away her doubts. Perhaps he really did want her as his wife, after all.

Angus looked down into her upturned face and smiled into her eyes. He was relieved to see a smile on her face and some measure of happiness in her eyes. Perhaps he was beginning to make some headway, after all. Blanche had become too important to him to chance losing her now. He tried to tell her with a look and the pressure of his arm around her waist what she meant to him—but he would have to wait until later to show her.

Sir Horace, meanwhile, was trying to send his defiant and unrepentent daughter to her room where she could reflect on her misbehavior in quiet solitude. Prudie, pouting and pleading and petulant, insisted that she would not go. Sir Horace was forced to give up and Prudie flounced off to the kitchens, saying she was hungry and wanted to have a word with cook to make sure that all her favorite dishes were served at dinner that night.

When Sir Horace's fury had receded somewhat, Angus explained that although young Waddle had eloped with Prudie, the boy deeply regretted that action and was coming to apologize to Sir Horace on the morrow. Angus went on to tell Sir Horace about how Bartie had then rescued Prudie on the homeward journey.

"You've confounded me," Sir Horace said, shaking his head. "How can young Waddle be a hero? I thought the young rascal ran off with my daughter in the first place."

"Oh, he did, Uncle—or perhaps it would be more accurate to say that Prudie ran off with him. But then he came to her rescue—twice, actually," Blanche said in the same unemotional voice she used to speak about the most mundane of everyday matters.

Eventually, Sir Horace extended his hand to Angus once more. "Seems I owe you an apology and a debt of thanks, Dalglish. You've saved my daughter. I think you will make a fine husband for my niece. As a matter of fact, I will settle a hundred pounds on her as a wedding gift."

"Uncle!" Blanche's hand went to her throat. "I promised Mister Dalglish that there would be a substantial reward if he would help me rescue Prudie and return her to you unwed. A hundred pounds is paltry when you think of Prudie's fortune. And I—I'm not at all sure a marriage contracted under such unusual circumstances as mine should stand—"

"Nonsense, nonsense, girl!" Sir Horace interrupted. "Of course it will stand. And perhaps I do owe Dalglish here a larger, um, financial remuneration," Sir Horace admitted after a few hemming coughs.

"I couldn't take a penny, sir," Angus spoke up. "Good of you to offer, though."

Blanche turned an amazed look on him. She had thought the promise of a large reward was his only reason for aiding her. "But that's why you agreed to help me."

"Was it?" He turned a glinting smile on her as he gazed down into her face. What she saw in his flashing black eyes told her that he had a reward other than monetary in mind.

"Well, I wondered when you would decide to join me," Angus said from his recumbent position on the small four-poster bed when Blanche came in.

He was lying on her bed with his arms behind his head, sprawling comfortably on top of the frayed, old coverlet in nothing but his breeches. The sight of that thick mat of black hair on his bare chest trailing down and disappearing under the fabric of his breeches was doing strange things to her breathing and making her legs feel shaky. He looked so dangerously beautiful lying there in such familiar homely surroundings—in her own room, on her bed. She struggled to maintain her composure.

"It must be close to midnight. Surely you haven't been talking to your uncle all this while? It seems like hours ago that he directed me up here to your room." Angus yawned and stretched his arms above his head. "I hope you don't make a habit of these late nights, Fleur. I must confess, after the last few days, I'm ready to spend the next week in bed."

"Angus—" Blanche began, then bit her lip. She turned away, unnerved by the sight of him lying there, to pace about the small chamber.

"Yes," he drawled.

When Blanche continued her restless pacing, keeping her face averted from him and her hands clasped tightly in front of her, Angus prompted, "I'm at your service, as always, my dear."

"Angus, we really must discuss how to—to come to some *arrangement* about this so-called marriage."

"Oh, I couldn't agree more, my dear."

"I suppose—I suppose we must seek an annulment."

"Must we, Fleur? Why?"

"Oh, Angus, I—I will not hold you to this marriage. You know that it is a farce."

"I know nothing of the kind," he said softly, but

Blanche didn't hear his remark. She had hurried on with her prepared speech.

"You are free to leave here tomorrow. I think—I think you should do so. Uncle Horace will finance your journey and repay what Prudie took. It would be the wisest course. To delay will only complicate matters further. You can have your solicitor forward the annulment decree to me here. I—I hope it will not take long." Blanche was not as coherent and composed as she had planned to be. She could not quite breathe properly and she felt so confused that it was difficult to concentrate on what she knew must be said. It was so hard to let him go, yet she knew it was what she *must* do, if she wanted to avoid a broken heart. If she gave in to his desire to consummate their marriage, she was sure he would tire of her in no time at all and leave her—leave her to long for him, with not even the shell of her former self, her long-cultivated pose of dispassionate serenity, to hide behind.

"Fleur—that's nonsense. You yourself have pointed out that you've been compromised in society's eyes by traveling with me for several days as you have done. I'm your husband now. I may not be the best of bargains, or what you expected to find in a husband, but why not make the best of the situation and stick to your vows?"

"Vows? What vows? I don't remember saying that I would take you as my wedded husband," she said in the icy voice that only provoked Angus's hot temper.

He leapt up from the bed and came toward her. "You have nowhere else to go. You heard what your uncle said—he was more than happy to have you off his hands. You must remain married to me."

"Oh, must I? You would keep me out of pity?"

"No!"

"Then I must remain your wife because you command me to? Why?"

"This is why." He took her by the waist and pulled her fully against himself. "Because I want a *real* marriage with you," he said before he lowered his mouth to hers and began kissing her with an intense longing. He was tired of her arguments—of her icy reserve, always holding herself aloof from him.

He had been holding back long enough. His nerves were frayed from all the understanding and consideration he had shown, all the restraint he had imposed on himself in the days they had traveled together. The hen-witted little minx had been restored to her father. The girl was no longer Fleur's problem. She would be his wife. Here! Now! Tonight!

He kissed her with all the pent-up frustration of a man who knew himself married, but who had yet to taste the fruits of that union. He longed for her with a fierce ache.

Blanche stood passive, making no move to push him away, but resisting his efforts to kiss her deeply. She let him press his lips to hers, but denied him entrance to her mouth, standing like a marble statue, stiff and unmoving.

She had kissed him properly during their second

night at the monastery and responded to his lovemaking with a hot passion of her own, Angus remembered. And, by God, he was determined that she would do so again.

He raised his head and asked desperately, "What must I do to shake you out of this infernal coldness of yours?"

"Why do you wish to do so?" Blanche asked.

"It's Guy Fawkes Day, bonfire night, you know—seems appropriate to celebrate by igniting a bonfire of our own," he said with a touch of humor breaking through his intensity.

She gave a half smile, and he continued, "It's an irresistible attraction, I think. We're opposites—you stand there cold as ice, while I'm on fire."

"I've learned to be cold. How else do you think I've survived?" But he was wrong, and she had lied. She was only trying to hide behind her defensive mask again—she wasn't cold at all, she was warm, so warm her skin burned under his touch, her body wanted to melt against him and she pressed closer to the heat of him, lifting her face up to his, aching for his kiss.

"Please don't freeze me out, Fleur!"

"I'm just not sure what you want of me," she whispered, looking up into his eyes, seeking to be reassured.

"Fleur—I want you to remain my wife!" he said, giving her an earnest, pleading, look and a little shake to emphasize that he meant his words. "If that infernal mix-up hadn't occurred, I would have asked you to marry me, anyway."

And he would have, Angus knew with complete certainty. It had started out as only another one of his adventures, but it seemed that the midnight meeting with his silver lady on All Hallows' Eve would be the defining moment of his life, for when he had leapt into her room, love had invaded his heart. He hadn't quite realized it at first, but he knew now he could never let her go.

"You're just being honorable, Angus," she said, but she was disarmed by the sincere note she heard in his voice.

"Honorable! Not half, my girl. I'm being selfish, possessive, and overbearing, maybe." He nuzzled her under her ear, teasing at the lobe with his lips while he ran his hands lightly over her back and hips. "Is it honorable to desire something I can't live without?"

She made a small noise, it could almost have been a sigh of pleasure, he thought, before she protested, "Oh, Angus, I know you only agreed to keep to this marriage for appearances sake—it was convenient when we were escorting Prudie home."

"Convenient? Yes, it's mighty convenient for me, because I've thought I would go mad with wanting you," he said, running his hand over her back, her waist, her hips, stroking gently up and down, warming her flesh through the thin material of her gown.

"I can't resist you, my flower. . . . Don't you like me at all? Just a little bit?"

"Oh, Angus, of course, I like you. I like you very much." He bent his head and kissed her fiercely.

When he lifted his head, she moaned, "Oh, I like you, I like you . . . more than is good for me."

"Show me then," he growled. For answer she put her hands up and pulled his head down to hers. She pressed her lips to his and began to kiss him with an intense hunger of her own. He was not slow to take up her invitation.

His mouth moved over hers, gently at first, touching, tasting, savoring. Take it slow and easy, he told himself, trying to impose calm on the blood pounding through his veins.

She put her arm up round his neck and wound her fingers through his hair. She did not object when he began to unfasten the buttons at the back of her gown. She could feel his fingers trembling against the bare skin at the nape of her neck, while he continued to place feather-light kisses over her eyes, her face, her neck and murmur passionate endearments.

His lips moved back to her mouth where his tongue teased at her lips until Blanche felt she would suffocate if she didn't give him entry. All clear thought vanished under the tumult of her emotions. Her gown fell open and Angus pushed the soft muslin material down so that it fell over her shoulders and down her arms so that his hands could stroke and caress the smooth skin of her back, her neck, her shoulders, her breasts, while his mouth was busy moving over hers. He released her lips and his mouth followed in the wake of his burning fingers, following the trail his hands had blazed. Blanche closed her eyes and sighed softly. She scarcely knew that one of her hands was entangled in his hair, and the other was trailing over the warm skin of his neck, his back, his shoulders.

He began to kiss her deeply again, his tongue stoking a fire deep inside her, as he moved her inexorably backward to the bed. She felt her legs give way as her knees hit the back of the mattress and then she was lying sprawled across the bed. Angus had come down to lie half on top of her with one of his legs pinning her to the mattress.

"I'm glad you finally decided to lie down, Fleur. I don't think my legs would have held me up another minute." Angus was laughing, his breath coming in short bursts. "Now let's just get you out of this gown," he said hoarsely, impatiently tugging the gown down to her waist and then down over her legs; then he removed his breeches.

Blanche's passion suddenly fled and panic took its place. She lay paralyzed with fear. What was she doing—giving in to a shameless adventurer who would probably leave her, wedded or no, as soon as he had slaked his desire—whatever his words to convince her beforehand.

It was just that Angus was so stubborn. The more she opposed him, the more determined he was to have his way. And the trouble was that she wanted him. Oh, how she wanted him. But she mustn't let him see that. No, no. It would be humiliating to let him see that she was as on fire with love for him, as he was with lust for her. She willed herself to lie still, when all the while she wanted to press herself against him, wind herself about him, and touch him as he was touching her.

Angus felt her stiffen beneath him. "I like my serene, sedate lady—but not in bed, love!" he said, laughing against her mouth and gasping for breath, as he sought to tease her into returning his passion the way she had been doing a few moments before.

But when she remained quiet and unmoving, he exclaimed in frustration, "My God, Fleur, I can't wait another minute!" Blanche didn't resist when he positioned himself between her legs. She didn't resist, but she didn't react, either.

"Don't lie there like that! I don't want to make love to a marble statue. You're making me feel like a devil . . . I can't stop now," he said a moment later, all control beyond him.

"I'll make you love me, by God, I will!" he swore raggedly. Then with one sharp thrust, he was inside her softness.

Blanche bit down on her lip and stifled her cry at the sharp pain. She tried to keep her mind blank, telling herself that she was, after all, his wedded wife. But she was not going to show any emotion. No, no. She would lose herself in this maelstrom of spiraling sensation if she did so. She would never be quite herself again, never be able to regain her mask of cool composure, if she let herself go.

"You're mine now!" Angus said triumphantly. "Now. Forever. Always!" he whispered against her ear.

He moved within her for a time, then shuddered, calling her name.

Blanche lay stunned. She was afraid to move an inch, not daring to breathe. Afraid almost to take a breath. If she did so, she wouldn't be able to stop herself from telling him that she was indeed his forever—and not just her body, but her heart as well.

Angus lay heavily on top of her, spent, continuing to draw in deep breaths through his parted lips. After a few moments, he rested his cheek against hers and whispered, "Oh, God, how I love you!"

Blanche was afraid to trust her ears. What had he said? He loved her? He really did? Oh, then—

"Are you—are you sure your affections are firmly fixed?" she whispered back, unsure even yet.

He began to shake with laughter, shaking her, too, as she lay beneath him.

"Am I *sure*? Of, Fleur, my darling—" he broke off, trying to stop laughing and catch his breath. "My affections are so firmly fixed, they haven't moved an *inch* since I met you."

"It's not just my—my proximity?"

He laughed even harder, pressing her to the mattress. "Oh, that, too, love!"

"And in truth you *really* love me?"

"I really, *really* do. . . . Do you not feel it, too? Beneath that mask of reserve, do you not feel it, too, my love? For God's sake, Fleur, don't freeze me out! I want you to love me as I do you!"

Something broke within her, something long suppressed, something that had been growing and seeking release since she met her black spirit of the night. He loved her! There was no reason to hold back any longer. She put her hands up to caress the sides of his face and smiled radiantly into his eyes. "Of course I love you, my dear cavalier. I've loved you since you leapt through that window into my room and into my heart!"

"Then don't lie still and passive, and make me fear that I'm taking you against your will, when I make love to you. Show me that you love me, too."

She gazed into his passion-filled eyes. She traced the light film of moisture on his cheekbones and chin with a delicate finger as he waited poised above her. She ran a gentle finger over his lips. They trembled. She touched them lightly with her own, feathering kisses along the outline of his firm lips, from one corner to the other. Then she ran the tip of her tongue over his parted lips as one of her hands entangled in his thick, black curls and the other ran over his shoulder blades, caressing the strong muscles of his back. He let her take his mouth as she became bolder in her explorations, daringly running her hand down over the small of his back and hips. She was kissing him deeply and he groaned as her legs gripped his slim, muscular hips. He wrapped his arms around her and rolled them over.

"Make love to me, Fleur! I'm on *fire* with love," he said with an urgency underlying his half-teasing comment.

"That's what I'm trying to do, my fiery spirit!"

she whispered against his lips, smiling softly. And together they gave themselves up to the secrets of the night.

Chapter 16

Angus awoke early. His eyes lit up as he looked over at Blanche who was still asleep, with her silver hair spread out over her pillow, much as it had been the first time he had seen her. He smiled tenderly as he remembered her initial nervousness the previous evening—that was all it was, he was sure—and how she had become a warm and passionate woman in his arms once she had overcome it . . . once she was certain that he loved her.

He leaned over and gently placed a kiss on her soft shoulder. His heart began to beat faster as memories of the previous night flooded through him. He was tempted to wake her for another round of lovemaking. But she looked so peaceful, that he sighed and decided to let her sleep. Carefully, he pulled the sheet up to cover her bare shoulders. His poor love must be exhausted, and not just because of their activities last night. He grinned. It had been a tumultuous past few days.

He was impatient to arrange matters so that they could leave Heywood immediately. He dressed quickly, looked back once with regret at the still-sleeping Blanche, and went off to ask Sir Horace for the loan of a hack so that he could ride into town. He wanted to call in at the nearest bank and make arrangements for a transfer of funds from his account in London. It was also necessary that he send off a letter to his uncle's man of affairs without delay.

He had to hang around until the bank manager arrived so that he could use his newfound influence to prevail upon that gentleman to advance him some cash on the spot. He was impatient to buy Blanche a ring. And he wanted to buy himself some new togs so that he could dispose of the travel-worn garments he had been wearing for the past four days.

While he awaited the arrival of the bank manager, Angus sauntered out, hoping to find a jeweler's shop so that he could at least select Blanche's ring, if not make the purchase just yet, and walked headlong into a gentleman he was extremely surprised to see. The man showed not a flicker of recognition when he looked straight at Angus and proceeded to walk right past him. Had he been recognized, it would certainly have added an unwelcome complication to his morning, Angus thought with a wide white grin splitting his dark face.

When Blanche first opened her eyes that morning, she looked over to the other side of the bed to see it empty. Angus was gone. She felt bereft. There was a sinking sensation in the pit of her stomach. Oh dear, she thought, she was his wife in truth now. What if he had left her, even after all his protestations? She bit her lip, but couldn't quite quell the warmth that enveloped her when she remembered how he had loved her last night—and how she had loved him. She smiled softly, gazing unseeing at the canopy above her head, seeing instead Angus's eyes blazing with love. How in the world was she to face him in the daylight? she wondered with great embarrassment and great eagerness.

But she didn't have to deal with that particular problem immediately, for when she went belowstairs there was no sign of her husband. She found her uncle in the morning room. He looked up from the newspaper he was perusing to tell her that Angus had ridden into town on some business or other. Blanche was dismayed. Had he left her so soon?

"Says here, the Duke of Sinclair has died," Sir Horace said to Blanche, reading an item from his paper. "Apparently his death was rather unexpected, despite the fact that he'd been in failing health for some time. His only son was killed recently and seems the blow was too much for him, finished him off, it did. Says a nephew stands his heir. Apparently the lad is the son of a third brother. Seems no one can find him, though. Quite a mystery surrounding the young man.

"The duke's man of business has been looking high and low for this missing heir for a week or more. No one knows if he's alive or dead. It's been rumored that the young man goes about in disguise and uses his mother's maiden name—an outlandish Scottish moniker instead of his own good English name. Humph! Imagine! Going about in disguise as a commoner when one is heir to a dukedom! The *ton* is in an uproar,'' Sir Horace reported with glee, savoring the gossip. He buried his nose in the newspaper once more and read on.

"Hah! The things these wild society bucks get up to! There's a cartoon here showing that cad Wolverton involved in a brawl over a card game." He tut-tutted.

"The Earl of Wolverton!" Blanche exclaimed before she could stop herself. Her uncle's words sent an unpleasant shiver of alarm coursing through her. "What has the earl done now, Uncle?" she asked in a more collected manner.

"You've heard of him, have you, niece? I suppose his notoriety is widespread, what with his habit of leaving debts and spreading mayhem in his wake wherever he goes. Why, the blackguard even owes me a pony. A bad lot, that one—gives the nobility a bad name," Sir Horace grumbled, shaking his head sadly. "The devil earl, he's called—and with good reason."

"Look at this cartoon." He lifted the paper so that Blanche could see. "You see, there's an overturned card table, with the cards scattered all over the floor. Shows the earl shooting at a fellow escaping out the window. His victim is in disguise. See how the fellow is portrayed—dressed all in black, all got up in the costume of a century or more ago."

Blanche stared at her uncle wide-eyed after he showed her the caricature. The Swan in Skipton had been teeming with London gentlemen, she remembered. What if one of them had recognized Angus and had informed the earl of the identity of the black-clad cavalier? Before she could mull this over further, Bartholomew Waddle was announced and Blanche was called upon to introduce the young man to Sir Horace and to smooth his way, praising his efforts to help her bring Prudie home.

Although he stammered somewhat, Bartie made his request to speak privately to Sir Horace with boyish dignity. Her uncle led Bartie off to his study whereupon Blanche was called on to soothe her cousin's wounded feelings. Prudie wondered, loudly and repeatedly, why she wasn't the one Bartie had come to see. Blanche distracted Prudie with a new issue of *La Belle Assemblée* that had arrived while they were away, showing her the latest style in ladies' fashions, some straight from Paris. The tactic worked. Prudie "ohhed and ahhed" and declared that she would have a copy of every outfit she saw made up at the earliest opportunity for her "London come-out," never mind that many of the gowns illustrated were clearly for older women, not debutantes. The fact that her father was still in a miff with her for her recent antics and had threatened to forbid any such London come-out, did not deter her enthusiasm in the least. Prudie knew she could talk him round.

Blanche escaped from Prudie when the housekeeper came in to consult her about the menu for the evening meal. As soon as Blanche left the room, Prudie tossed the magazine aside, picked up her skirts and skipped from the room. She almost ran to her papa's study, where she set her ear against the closed door. When she could not make out anything that was being said inside, she paced about in the hallway outside the study, waiting to intercept Bartie when he should eventually come out. She didn't dare interrupt. Sir Horace had actually denied her the treat of attending the local assembly rooms when she had burst into his study unannounced last summer while he was entertaining a visitor. He had warned her that worse would follow if she ever pulled such a stunt again, and Prudie had believed him.

Sir Horace and Bartie emerged looking pleased with one another some half an hour later. Sir Horace shook Bartie by the hand and said with a wink at his daughter, "Ahem, I suppose you want some conversation with this young man, Puss." He laughed jovially and took himself off to the back of the house.

Bartie stood looking at Prudie with his head a little to one side. She looked flushed and petulant, but as lovely as ever. "Well, Miss Wilmont," he said eventually.

"Well, Bartie Waddle. If you've come here to ask me to marry you, don't think for a minute that I will accept!" she said energetically. When he just grinned at her, Prudie had the sudden maddening suspicion that he was beginning to treat her like a child.

"Oh, I don't," Bartie said eventually.

Prudie looked at him in openmouthed astonishment.

"But I'll see you in town next spring when you make your come-out . . . brat." He daringly used Angus's term for her as he reached forward and tweaked one of her guinea-gold curls. He walked to the table near the door, picked up his brand new curly brimmed beaver hat and clapped it on his head, swung his gold-tipped malacca cane jauntily, and strolled out the door, leaving Prudie speechless—or almost so.

"Well . . . well," was all she could manage to say as she put her hands on her hips and resisted the childish urge to stick out her tongue at his retreating back.

A few minutes later Sir Horace joined his daughter in front of one of the windows in the drawing room where she stood looking out, watching Bartie ride away down the drive while she twisted the tassel of one of the drapery cords between her fingers.

"There goes a fine young man, my dear," Sir Horace said, setting an arm about Prudie's shoulders. "Only nephew of a bachelor earl, he says. The title will be his one day," he told her with satisfaction.

Prudie gasped.

Very much later in the afternoon Blanche was passing through the front hallway intending to go upstairs to speak with Angus, whom she learned had just returned from town, when the butler opened the front door to a rather burly looking gentleman. "The Earl of Wolverton, Miss Charolais, er, pardon me—Mrs. Dalglish," the butler said as he handed the man's card to Blanche.

Blanche concealed her shock as well as she could and quelled the urge to turn on her heel and rush away. "Who is it you've come to see?" she asked stiffly, but with her heart in her mouth.

"I have some pressing business with Sir Horace Wilmont, ma'am. If you would be so kind as to inform him I am here—" Wolverton's reply left her giddy with relief. It seemed he had not learned of Angus's presence in the house, then.

The Earl of Wolverton had come to call on Sir Horace in order to repay an old debt. Sir Horace told them all later that the earl had recently had an amazing streak of luck, starting with a successful wager on a pugilistic contest held several nights previously, and had been able to bring himself about somewhat—at least he had been able to win enough to pay his most pressing debts of honor.

Sir Horace also told them that Wolverton had spotted the newspaper, folded open to show the cartoon of himself. The earl had given a snort of laughter, saying that the villain had not been shot at all, as far as he could discover, for no trace of blood was found. There had been a hue and cry out after the man for more than a day, but it seemed that the rogue had had

307

a lucky escape. It was too bad no one had been able to penetrate the fellow's disguise, Wolverton had said with an ugly sneer. Although he had tried, the earl admitted that he had found no one who had the least idea who the man was or what the "Black Cavalier" looked like under his concealing costume, wig and mustache.

But Blanche did not learn all of this until later— much later.

She directed the butler to announce the earl to her uncle. When he was out of sight, she picked up her skirts and flew up the stairs in a fashion most unlike herself in search of Angus. She had learned he had returned from town and had gone upstairs to change out of all his dirt, as he had told the butler.

She opened the door to their room and rushed in exclaiming, "Angus! The Earl of Wolverton is below, closeted with Uncle Horace! Whatever are we to do?"

She had been about to fly across the room to him when she came running in, but was brought up short by the sight of him standing shirtless, his hair looking slightly damp around the edges. It was evident that he had just emerged from the bath. Blanche blushed and folded her hands together in front of herself, looking at him a little uncertainly as he stood near her bed—the bed where they had enjoyed such a wonderful night.

"Wolverton! Here!"

"Yes. He asked to speak with Uncle Horace," she

308

was able to tell him in a less agitated voice after she swallowed against the constriction in her throat.

"Oh, I don't think the visit need concern us, then."

"Are you sure he hasn't come in search of you?"

"Fleur, there is no way the man could have recognized me. Why, I wager that my own mother would not have known me. Don't worry. We shall just stay up here, out of sight, until he leaves, if it will make you feel safer. . . . Though I must confess, I would enjoy coming face to face with that ugly customer." His eyes flashed dangerously as he considered going belowstairs to confront the earl.

"Oh, no, my dear! Don't think of doing so even for a minute!" Blanche put her hands up as though to prevent him from leaving the room.

He smiled a bit crookedly to see such an expression of concern for him on her face, feeling the strength of her love, though she was still trying to hide it from him. "It's all right, my dear. I ran headlong into the earl in town this morning and he didn't recognize me then. There's no chance he would have come in search of me now," he said with a flicker of a smile, trying to assure her that he was in no danger.

"If you say so, Angus."

He noticed that her clear, alabaster skin appeared quite flushed. She looked very lovely with the high color in her cheeks. She was avoiding his eyes, but he could see a warm glow shining from her eyes when she could bring herself to look at him directly.

"Hand me my shirt from the back of that door you

seem glued to, would you, my love?'' he asked in the blandest of tones.

This request brought her eyes up immediately to his, but she didn't move to do as he requested. She just stood there looking at him. ''Like what you see, my flower?'' he asked playfully, biting back a grin.

Angus's provocative words caused Blanche to turn quickly and jerk the shirt from the hook where it hung on the back of the door she had just closed. She took it over to him, feeling inordinately shy. He turned his back to her, inviting her to assist him with the shirt. She slipped one sleeve over one outstretched muscular arm—the memories of the previous night stirred so strongly that she couldn't resist the temptation to stretch up and set her lips against the back of his neck, just where it joined his shoulder. Her breath sent the damp ends of his curly hair tickling against his ear as she did so.

''I don't think that's at all prudent, Madam Wife,'' Angus said, shaking with silent laughter, ''if you expect me to take *that* without retaliating in kind.'' He swiveled round, set his hands at her waist, and pulled her into his lap as he sat back on the bed. Without giving her a moment's pause in which to utter a protest at this high-handed treatment, he brought his mouth down to hers and began kissing her deeply, one hand playing over the front of her gown, lightly caressing her breasts through the thin fabric of her gown.

Blanche dropped her hold on the shirt to put her arms up about his neck. The shirt fell to the floor, still hanging off one of his arms. Angus raised his lips from hers and shook his arm out of the dangling sleeve. "A fine way to assist me to dress, Madam Wife! I have no objection to you removing the rest of my clothes, however, if you'll let me perform the same office for you."

"Oh, no, Angus. We can't," Blanche said breathlessly. Angus continued to kiss her, planting little nipping kisses all over her face and neck as she uttered this token protest, making it difficult for her to speak.

"Why not?" he asked, continuing his actions, not deterred one whit by her mild demur.

"The Earl of Wolverton is below."

"Well, that's no impediment—we can lock the door." His hands went to her hair. He drew out the pins, one by one, and scattered them on the floor.

"But it's still light outside!—or almost. And we—we'll miss our dinner."

He kissed her ear and ran one hand down over her leg, pushing the material of her gown up as he went. "Umm. Think I'll pass on dinner tonight."

"What!" She laughed against his mouth. "Surely you can't mean that you would forego your dinner! With your insatiable appetite?"

"I have another appetite that craves fulfillment at the moment."

Blanche wanted to taste his kiss on her lips again. She reached up, put one hand on his shoulder and the other behind his head to hold it still. Then she set her

311

mouth against his, kissing him the way he had kissed her, trying to pry his lips open as he had hers.

"Are you, by any chance, trying to seduce me?" Angus laughed against her mouth.

"Am I? Hmm. Yes, I do believe I am!"

"Think I'll let you," he said huskily.

"How does a lady go about such a thing?" she asked with a soft laugh. "Perhaps I need lessons."

"Oh, I think you've set about it quite successfully. Ye gods, preserve me, if you have any more lessons!"

She hushed his laughter with another kiss while her hands found those sensitive spots on his body that she had discovered last night.

"Are you trying to drive me out of my mind, Fleur?" he whispered raggedly.

"Yes."

To her satisfaction, his breathing was out of control now. "God! I love you! My beautiful, beautiful wife!"

And soon he was showing her how much he loved her, and she was showing him, glad to leave behind the reserved, inhibited, sedate Blanche Charolais forever—at least when she was with him. She was Blanche Dalglish now, a far different woman, free to express all the love and emotion she had suppressed for so long.

"I'm afraid you're stuck with me now, Angus," Blanche said sleepily, a good while later.

"Stuck to you is more like," he quipped.

She laid the back of her hand against his cheek. "Oh, Angus, this is madness. We have no funds between us to set up our household. However are we to live on love?''

''If it's madness, it's a divine madness. Not to worry, love. I've told you, I've investments. Besides, I can always go back to gaming, if it becomes absolutely necessary—if you wouldn't object, that is.'' For just a moment, he didn't want to reveal the news of his uncle's death and his new status, wanting her to accept him for himself, wanting to savor having her love him for himself alone, before he set the world at her feet.

''No. I suppose I wouldn't object. But only if it's absolutely necessary, mind.''

''Before we retire to that marshy estate I inherited from my father and try to make something of it, I want you to go with me to London for a time.''

''London! Whatever would we live on *there?* However would we manage?''

''We'll manage.''

''Will we? If you don't take up gaming again? I'll probably have to go on the stage and wear short skirts,'' Blanche said with a twinkle lighting up her silver eyes, making them sparkle in the darkened bedroom.

Angus ran his hand down one of her long, shapely legs. ''By my sword, no one will *ever* see these legs but me!'' he said fiercely. ''My God, they'll still be beautiful when you're eighty!''

''Eighty! I'll only promise to live that long if you'll be here with me.''

313

He laughed. "I daresay you'll have worn me out long since." He leaned over and kissed her.

"Oh, one thing I forgot to mention," he said several minutes later. "As my hostess, I hope you'll help me launch my sister Fanny into the *ton* next spring." He let his fingers play with the fine hairs at the base of her neck, sending a warm tingling sensation all the way down to her toes.

"Into the *ton?* But I know nothing of the *ton!*"

"Why, considering what a fast learner you are, you'll manage in a twinkling . . . your grace—" Angus drawled, moving even closer.

"Your *grace!*" Blanche exclaimed in consternation, her silver eyes wide.

"Why, yes. It's the customary mode of address for a duchess," Angus said blandly.

"A *duchess?*" Blanche asked in disbelief. "You're roasting me!"

" 'Fraid not." He brought one of his legs up over hers. "And by my troth, there's not a woman alive who would 'grace' the title more than you, my lovely white flower."

"That article in the paper Uncle Horace told me about this morning—the Duke of Sinclair was your Uncle Maurice?"

"Yep."

"Angus Dalglish—Sinclair! Whyever did you not tell me? Letting me believe you were a penniless adventurer like that."

"I was."

"Whatever am I to do with you?"

314

"Oh, Fleur! I think you know the answer to that one." He laughed, running his warm fingertips over her bare breasts as he kissed her deeply once again.

"Well, my swashbuckling cavalier of the night, or should I say my swashbuckling lord duke," Blanche said teasingly when she emerged breathless from his kiss and his touch. "You've missed your chance to be a free man. There's no backing out of this marriage now. I'm afraid I'm thoroughly compromised."

"Oh, not quite *thoroughly,* my love!" Angus said huskily, reaching for her again. "I've only just begun."

THE END

A Memorable Collection of Regency Romances

BY ANTHEA MALCOLM AND VALERIE KING

THE COUNTERFEIT HEART (3425, $3.95/$4.95)
by Anthea Malcolm
Nicola Crawford was hardly surprised when her cousin's betrothed disappeared on some mysterious quest. Anyone engaged to such an unromantic, but handsome man was bound to run off sooner or later. Nicola could never entrust her heart to such a conventional, but so deucedly handsome man. . . .

THE COURTING OF PHILIPPA (2714, $3.95/$4.95)
by Anthea Malcolm
Miss Philippa was a very successful author of romantic novels. Thus she was chagrined to be snubbed by the handsome writer Henry Ashton whose own books she admired. And when she learned he considered love stories completely beneath his notice, she vowed to teach him a thing or two about the subject of love. . . .

THE WIDOW'S GAMBIT (2357, $3.50/$4.50)
by Anthea Malcolm
The eldest of the orphaned Neville sisters needed a chaperone for a London season. So the ever-resourceful Livia added several years to her age, invented a deceased husband, and became the respectable Widow Royce. She was certain she'd never regret abandoning her girlhood until she met dashing Nicholas Warwick. . . .

A DARING WAGER (2558, $3.95/$4.95)
by Valerie King
Ellie Dearborne's penchant for gaming had finally led her to ruin. It seemed like such a lark, wagering her devious cousin George that she would obtain the snuffboxes of three of society's most dashing peers in one month's time. She could easily succeed, too, were it not for that exasperating Lord Ravenworth. . . .

THE WILLFUL WIDOW (3323, $3.95/$4.95)
by Valerie King
The lovely young widow, Mrs. Henrietta Harte, was not all inclined to pursue the sort of romantic folly the persistent King Brandish had in mind. She had to concentrate on marrying off her penniless sisters and managing her spendthrift mama. Surely Mr. Brandish could fit in with her plans somehow . . .

Taylor—made Romance From Zebra Books

WHISPERED KISSES   (3830, $4.99/$5.99)
Beautiful Texas heiress Laura Leigh Webster never imagined that her biggest worry on her African safari would be the handsome Jace Elliot, her tour guide. Laura's guardian, Lord Chadwick Hamilton, warns her of Jace's dangerous past; she simply cannot resist the lure of his strong arms and the passion of his *Whispered Kisses*.

KISS OF THE NIGHT WIND   (3831, $4.99/$5.99)
Carrie Sue Strover thought she was leaving trouble behind her when she deserted her brother's outlaw gang to live her life as schoolmarm Carolyn Starns. On her journey, her stagecoach was attacked and she was rescued by handsome T.J. Rogue. T.J. plots to have Carrie lead him to her brother's cohorts who murdered his family. T.J., however, soon succumbs to the beautiful runaway's charms and loving caresses.

FORTUNE'S FLAMES   (3825, $4.99/$5.99)
Impatient to begin her journey back home to New Orleans, beautiful Maren James was furious when Captain Hawk delayed the voyage by searching for stowaways. Impatience gave way to uncontrollable desire once the handsome captain searched *her* cabin. He was looking for illegal passengers; what he found was wild passion with a woman he knew was unlike all those he had known before!

PASSIONS WILD AND FREE   (3828, $4.99/$5.99)
After seeing her family and home destroyed by the cruel and hateful Epson gang, Randee Hollis swore revenge. She knew she found the perfect man to help her—gunslinger Marsh Logan. Not only strong and brave, Marsh had the ebony hair and light blue eyes to make Randee forget her hate and seek the love and passion that only he could give her.

Available wherever paperbacks are sold, or order direct from the Publisher. Send cover price plus 50¢ per copy for mailing and handling to Zebra Books, Dept. 4336, 475 Park Avenue South, New York, N.Y. 10016. Residents of New York and Tennessee must include sales tax. DO NOT SEND CASH. For a free Zebra/Pinnacle catalog please write to the above address.